Born in Scotland in 1910, Jane Duncan spent her childhood in Glasgow, going for holidays to the Black Isle of Inverness. After taking her degree at Glasgow University she moved to England in 1931, and when war broke out she was commissioned in the WAAF and worked in Photographic Intelligence.

After the war she moved to the West Indies with her husband, who appears as 'Twice' Alexander in her novels. Shortly after her husband's death, she returned to Jemimaville near Cromarty, not far from her grandparents' croft which inspired the beloved 'Reachfar'. Jane Duncan died in 1976.

Also by Jane Duncan

MY FRIENDS THE MISS BOYDS
MY FRIEND MONICA

and published by Corgi Books

MY FRIEND MURIEL

Jane Duncan

CORGI BOOKS

MY FRIEND MURIEL

A CORGI BOOK 0 552 12875 9

Originally published in Great Britain by
Macmillan London Limited

PRINTING HISTORY
Macmillan London edition published 1959
Macmillan London edition reprinted 1959, 1970, 1972,
1977, 1983
Corgi edition published 1986

This book is set in 10/11 pt Plantin

Corgi Books are published by Transworld Publishers Ltd.,
61-63 Uxbridge Road, Ealing, London W5 5SA, in Australia by
Transworld Publishers (Aust.) Pty. Ltd., 15-23 Helles Avenue,
Moorebank, NSW 2170, and in New Zealand by Transworld
Publishers (N.Z.) Ltd., Cnr. Moselle and Waipareira Avenues,
Henderson, Auckland.

Reproduced, printed and bound in Great Britain by
Hazell Watson & Viney Limited,
Member of the BPCC Group,
Aylesbury, Bucks

For the oldest of all my friends,
that great teller of stories,
GEORGE
who used, modestly, to preface his tales with the words:
'Was I ever telling you about the time when —?
It is a foolish kind of story, but —'

CONTENTS

Part I

Part I

Often at night, when I take rather a long time to go to sleep, I think of My Friend Muriel.

And now that I look at that, written down there, that sentence that says that I think of My Friend Muriel is a whopping great lie, for at these times I do not think of Muriel at all — I do not think of my friend. What I think is something like this: 'I wonder what would have happened to *me* if I had never met Muriel? What would the course of *my* life have been? If I hadn't met Muriel would I ever——?' It has endless ramifications and in the end I go to sleep, but it is not 'thinking about My Friend Muriel.' What is Muriel to me and what am I to Muriel now? For that matter, what were we to one another ever? If one thinks, really *thinks* that is, about this word Friend, one thinks, if I am the one — and of course I am the one who is writing this — one thinks in terms of David and Jonathan and people like that. Muriel and I were not like that, not at all like that. At least, I do not think so. For I feel that David liked, not to say loved, Jonathan, while, truly, I did not even like Muriel particularly. She was just someone I knew a little — a very little — once upon a time, that is all. But I often think about her at odd times, as I said at the beginning, really because I wonder what the pattern of my life would have been if I had never met her, so that it is not really thinking about her at all, but about *me*, which brings me to the conclusion, for, after all, one can only speak as one finds, that oneself is the most popular and recurrent thought with every last one of us except, maybe, the Davids and Jonathans, and they are rare enough to be marked men in the long tale of history.

Muriel came into my life trailing no clouds of glory, but enshrouded in a patchy miasma of petty disadvantages, not the least of which was this Christian name of hers, Muriel. My family, which is a Scottish Highland one, has a large number of fixed ideas about all sorts of things, and as a young person my mind was like a badly-made, partly-set jelly — a wobbly dollop with, scattered through it here and there, a few hard lumps of fixed ideas that my father, mother, grandparents, uncles and aunts had dropped into it and which had been somehow trapped in the jelly without falling right through into the nothingness of the unremembered. These fixed ideas that my family had, embraced all sorts of things from the great moral issues of right and wrong down to the 'right' way to scoop jam from the storage jar into the dish to be served on the tea table, and somewhere along the line my family had a code of rules about names, especially Christian names. Roughly, these names fell into three classes:

(a) Names that ordinary people like us could have.
(b) Names that were for the gentry.
(c) Names that were just plain silly and outlandish and borne by a class that was somewhere between us and the gentry and did not know its own place, anyway.

The word 'bourgeoisie' was not in my family's vocabulary. And now, to clarify matters for you, I shall classify some names as my family would have classified them.

(a) Names for people like us:
    Janet (my name).
    Elizabeth (my mother's name).
    Catherine (my grandmother's name).
    Isobel (an aunt).
    Duncan (my father).

12

George (an uncle).

John (my grandfather).

(b) Names for the gentry:

Victoria (the only queen my grandmother ever recognised).

Alexandra (the reigning queen at the time of my birth, recognised by father, mother, uncles, etc.).

Lydia (the name of the wife of the local baronet who was the Lady Lydia M — in her own right).

Deborah (or other biblical names — all right for the gentry but presumptuous for people like us).

Edward (the husband of Alexandra above).

Torquil (the local baronet).

Anthony (son and heir of the above).

Michael (see biblical reference above).

(c) Names silly and outlandish:

Gladys, Wendy, MURIEL, Doris, Victor, Barry, Robin, Albert.

The above tabulation is only the bare bones, the slender skeleton framework, of a sort of Chinese-pagoda-like structure of opinion which branched away into all sorts of over-hanging eaves, intertwinings of scrollwork and dangling bells at the corners. For instance, people like us could have names that the gentry were not using at the moment, so that I was christened Janet Elizabeth in 1910, presumably because Queen Elizabeth had died over three hundred years ago. Also, it was quite in order for the gentry to take a notion to call a girl Jean although this name was truly the property of people like us, for the gentry had all sorts of licence, but it would not have been the thing for me to have been named Eleanor or Eve. The main feature of the whole complex business, though, was the apartness of the silly and outlandish section of names. People like us would never even *think* of names like these if we had any sense, and the gentry, of course, had so *much* sense that they did not recognise them as names at all, even for horses.

Now you, Gladys or Robin, who have picked up the book that your friend let the girl at the library choose for her and which you have found lying on the hall table while you wait for Doris or Barry to get ready to come out for a round of golf and are reading this and saying: 'A lot of stupid prejudice!' and feeling indignant — to you I say: 'Certainly, it is prejudice!' Please note that I am not saying that my family was right. I am merely writing down here how my family *was* — and *is*, for that matter. 'What's in a name?' Indeed! My family could have told you. There was nothing of the shifting sand about my family's ideas. They were based on and embedded in the solid rock of the Highlands, and no man could go calling his infant daughter Coral without being asked how he came to think of such a silly and outlandish name. Coral, for pity's sake! When the boy comes along call him Great Barrier Reef and be done with it. That was my family's attitude.

So, out of the great universe of chances and cross-currents, accidents of time at places and places in time and this and that that forms the terrifying web of human experience — out of this great *universe*, I repeat, before I lose myself and you entirely, Muriel came floating towards me in the grey cloud of the unattractiveness of her name.

To say that Muriel floated — light and ghost-like — is, actually, the height of nonsense, for Muriel was a hefty piece of womanhood who would have been hard put to it to float even on the Dead Sea, but at this stage Muriel is not an actuality in my life or in this story. She is a nebula, a thickening of the mists somewhere in my future.

At this time, I was about twenty years old and a student at the University of Glasgow and I had lodgings with friends of my family in a village on Clydeside between Clydebank and Dumbarton. So it was 1930 and the big Trade Depression was at its nadir and I used to travel daily by motor bus up and down from this village to the university. And the bus rattled and clanged up and down through the dreary western suburbs of Glasgow where it always rained and the smell was of fish and chips and noxious fumes and wet human clothes, and the yellow lights of the shops wavered in a sulphurous fog of deadness, and the noises were not the right noises for

Clydeside, for instead of the cheerful clang-clang of the riveters there was only a low grumble of cold, hunched, disgruntled men who hung around the street corners and busstops, watching with dull eyes the road to nowhere. And now and then there was the wailing cry of a child, a weak, hungry cry, not the lusty shout of a riveter's son who should be born with a voice that means to be heard above the busy hammers of the ship-builders. And dominating all the sounds and smells and earth-bound sights were the great steel ribs of John Brown & Co.'s No. 534, the skeleton of the great ship whose keel had been laid down, whose gigantic thorax of curved steel had been set in position before the descent of the great deathbird known as the Big Depression over Clydeside. For many months now no hammers had sounded, no carpenters had whistled the latest song-hit in time to the sweep of their planes, no cries of 'Take her away, Jock!' had come from the shipwrights as the slung steel plates swung away and up into the smoky air. Clydeside was silent, and the arms of No. 534 stretched upwards to the sky in silent prayer. Day after day I saw that skeleton from my rattling bus and I was young and full of the lost unhappiness of youth that sees no future, for I did not know then that one evening I would see that skeleton, clothed with the majestic flesh of a great ship and hung about with necklaces of jewelled light, sail down the Hudson River so that Martha, my friend who lives in Brooklyn, would call out to me: 'Hi, Jan! Come quick to the kitchen window! The *Queen Mary's* going by! Gee, isn't she *something* at dusk, huh?' And I told Martha that at dusk or in the morning or at high noon the *Queen Mary* and ships like her were always *something* and how this one had been something when she was known as 'the five-three-fower' and Martha knew what I meant and the tears came into her beautiful eyes at the thought, for Martha, come to that, is *something* too. One day, maybe, I will write about My Friend Martha, but I have to remember that right now I am busy with My Friend Muriel.

So here we are at this place Clydebank in this time 1930, with the praying arms of the Five-three-fower reaching to the unresponsive sky and the bus standing at a stop and it is raining and the idle men are hunched up under their shabby overcoats and I am twenty years old and in almost my finals at the university and it is all leading nowhere for in Big Depressions there are no jobs for the newly qualified and I am in a muddle about a young man who wants to marry me and, finally, I have toothache. And so on a pillar by a doorway I see a greasy-green brass plate that says: 'Dentist. Somebody, L.S.D.' I had never had toothache in my life before, I had never been to a dentist in my life before, and I decided that it would be 'experience is an arch wherethrough gleams the untravelled world' (Did I say that I was a student of English literature?). So I got off the bus and went up the stairs beyond the portal with the brass plate. The said portal turned out to be something of a magic casement opening on a perilous sea (if be literary we must), for at the top of the stairs I encountered a little fat man in a white coat who had all the aspect of a legendary Scots character called 'Cockabendy' as I had visualised him. He was round all over: a round head on a round body, and round of movement, somehow, for in motion he looked like a rubber ball. I remembered, when I saw the waiting-room and the rather shabby magazines on a table, that these were what the Business Course, in which I was interesting myself as a diversion from my more serious studies, called 'overheads', and I remembered simultaneously that it was nearly the end of the week and that my allowance of cash in purse was standing at five shillings and sevenpence.

'Good evening,' I said. 'I have a toothache. How much does it cost to take a tooth out?'

'Out?' he said, giving a little bounce. 'Nonsense! I'll look at it. In a minute.' Another little bounce. 'Maybe quarter'f'n hour. Busy now. Sit down.'

Before I could indicate that I had no faith in being looked at he had bounced a hand in the direction of a chair and had bounced himself out of the room, so I sat down at the table, and there were the magazines, all designed to be ever so cosy and homey and lie on polished tables in little rooms called 'lounges' and all equipped to tell the little 'wifey' how to 'hold her man' and how to deal with her 'little ones' and how to crochet those 'little mats that make all the difference' (what kind of difference?) to that 'little table' and with titles like *Fireside Chat* and *Homey Hearth*. But they were all very tatty and dog-eared, poor things. But also, forbye and besides, to use the pet idiom of a Highlandman I know, the born reader will always read the printed word no matter in what guise it may appear, so I opened *Fireside Chat* — or was it *Homey Hearth*? — and began to read the words that lay before me. I do not remember all that I read but there was a page headed 'Are You Lonely?' and in the corner of it was a picture of a woman with white hair, sitting at a writing-table with pen poised, and the purport of the article was that to have pen-friends scattered about the earth was a wonderful antidote to loneliness and this woman with the white hair, who had written the article, was apparently willing to find these pen-friends for one, free, gratis and for nothing, because she believed that if all the countries on earth were full of people who had pen-friends in all the other countries on earth there would be no more war and man to man the world o'er would brothers be for a' that.

Now, what I have written up there may look to you like the ordinary, careless sentence that an illiterate like me might say or write all the time, for I do not set up to be a literary stylist like S. Maugham, whose work I happen to dislike, or Eric Linklater, whose work I happen to admire, nor am I a poet even when I write in prose like Osbert Sitwell, but that sentence up there is subtler than you may think.

Please notice, you who read, that at the end of that sentence I went into unacknowledged (at the time) quotation from a poet (and not a bad poet, off and on) called Robert Burns, which gave me the phrase 'man to man' which *you*, you careless thing who read in a hurry, slipped over unnoticed because you know the phrase, anyway. But that little phrase 'man to man' was the crux of this white-haired lady's panacea for the world's ills. In other words, a woman could get a *woman* pen-friend, and a man could get a *man* pen-friend, but not, nohow, never in this world chain of friendship was sex to be allowed to rear its ugly head. And, maybe, she had a good idea at that, but I do not intend to argue the point here, for which you may live to be thankful, for I am a heller for an argument.

I had read right to the end of this page in this magazine, right to the part where it said that if you were interested in the brotherhood of man (or woman), or if you were lonely, you should write to:

> Mrs. Whitely-Rollin,
> Hon. Sec. The Chain of Friendship,
> Whitely House,
> Somewhere in Kent,

when the little Cockabendy in the white coat bounced in and said: 'How's the tooth? Still sore? Sorry I'm delayed. That's right — read a book, take your mind off it!' and bounced out again. If you are lonely, the article said. Still sore, said Cockabendy. God knows, I thought, I am lonely, for I was not then old enough to know that youth is always lonely. God knows, I thought, it is still sore, for I was not then old enough to know that in this world something is always sore and that you are lucky if it is only a tooth. But I was also a daughter of my family, who were a lot of people who knew, beyond a shadow of doubt, what was what, and they had imbued me with the idea of if you are lonely and your tooth is sore don't sit down and make a fuss, why don't you *do* something about it? — so I decided to wait for the dentist to look at my tooth, and while I was waiting I would write to this Mrs. Whitely-Rollin and see what she was prepared to do for my loneliness.

Like most students of my era, I carried always with me a little leather case which contained a book for lecture notes, a pen, some odds and ends of writing paper, an envelope or two, a few stamps, a dirty handkerchief, a battered cigarette, a box with three matches, a rather soiled—— Well, anyhow, I had paper, envelope, pen and stamp and I wrote to this woman 'Dear Madam' in my best Business Course style and stuck a stamp on the envelope, a stamp worth a penny-halfpenny, and at that reckless moment Cockabendy came in again and said: 'Well, let's see this tooth that has to come out, ha-ha!' So, with life closing in on me like this, I got up and followed him and

18

left writing-case, stamped letter and all lying among the cosy dog-eared magazines on the table.

All dentists' surgeries will always be for me that room of Cockabendy's. I have no fear, now or ever, of the dentist's big comfortable chair with its place for your head and its place for your feet and the Cockabendy's hands that smell of disinfectant.

'Open, please! My God, beautiful teeth! You lucky girl! Pull it out indeed. Nonsense. Nasty little hole though. Should have come to me long ago. Steady now — this is noisy but it won't take long.'

He thrummed with his drill, he made his little mix of concrete on a tiny mortar-board, he filled my tooth while intoning a panegyric to all my teeth, and then he said: 'There now, young lady — no more trouble for years I bet', and I pushed with my tongue at my miracle patch where there was no pain now and said 'Thank you. Thank you very much. How much do I owe you?'

'Out, you said,' he replied with a bounce and a smile. 'So out it is. Price for extraction is half a crown.'

'Oh, but — I meant — well, I didn't know —'

'No. Lucky girl! You didn't know!' He bounced through to the waiting-room with the magazines on the table. 'No. Beautiful teeth. Lovely. Time I went home for my tea. Half a crown's the price. Here, don't forget your case!'

He pushed my little writing-case at me and I proffered half a crown.

'Thank you,' he bounced. 'Take care of them. Brush them. That's a good girl. Goodnight. Goodnight!'

He bounced me out on to the stairs and I heard a bolt slide home on the inner side of the waiting-room door and all the cosy, homey magazines and my letter with its stamp and all were left inside. Oh, well, my tooth did not hurt any more. I felt grand. That is the sort of person I was at twenty — either feeling terrible or feeling grand. There is nothing unusual in that. I believe that most people of twenty feel like that. They are either conscious of far too much excessively dreary future or they are raptly, blissfully conscious only of the present and have no time to think of any future at all — anyway, that is how I was at twenty and you can only speak as you find.

I caught another bus in the dreary, Big Depression, Clydeside evening and went to my lodgings, and in the human way of benefits forgot I did not think again of Cockabendy and how he had rid me of all that pain for half a crown until four days later when I found a letter by my breakfast plate which said: 'Dear Miss Sandison, I was so glad to have your letter, and although you tell me very little about yourself except that you are an undergraduate at Glasgow University, I hope you will enjoy writing to this girl who studies at the University of Sydney in Australia and who is just about your own age. Her name is so-and-so and her address is so-and-so. I shall be glad to put you in touch with other pen-friends in other parts of the world as soon as I find suitable girls among my applicants. Yours sincerely, for Mrs. Whitely-Rollin, M. Thornton.'

Very unfairly, I dratted Cockabendy for having posted the letter which he must have found on his magazine table, for here I was, on my thin pocket-money, committed to buy stamps and paper to write to this unknown in Sydney, besides having to write to 'For Mrs. Whitely-Rollin, M. Thornton' to thank her for something I did not really want.

I am not much of a one for bawling about the unfair inequalities between the sexes, but it does seem to me that women are more frequently victimised than men in this way of having to thank people for things they do not want. I suppose that, quite often, men are presented with neckties that they hate and still have to render thanks for them, but at least they *are* neckties, and even their particular pattern, which may be repulsive in the extreme to the recipient, may be a pattern that would have untold appeal for another man. But if you are a woman, and are given a handkerchief sachet, pink satin, with hand-painted flowers, there seems to me to be no 'out', as My Friend Martha would call it. Who *wants* a handkerchief sachet, hand-painted or not? Again, as Martha would say — God bless America, Martha and their succinct bastardisation of the English language — I take a rain-check on handkerchief sachets and returning thanks for them. And while I am taking rain-checks, I wish to record that I take a string of three of them, straight out of the machine, on the following: coloured witch-balls that hang in windows, mass-produced china figures of people or animals, and any darned thing for eating out of that is made of what this era in which I live calls 'plastic'. Oh, and while I am about it, I take the most expensive seat in the rain-check stadium for anything that tries to masquerade as anything else, like a crinoline lady with a telephone under her skirts (the coarse trollop) or a literary-looking volume entitled *Scotland's Pride*, which conceals between its boards a bottle of whisky (the palateless illiterate).

Well, there I was, before I became garrulous about rain-checks, faced with a pen-friend and a letter signed 'M. Thornton' through the mistaken but good intentions of Cockabendy; and my family being the sort that never started anything it could not finish, it never entered my head to ignore my new responsibilities, so I wrote to the girl in Australia (to write a screed to almost anyone about almost anything has never caused me the slightest trouble), and I wrote a polite note to Mrs. Whitely-Rollin thanking her for her kind attention to my letter and telling her that one pen-friend would be quite enough, thank you.

But — ha ha! — and other expressions of scorn. I did not know Mrs. Whitely-Rollin. Ah, no. She was one of the bull-dog breed. Seemingly this girl in Australia, who was really very nice and sent me a book of poems by Banjo Paterson and a needle-book with a Koala bear painted on it for Christmas, wrote to Mrs. Whitely-Rollin and told her about the 'wonderful letters' I wrote and as a result of this I found myself swamped, inundated and overwhelmed by pen-friends all over the world. Letters came from France, Belgium, Canada, New Zealand, Ceylon, India, South Africa, Martinique — but why this list? The letters were from 'a' airts an' pairts', and I, with my final degree examinations coming up, not to mention my attempts to attain a reasonable typewriting speed on my old second-hand machine for my Business Course, was surrounded by letters from enthusiastic young women whose grandmothers' cousins four times removed were all from Scotland and who were so pleased to find a friend in the 'dear old home country'.

At first, when the letters from Mrs. Whitely-Rollin began to come in with more and more addresses of pen-friends I ignored them, but that did not work, for every time that Mrs. Whitely-Rollin wrote to me she wrote to the pen-friend also, giving her *my* address, so there it was. My allowance would not have covered the cost of the paper and stamps even if I had had the time and the inclination to deal with them all, and many a few minutes I spent in cursing the well-intentioned dentist Cockabendy. And all the time, behind it all, was the voice of my family saying: '*You* started this, *you* finish it!' So I made a gallant attempt. I wrote to this 'M. Thornton', who signed everything in a thin, indeterminate hand in light-blue ink, and told her with frankness as polite as I could make it that I could not cope with all this, that I was willing to continue with my first pen-friend, the girl in Australia, but that the rest were *out*. I received by return a very civil letter written throughout in the thin, indeterminate hand which told me that my position was quite understood but it was hoped that I would keep in touch with the office, as the writer herself and Mrs. Whitely-Rollin, 'who is a wonderful and delightful person', would not like to lose sight of me, and this letter was signed 'Yours sincerely, Muriel Thornton'. So, with a fanfare of trumpets and a rat-a-plan on the big drum, here enters My Friend Muriel.

Now don't you run away with the idea that from here on all this writing that lies spread out over all these pages in front of you is all about Muriel, because it is not. I do not *know* that much about Muriel. I question if anybody knows that much about anybody except himself or herself. I think people are the most difficult things in the world to know about and to know oneself is not all that easy either. Wasn't it St. Paul who commanded 'Know thyself!'? Well, he knew a packet about commanding, anyway, if commanding means telling people to do things they would not even dream of trying to do unless they were commanded, like presenting arms and changing step on the march and that.

Just because a book is called *My Friend Muriel* is no reason for thinking it is *all* about My Friend Muriel — not if I write it, anyway. She could not be my friend at all except for *me*, so I have to come into the thing somewhere, don't I? And if *she* wanted to hog the whole thing, why didn't *she* write it and call it *My Friend Janet*? Ha! I'll tell you why not. Just because Muriel would never think of doing anything so darned silly, that's why. It would never occur to Muriel to think about writing a book about me, for she would never imagine anyone wanting to read it. Muriel is not like me. Now, if I want to write a book, I write it whether anyone wants to read it or not. I have written dozens of books. I think I am interesting, and I think Muriel is interesting, and I think everybody is interesting, and if other people don't agree I am going to write about myself and all the interesting people, anyway — people can take it or leave it. Now, this is where Muriel would say: 'Why write a book that nobody wants?' and I would say: 'But I want to *write* it!' and Muriel would say: 'I never *heard* of anybody doing a thing like that!', and we would not say any more on the subject. It would be closed at that.

But do not let me get away into 'telling' you things about Muriel. My idea of a book about Muriel is to tell you the things I saw Muriel doing and heard her saying and let you judge for yourself what sort of person she was, for if there is one thing in the world that I distrust more than another it is someone saying to me: 'So-and-so is a fool.' It is never true. So-and-so may be an awful fool to the person who told me that he was, but that does not mean that So-and-so is a fool to *me*. Like beauty, foolishness is in the eye of the beholder and it is no use my saying to you: 'Muriel was thus and so', for you may not have thought so at all. But what I *can* do, and will try to do to the best of my ability, is tell you what Muriel looked like, the things I heard her say and the things I saw her do, and after you have read about that you can make up your own mind what sort of person she was. A book about people is not the same thing as a book about algebra or cookery. In algebra or cookery you obey the rules the book lays down and you get either an equated equation or an omelette, but with people there are no rules and it is a case of every man for himself.

So, even before we get to Muriel at all, I am going to write a few pages about myself and the devious route by which I finally met her in the flesh, so that when you begin to read about her you will be acquainted with the person who saw her, heard her and is telling you about her, which should remind you that, in this book, you are seeing Muriel through my eyes and that should cause you to make certain allowances, for I do not set myself up to be the goddess of cold, impartial justice at the Old Bailey. Also, we have plenty of time. You and I are in this book-reading, book-writing business for fun, I hope, and, frankly, it is not a matter of life and death if we *never* get to Muriel — she was not a Cleopatra or anything. So, I am not going to tell you either that *I* am thus and so. I think that is a very difficult thing for anyone to do, for few people can see themselves as others see them. No. I am not going to say a lot of 'I ams'. I am going to tell you what happened to me, in a brief way, between getting the letter signed 'Muriel Thornton' and actually seeing Muriel in the flesh, for I have always found the 'I am——' suspect and usually my suspicions have been well-founded.

All this is, of course, a long way from My Friend Muriel, but let us not get back into that comic argument again. We are in a village on Clydeside, which is a long way from Kent where Muriel is, and a long way, too, from my home in the county of Ross, away up in the Highlands, and although 'Aunt' Alice and 'Uncle' Jim, my host and hostess, are kindness itself, I am still a jelly-minded young thing of twenty, full of ups and downs, and there is the Big Depression and there is this trouble with my young man and it keeps raining all the time. So I do not bother very much with this letter from this Muriel Thornton and this Chain of Friendship, and Australia is a long way away and the airmail is not in common use yet, so I write a screed to this girl in Sydney and throw it into the post with a 'Thank heaven for ten weeks' respite' and that is that. I reserve what bothering I have for this young man of mine whose name is Victor.

Now this young man called Victor is about twenty-five years old and is something in one of the banks where his father is also quite something senior, and he has one brother who is in America, and a mother too, but she is very much at home, thank you, in a semi-detached villa on the hill that rises behind this village. At this time that I am telling you about, Victor has already told me that he is fond enough of me to want to marry me, and Victor's father, although he has not told me, is very fond of me too and likes Victor's idea of bringing me into the family, but Victor's mother is different. She, although she has not told me anything either, does not like me at all, and she does not like Victor liking me, and she does not want me anywhere near her family, much less in it.

But I am here to tell yee-ewe, to quote the words of an American Jewess I met once, that Victor's mother was not the only disapprover in the field. Oh no. Sitting up on our croft, by which I mean our small farm, in the county of Ross, was a whole heavy battery of disapproval, consisting of five guns, all of them big — to wit, my grandfather, my grandmother, my father, my uncle and my aunt (my mother was dead by now but in spirit she was with them) — firing salvo after salvo of this sort by letter: 'This Victor, we gather that he is some sort of counter-jumper——' and 'This Victor Halloran, it sounds Irish — an unreliable lot——' and although Old Tom, who was our odd-man and my familiar up there, did not put his views in writing, I could imagine them, like the after-blast of the family guns; 'Also, forbye and besides, thiss fellow Veector, he iss twenty-fife they'll pe tellin' me an' him still livin' at home with hiss mother, the poor craitur!'

It was not that my family disapproved of my marrying, in spite of their advanced views on the Higher Education for Women. Indeed, I knew without being told that they hoped that in due course I *would* marry and have children and pursue the normal course that women of families such as mine had always pursued and that, in the meantime, they were giving this Higher Education thing a whirl just to show themselves and the world at large that they were not backward in thought or averse to being abreast with the times. No. They disapproved of my marrying Victor for no definite reason that they could put into coherent words. They disliked the 'silly and outlandish' name Victor; his surname had an Irish flavour; he was a counter-jumper whatever that may have meant; and they had never seen him. Also, forbye and besides, they had no wish to see him, and if forced to see him were not prepared to alter their views by one jot or tittle. They contrived to indicate all this without saying it in so many words, and in a similar way they contrived to suggest that it was a pity that I had absorbed a lot of money, was about to attain a creditable degree and a reasonable diploma from university and business college only to throw the whole lot away by settling down with a creature called Victor, in a semi-detached villa, overlooked by Victor's mother, to a lifetime of the fog of Clydeside.

While war was rampant in the central plain of my mind between Victor on one side and my family on the other, with Victor's mother as an uneasy, distrustful ally of my family skirmishing in the foothills, Aunt Alice, with whom I lived, was carrying out a series of guerilla raids on Victor's side as she sat comfortably by the fire with the sock she was always knitting.

'I'd have thought you and Victor would be off to the choir dance tonight. He told me he had tickets.'

'I know, Aunt Alice. I didn't want to go. I don't know any of the Church crowd of people.'

'Humph! They know *you* though! That Peggy Fletcher would jump at the chance of going to the choir dance with Victor. He's a fine, steady fellow. A lassie could go a lot further and fare a lot worse!'

And so it went on. The cinema with Victor and a box of chocolates; Sunday tea at Victor's home, and his mother's: 'Of course, you are very young for your age, aren't you? I suppose it's being brought up away up there at the back of beyond'; and Tuesday, and the letter from home that had been written on Sunday: 'I suppose this fellow Victor is taking up all your time when your last letter was so late'; and Wednesday and Victor suggesting the Freemasons' Ball on Friday and Aunt Alice saying: 'And I'm going to put a broad crimson sash on that white taffeta frock of yours — it's too young-looking for the Masons' Ball with Victor, the way things are——' and so on and SO ON, until one evening, when Victor had tickets for

26

something and Aunt Alice was planning an alteration to the collar of my coat and, as it was Tuesday, the letter from home had been fretting me all day, I said: 'Oh, the coat's all right, Aunt Alice.'

'All right!' She laughed indulgently. 'Hark at her, Victor! It's not a *vain* wife you're getting, anyway!'

Victor said something, but I did not listen and I said again: 'The coat is all right.'

That is how it was. One had to keep on saying something, something harmless about coats and things like that, but *something* all the time.

Aunt Alice laughed again. 'But Victor says——'

'To *hell* with Victor!' I heard myself say, quietly, as a snake might hiss. 'To hell with Victor and his mother and me and my family *and* the coat! To hell with the whole bloody lot of it!' And I turned to Victor. 'Go away!' I said. 'Get out of here! Go on! Get out!'

And Uncle Jim, who was not my uncle any more than Aunt Alice was my aunt and who had been reading about the Rangers-Celtic football prospects for the next Saturday in his evening paper, laid the paper down on his knees, watched Victor drift awkwardly out of the house, bumping into the door-lintel like a twig caught in a torrent, and said: 'And to hell with you too, Alice! Why the devil can none of ye let the lassie live her own life in her own way? Her life is all she has! Make a cup of tea, woman, and haud yer wheesht! Sit ye doon lassie — that Victor was a white-collared poop o' a fellow, anyway!' Uncle Jim took up his paper again and gave it a good shaking. He was a shipwright by trade, with beautiful, broad, sensitive but strong craftsman's hands, and when he shook a thing it shook. That shake of his newspaper was the last salvo fired in the battle of Victor. Shortly after that, I went up to my home in Ross, degree, diploma and all, and heard no more of Victor and little, indeed, of kind Aunt Alice and Uncle Jim, who are both dead a long time ago.

I remember little of the Clydeside village or of the people there, with the exception of craftsman Uncle Jim. I remember little about the university except for vivid details of some of the great men I heard speak there, and what they said, and the

27

books I read. Oh yes, I remember the books. I think perhaps I am a person like this: I remember all the things I liked and forget all the things I did not like. It is very comfortable. And I think I remember the evening of the exodus of Victor so vividly because I liked it as much as I had ever liked anything in my life up to that time. My family, you see, is a peaceful family. We do not Have Rows, or situations where people Don't Get On with their mothers-in-law or fathers Show Daughters the Door or things like that. Oh no. My family has an even tenor of its way and moves along without fuss or fume, and if at times it is a little like a road-roller that mistakes somebody for an ant-hill it shows no cognisance of the fact.

'I am a plain woman,' my grandmother used to say, 'and I speak plainly.'

(Remember how I told you earlier that the 'I am' is nearly always a lie?) And so, at times, like most people, my grandmother was a liar. She had never spoken really plainly in her life. I question if she had ever *thought* plainly, even. Always, speech and thought were coloured, tainted, lightened or darkened by something else, and I had acquired the habit of this kind of speaking and thinking too, but that night, over the symbol of Victor, I broke through it. I felt as Beethoven must have felt as he built up the climax of the Ninth Symphony or as Cortez must have felt in his first moment on his peak in Darien. They were greater people than I, those two, so their moments were greater than mine, but mine was a Fine Thing from my low standpoint. With that final 'Get out!' to Victor I drew a deep breath and thought: 'By golly! For once I have really said exactly what I mean!' and so I said, over again, to myself: 'To hell with the whole bloody lot of it!'

And so My First Early Love, that love that Never Comes Again, was Blighted. Oh, willy-waly o'er the hill and waly down the meadow! Oh, in fact, fiddlesticks! Or, if you prefer it, horsefeathers! At twenty or so I was a young girl like this: I was a young girl who was incapable of loving anyone, and I will take on all comers with the argument that ninety-nine per centum of young girls of twenty or so are exactly as I was.

There was Victor. I do not even remember what he was like, and if he happens to read this at this late date I can only say that

I hope he is honest enough to admit that he does not remember what I was like either. And when I use that phrase 'was like' I mean precisely what I say. In the words of a West Indian friend, I mean that I cannot remember the 'this that Victor was a person like'. Do I make myself clear? And this, if I am not mistaken, proves conclusively that I did not love him. When a personality has impressed itself on you to the extent that you feel even a glimmering of affection for it, you remember and know always at least the facet that has caused that glimmer in you, for it has become an integral part of yourself.

No. Young girls of twenty do not love. I do not know about young men. I have never been a young man of twenty. But girls of twenty are hellers for responding to suggestion, and in my day a great deal of suggesting about how to behave in a Nice Way that Might Lead to Something and about cosy little homes and dear little babies and how to cook to Please the Brute and this and that went on. But there was a worse thing than that. Around 1930, although Higher Education for Women was a common run-of-the-mill affair, it was made very clear by the older women to the girls of twenty that it was still a Man's World and that the safe thing to do for decent survival was to obtain a position by legal contract of marriage as a parasite on some man in the world at the earliest possible moment. Put bluntly like that, in my inartistic way, it all sounds highly immoral, with the basic immorality of parasitism. Well, it *was* immoral. But it was never put bluntly — it was put in the form of romance, in books and magazines and plays and films and all that, but behind it all was the truth that the complete emancipation of women coupled with the post-war outbreak of reckless living which had characterised the 1920's brought a hunted, panic fear into the minds of the parents and guardians of girls, a fear that urged: 'These young ones are going to break out into recklessness! Get them married before they start on the downward path and maybe they'll be forced by circumstances to settle down. The old ways are best. We should never have subscribed to that education nonsense for them!' Happiness or honesty did not come into it. The pendulum was on its backward swing; and although I never expected to say a word in praise of Hitler,

Mussolini and the warlords of the 1930's, I do not know where the world's attitude to women would have fetched up but for their shocking intervention.

But to return to Victor. Having had my moment of revelation as to the shibboleth in which I had been enmeshed, and having realised what I had escaped, I went haywire (oh, descriptive word!) among all the shibboleths, and up at home on the croft where the clear winds blew across the heather I went around and about the house and land outwardly composed but inwardly dancing a fandango in celebration of the fact that no shibboleth-thinking in the world could make me do anything else that I did not want to do, either.

One of the reasons why this book is called *My Friend Muriel* is that I am at a loss to understand why such apparently unimportant things should exercise so much influence on one's life. No one could have looked so unimportant as Muriel, but she seems to have had a curious space-time effect on my life. Well, in the same way, Victor was a fearfully unimportant thing, really — I mean you could hardly imagine anything so null and void as Victor and conceive that he was one of these specks of dust that the divine breath had gotten breathed into, and yet, you know, if it had not been for Victor and the muddle I got myself into over him I would now be a completely different person. Being a very happy, fortunate person right now, the thought of what *might* have happened to me appals me. God bless Victor!

Talking about shibboleths, though, I think that shibboleth is a lovely word. I am very keen on words. Yes, I am a person like this: I am very keen on words. But I like words in a particular way — I like them 'for queer' as they say in parts of east Scotland, and the queer words form themselves into a picture in my mind.

Do you know this stuff called 'umbrage' that people are said to 'take' now and then. I have never taken it myself and have never understood why some people do, for it looks to me like a bundle of greyish-brown stuff, about the size of a bundle of asparagus (but not succulent at all) and, indeed, in texture like the dried herbs you may have seen hanging in a good French kitchen (but not aromatic at all, as the herbs are). When people take it, they take the bundle in both hands and go away into a dark corner where you cannot see them, so I have never been able to find out what they do with it. I once enquired of My Friend Monica (she is a new one on you and very nice, although a little short-tempered), who, although not an umbrage-taker herself any more than I am, had known a number of addicts to it, and she said that it was not this bundle of stuff that I am telling you about at all. No. Monica said she was sure that they got it in bottles of blue ribbed glass from the chemist's shop and that they took it in private, in their bedrooms or in the bathroom, without measuring it with a spoon or anything but just by tilting the bottles to their mouths. That, she said, was very important, this thing of there being no regular, prescribed dose. In the end, after a long discussion which cost over a pound in Dry Martinis at 1939 officers' mess prices, Monica and I decided that the umbrage-takers she had known were more confirmed addicts than those I had known and that her lot were taking the distilled essence, put up in blue bottles, of these bundles I was telling you about.

This reminds me that I was telling you about having gone up home to Ross with my degree and everything, leaving Aunt Alice and Victor down on Clydeside and I was dancing fandangos like a mad thing, all in secret, when I received a rather umbrage-taken letter from Aunt Alice saying would I please give my correspondents my proper address as she was tired of redirecting letters. The redirecting that had made her so tired consisted of two letters from My Friend Muriel, one of which was to say she had heard from the girl in Australia again about how nice I was and the other of which was to ask me why I had not replied to her (Muriel's) last letter. If Aunt Alice had taken a proper full dose of umbrage she would not have written to me at all and she would not have redirected Muriel's letters, which just goes to show how a half-dosage of umbrage on somebody's part, or any other small accident, can have an out-of-proportion effect on the life of some other person. I wrote to Muriel giving her my home address; and my family being the permanent kind of institution that it is, this meant that Muriel could find me somehow, sometime, for ever after for as long as she wanted to, which was a great big long number of years as it fell out.

So I wrote a letter to Muriel telling her that I had finished my education now (silly phrase — only the living dead ever finish their education) but had not found a job yet and was at home for the present; and, of course, Muriel wrote back to say that was nice. Muriel was what was known as 'a great letter-writer' and always remembered people's birthdays and to ask after the health of their cats and things like that, and only in one letter at this time did she say anything that I remember word for word. She said: 'From its address, your home sounds very remote and lonely!!!!!' She was also a 'great user' of exclamation marks.

My home was remote, but I did not find it lonely. Better pens than mine have described the Highlands of Scotland, notably, in my opinion, Eric Linklater's, Seton Gordon's and Neil Gunn's in these modern times, and I do not propose to give what would be a poor imitation of them here, but in high summer I spent enchanted hours on a stretch of heather moor, sparsely studded with fir trees, with a floor of moss that was bejewelled with wild orchis and those greedy insect-eating plants, the butterwort and the sundew. And the sun slanted gold through the trees, and the bees hummed, and on the ridge of dry stones between moor and arable land, that 'strip of herbage strown, which just divides the desert from the sown', the wild thyme marched its purple legions across the grey boulders while the wild yellow broom popped the heavy artillery of its seed pods in the heat of the sun. And all this was on top of a hill, while below, the broad Firth, with its lesser firths reaching in between the hills, looked like a ragged cloak of silver-blue satin that some giant had thrown down, discarded, as he strode across this world full of summer heat.

No. I was not lonely. My family was there, and all their friends and neighbours, and everybody was very interested in what I was going to do now that I had a degree and a diploma and all. I tried to go on with, and hold on to, what I had there, with my gleams of poetry flashing across my brain as rapidly and brilliantly as kingfishers over a stream. I was not clever enough, or quick enough, yet to catch these kingfishers and find words to record their beauty for ever and ever before letting them fly away again, but given a little time I felt that I might attain some of the skill of that hunter who is a poet, that explorer who can go out, intrepidly, to remote places that most men cannot reach, and bring back for them, caught in a web of words, the strange, the exotic and the beautiful that are the inhabitants of these far, faery countries, like a Marco Polo returning from a spiritual Cathay.

In some islands of the Caribbean — this is a New Paragraph and has no obvious connection with the firm next door, for Caribbean Islands are not faery countries no matter what the travel agents may say — there is a plant called the sensitive mimosa. It grows by creeping along the ground, sending out from a central root long, thorn-laden, tendril-like branches which have little ferny leaves and which bear a blossom, a round fluffy ball, like the yellow mimosa balls that sell in the London shops, except that this ball is the pale purple colour of cottage lilac. If you walk across grassland where this mimosa grows you must tread on it — its very habit of growth renders it vulnerable — and the second it is touched, the feathery, ferny leaves shrivel up into dead-looking brownish twists and not for some hours will they open up into pretty leaves again. It seems to me that often young people are like this plant. By their very youth they are in a position to be trodden down by the generations, by their very nature they shrivel up when the heavy foot descends, and sometimes there are so many feet, one after the other, tramping along, that the wheel of time has turned too far before the leaves can open and then it is autumn and the frail leaves die for ever.

This treading-down process is seldom deliberate. Only a brute, or an eccentric with a morbid twist, or a child with its often brutal curiosity, would go out about the grasslands to look for sensitive mimosa with the purpose of causing it to shrivel, but in the wear-and-tear of day-by-day the mimosa suffers and quails. The peasant, after a long day in the banana cultivation, takes a short cut home across the grass and the mimosa shrivels where he steps; in the early morning, when the cool night has brought courage, it opens again, only to be trampled back by the cattle as they come grazing along; at high noon, when the leaves open again to the hot sun, the heavy wheels of the sugar-cane carts, grinding on their loaded way to the milling-house, leave new devastation in their wake. The mimosa does not die. It holds on, grimly, to the character with which nature has endowed it, but only seldom can it show itself in its full purple-tasselled, feathery-leaved beauty of small intricate tracery set in a broad spreading pattern of fantastically interwoven strong brown branches.

But I, bless your soul, was no mimosa plant. By nature I had been equipped with bigger, better thorns, and for a while I thought they were going to afford me complete protection. I knew that this strip of marginal land on a Ross-shire hillside was my mental climate and I wanted to stay there, and I spread my thorns which were in the form of a deep, low cunning. In my family it was impossible to say: 'I think I have it in me to become a writer.' If one had said that it would have been the equivalent of saying: 'I am Marie Antoinette.' My family would have sent for the doctor, had me certified and taken away in a plain van and hung their heads in the sight of their neighbours for ever afterwards. Or if the doctor by any chance had declared me sane enough, although a little odd, and I had persisted in my delusion, they would have sighed in a pained way and wondered aloud and by gesture and by implication why I should expect to be fed and clothed 'in idleness'. Either way, the mental climate I was trying to preserve for myself would have been lost.

So with the cunning of the fox I brought the conversation at meals round, as often as I could, to the Big Depression and the columns and columns of well-qualified people in the *Glasgow Herald* who were asking for employment, and I sighed and asked of the air around what sort of chance an inexperienced person like myself could have. All day I cleaned the house, cooked meals, washed clothes, made butter and milked cows with unflagging energy, for my grandmother was getting old and I knew that my aunt would get married and go away if only her conscience were clear about the welfare of her parents. And at night I wrote and scribbled by candlelight, and in the morning explained away this activity by 'this correspondence club that I am a member of' which was pronounced to be 'a harmless enough hobby', and so My Friend Muriel was brought into the thing, for I wrote to her occasionally to give colour to this lie about my nocturnal activities.

I spent a strenuous six months, but it was all to no avail. As far as the writing was concerned, I did not know my trade, and I think I was a little too tired physically to learn it in the night hours; but quite apart from that, the feet of the world were tramping very heavily and persistently. My aunt had dilly-dallied too long and her Malcolm went for a month's holiday to Edinburgh and came back married to his second cousin. Local sympathy was on the side of my aunt, but — have you ever lived with a proud-natured aunt who was being sympathised with against her will? Probably not, so I will tell you what such aunts try to do by way of finding an outlet for irritation, humiliation and all the other things they feel. They turn to *you* and say, a million times a day, directly and by implication: 'If *I* had had the chance *you've* had, *I* wouldn't be stuck here on this hill like a crow in a mist!' If I got around to it, I could write a book called *That Man Malcolm* and tell you about what he did to my aunt — or do I mean what he did to *me*?

Then, one day, the final tramping feet came along in the form of the well-polished, hand-made, brown brogues of Lady Lydia, between whom and my grandmother there was a long-standing, dignified friendship, so that when the one had a trouble or a joy she automatically turned to share it with the other.

It was a cold, frosty afternoon in January, or maybe February, when Lady Lydia tramped into our kitchen, stood her walking-stick in the corner by the window and came over to a chair by the fire, stripping off her hand-sewn hogskin gloves as she came, her beautiful fair skin flushed from the cold and the sudden warmth of the kitchen. My grandmother was baking scones, I remember, for she always had to be 'at' something and would bake whether we needed scones or not.

'I am in trouble, Mrs. Sandison,' said Lady Lydia.

'It's myself that's sorry to hear that, Leddy Lydia,' said my grandmother. 'Janet, be making some tea.'

I did as I was told, listening the while to Lady Lydia, for I liked her and admired her from her beautiful and open countenance to her pleasant voice and well-made clothes. The trouble, when explained, was that Lady Lydia's daughter Grace, who was married to a man who had a country place somewhere in Hampshire, was having a crisis among her domestic staff, to wit: the nurse that looked after her only baby, which was a three-months-old boy, had slipped on an icy puddle and broken her ankle and there was poor Grace, in the middle of the hunting season or something, with no nurse. It did not seem to me to be cataclysmic, but I had not learned then that troubles are very particular, personal things. What might be a devastating trouble to *you* in your life might be a mere flea-bite to *me* in my sort of life. People's lives are different and people's troubles are just as different as their lives. My grandmother was a wise old woman and she sympathised genuinely and from the heart with Lady Lydia and poor Grace — although she herself had brought up all her own children without benefit of nurse at all — and she was also a practical old woman and she at once began to cast around the countryside among the daughters of ploughmen and cattle-men to think of a girl who would go down to Hampshire for three months until Grace's nurse's ankle was better. But this girl that they thought of was too flighty and interested in the men and that one had hardly the appearance for a house like Lady Islington's, and the other one was 'a very nice lassie but terribly rough-spoken' and so on — but, standing by was one that was not (as far as *they* knew) flighty, who was tall and well-built with good teeth and who could be as 'smooth-spoken' as Uriah Heep if it would take her out of the orbit of her aunt and the devastation left by Malcolm. And this baby would go to bed at six at night or so and not have to have things fetched and carried for it all the time and have its hens fed and its cows milked like some people. So I said: 'Lady Lydia, would *I* do?' just bang-off like that and then waited for the heavens to fall. The heavens did not fall, but in the few seconds that elapsed after my question I learned more about my family than I had become aware of in all the nearly twenty-one years I had known it. The first astonishing fact that I noticed was that Lady Lydia, the wife of the local land-owner and terror of many county organisations, was far more afraid of my grandmother than I was. In her fear she went so far as to exhale her

36

breath in an involuntary whistle through her teeth as she cast her eyes upwards at the impending heavens. My family fell into an unexpected place in the Highland scheme of things. Lady Lydia belonged to what was known as the 'aristocracy', but it came home to me with a crash of thunder that there are all kinds of aristocracies — that Lady Lydia was of one kind and my grandmother of another kind, and that I was listening to a throne speaking to a throne. Gone were the tones in which they had discussed the ploughmen's and cattlemen's daughters, these beasts of the field to be used in the service of their natural masters should they be deemed suitable for the task to be done. My grandmother swung her girdle to the side of the fire, removed from it the last of her scones and sat down in her armchair.

'We could be considering that, maybe,' she said, as a great queen might direct that negotiations might be opened with some foreign power.

'It would be a wonderful solution,' said Lady Lydia tentatively, for she, after all, was the one who had sued in the first place for this discussion.

By the end of the week I was off to Wyke Hall, completely disguised as a children's nurse in a neat grey suit and overcoat and a suitcase full of blue dresses and white aprons and very becoming white veils (these last chosen by Lady Lydia), the whole weighted down with a large loose-leaf book of clean white paper and two fountain pens.

As a children's nurse I was a *succès fou* in what I choose to think is the literal, true, full sense of the phrase. I was a success at a job that any fool could have done and everyone behaved with a joy amounting to folly that I was such a success. Everyone congratulated everyone else and complete satisfaction was felt by one and all except me, but that did not matter because I was having a wonderful time in this strange new place. It is possible to be very happy without sitting back and clasping your hands over your paunch in a glow of satisfaction and I had all the world and time spread before me and it was a lovely world, far bigger and more beautiful and more full of all sorts of people and things than I had ever thought.

I lived in a very big room and a smaller room on the first floor of the house, with windows looking across a rolling park with big, fat trees in it, and spring was coming a little closer every day to that part of England. The baby sucked its bottle and wet its napkins, and a little maid called Ivy washed the bottles and the napkins and I washed the baby and took it out for walks in its perambulator and patted it on the back to make it belch. I enjoyed the walks very much although I cannot speak for the baby, for it was not a very communicative companion, but I did not object to that. I was not a very chatty or what is known as 'companionable' person myself, so the baby suited me very well. Its name was Adrian, after its father, and it was the fourth of a dynasty that had started about a hundred years before with old Hadrian Islington, who was born somewhere in Northumberland or Cumberland and had made a fortune in, I think, the wool trade. It is my fancy to think that this old man had probably been called after Hadrian's Wall but had pronounced, and consequently spelled, his name as 'Adrian' and had thus established this distinguished dynastic name but I have no proof of this. But this fourth Hadrian-Adrian that I was paid good money to feed porridge to as he began to outgrow the milk-bottle stage was the literal 'spitting' image of the first Hadrian on the dining-room wall, all except for the whiskers.

It is my considered opinion, formed at this time and consolidated in the time since then, that what My Friend Martha would call 'no ordinary amount' of nonsense gets talked about babies. In fact, there are more shibboleths about babies than about almost any other commodity — except maybe psychology — weight for weight. In fact, if you can build up a really good stuffed shirt of a shibboleth about babies you can make a packet of money out of it if you are that amoral sort of person. There are the feeding shibboleths and the routine ones, and dozens of good-going psychoanalysis ones, and all the other ones about the colour of the wall-paper and the patterns of curtains for them. Now, Martha's laundry-man, who is another friend of mine and has a lot of sense, would call this a 'lotta hooey', and so do I. No baby that is physically normal cares one damn about anything as long as you feed it at regular intervals. It does not care where it sleeps, for it is going to sleep, anyway; it does not care a hoot about the dear lickle woolly bunnies on its bed-cover because it can't eat them and it does not care tuppence if it is filthy dirty. Left to itself, it would stay in one place until the dirt and wet got uncomfortable and then it would roll to another place and get that wet and dirty too. And don't tell me that they can't move or do anything for themselves, babies. You try laying quite a small one down on quite a large bed while you go to the bathroom for a minute. You go putting a napkin on one that wants to be free to do things its own way and get a kick in the teeth for your pains.

Now, I do not dislike babies. I think babies are very sensible people who know exactly what they want and do not care whose feelings they hurt in order to get it, and this is much more sensible than being like many grown-up people who sacrifice themselves to suit other people and finish up in mental homes seething masses of frustration. When I think about how sensible babies are, I could write an ode about them, the selfish, egocentric little brutes.

But how I dislike with my whole crawling flesh the shibboleth of the Dear Little Stranger that every woman Who Is A Woman must lehrve googly-googly-goo and see how clever he is taking his nicey ottley-bottley when anyone in her sane senses can see that the creature is sucking in a frenzy of good, honest, primitive lust for food, which is a fine thing and damned healthy.

Young Adrian and I got along together very well. He was a normal healthy baby and I had been brought up to do as well as I could the job that came to my hand, so I gave him the care and attention that I was well paid to give him and he responded by thriving and, which was polite of him, appearing to prefer my knee and arms to any other knee and arms; so because Adrian responded in a normal way to reasonable treatment and preferred the armchair he was most used to to any other, it was decided that I was 'a born nurse' and that the baby 'adored' me. All this used to make me feel slightly queasy in my stomach, but the life, apart from the baby, had so much in it that was of fascinating interest to me that I did not annoy my employers by vomiting in front of their faces — or 'fornenst' their faces, as the Scottish Border would say with such telling effect.

The life of the house was divided into four parts, namely: 'the House', which meant Sir Adrian and Lady Islington; 'the Nursery', which meant Adrian, me and Ivy; 'the 'All', which meant the butler, his wife the cook and all the house servants; and 'the Outside', which meant the gardens, stables and garage, this last being a permanent battle-ground on which McNaught, the old head gardener from Fife, fought a running fight for domination against Molloy, the old head groom from County Cork. The entire population of the Hall, from Sir Adrian down to the youngest stable-boy, must have numbered some forty people, thirty-seven of whom were there because of three whose names were Islington — this was about the first fact that struck me and I noted it, baldly, as a fact, in a letter to my home. In his reply my father commented that 'Sir Adrian must be a valuable man to the district, in a position to provide so much work' and that 'It was a pity that so many of the big establishments were dying out of the countryside'.

I gave a great deal of thought to this. I could not see that work for its own sake was any true gift to any community. At the Hall, servants cleaned rooms that were used for nothing except to lie in half asleep after a hard day's golf, before having a meal and drifting off to bed. Maids polished furniture of hideous design and no value and dusted pictures of dead grouse whose canvas would have made excellent potato sacks. Gardeners grew grapes and peaches until everyone was sick of eating them and grooms polished the hides of horses that nobody bothered about out of the hunting season. Never have I seen so many people work so well and so conscientiously to no end except their weekly pay. I was troubled by all this human activity, some of it highly skilled, that went for naught by being non-constructive. All this work was contributed to Sir Adrian and his wife, and, reaching them, it reached the fire that consumed, the dead end, for these two did nothing. My only former experience of people in a like position was of Lady Lydia and Sir Torquil. Their establishment was smaller than that of the Islingtons, but there was a similar pyramid of labour designed towards the well-being of two people at the top and here the result was very different. Sir Torquil was a power in local government at home, and no muddle-headed power, but a man who knew well the people and the county that he helped to administer, while in private he was a naturalist of some distinction whose published works were of greater than mere local value. Lady Lydia, too, made her contribution to the world in the form of a great deal of interest in the tenantry and in the friendships which she established with people like my grandmother. She also took a vital and valuable interest in the workings of the local hospital, but apart from all these things, she had her own near-art or near-science, for she was something of an authority on needlework, both as a craftswoman and as a historian. Sir Adrian and Lady Islington, therefore, were something quite new to me. They were not useful, they were not decorative — indeed, they were a very mean and ornery (God bless America!) looking pair of people; they were not functional and they were not amusingly eccentric as was old Lady Ishbel, another neighbour of ours up at home. Lady Ishbel, in My Friend Martha's phrase, was *really* something. She invariably wore a long string of real, perfectly matched pearls when she went to feed her hens in order to indicate to them that they were required to lay eggs of a uniform, Grade A shape and size. The upkeep of Lady Ishbel, her pearls (which she was always catching on something and having to have re-strung) and her hens (which were always getting yaws or kindred complaints and dying) was considerable, and she required a lot of people to look after her, the pearls and the hens; but look, my friend, *look* at the entertainment and interest she provided. Lady Ishbel was value for every penny.

The Islingtons, as far as I could see, which might not have been very far, had no value for anybody or any penny. Now, I am a person like this: I am not a moralist or anything like that. I do not *care* about the ultimate end of the Islingtons one way or another — and do not know about their ultimate end either, come to that — but they were an infinite and sterile bore for anyone who had anything to do with them, which I *do* think is just about the *bottom*, don't you, dear, as the man said about the artesian well that was such a failure. What I am getting at really is that this house, Wyke Hall, was just about the most sterile hole I have ever lived in. The only one that was more sterile was the hole that took the place of the hut I had been living in on an airfield in 1940 when the landmine came down. The only difference was that the bomb-hole did not have two people sleeping in it after a hard day's tennis.

It seems to be that the essence of life is change, growth, development — call it what you like — and that the only things which man should leave untouched, make no effort to improve but preserve as they are, are the great works of art which rise from time to time, for no reason that I can see, like lilies out of a dung-hill and are true for *all* time. This does not mean that I am an advocate of change for its own sake. I should have told you, when I was taking rain-checks a few pages back, that I take a permanent rain-check on the cliché, especially the one that says: 'It is a nice change.' Have you noticed how this phrase is always spoken with bored sighs for punctuation? Thus: 'Sigh I like a kipper occasionally sigh it is a nice change from fish and chips prolonged sigh.'

The trouble with change is that you have to be very, very clever indeed to do it deliberately without doing more harm than good and you have to be much cleverer still to do it suddenly. Sudden change is the surgeon's knife of life and is justified only in cases of acute appendicitis, cancer and horrors of that kind. So I do not advocate that all occupants of 'halls' and great houses should be lined up against walls and shot before razing their homes to the ground. Oh no. I would go so far as to say that I would almost be prepared to shoot personally anyone who attempted to raze to the ground Chatsworth in Derbyshire, which is one of the largest and richest houses in England. No. No razings or mass shootings. No. And I say this not because the owners of Chatsworth will allow me to walk through some of their rooms and look at their beautiful possessions on payment of a small fee in these heavily-taxed times. I would be in favour of preserving Chatsworth and many others of its kind merely to know that they were *there*, for unless a vast number of artists and craftsmen have laboured in vain, which I flatly refuse to believe, all that stored beauty must be an influence for good, even if the influence is felt directly by only one or two people who own and live in each of these houses.

The house where I 'nursed' Adrian and the people who lived in it were horses (there was a deal of emphasis on the horse) of quite another colour, and I think and hope that the gradual change of the last twenty years is quietly eroding them away. No razing, mark you. They are disappearing by a smooth-running but deadly economic progress and that is very fitting, for from deadly economics were they made and to a deader than dead economic grave they will return. They were not all 'halls' exactly similar to that of the Islingtons. Some of them were castles and some of them were villas, cringing behind iron railings and laurels in their attempt to avoid the dust of the busy city streets, but from castle, through hall, to villa they were all the product of wealth controlled by the wrong hands, hands without sensitivity or taste, hands of two uses only: to grab and to hold down, with the grip of death. These were the hands that grabbed the wealth produced by other men's work and used it to build their architectural monstrosities. These were the hands that held down in a death grip the people who worked for them until they had killed the dignity of work even among their intimate servants, so that 'good service' is now, regrettably, an obsolete phrase for a commodity that no longer exists. These were the hands that came from shirt-sleeves and are going back to shirt-sleeves in three or four generations — and a good thing too.

My Friend Muriel — here we go again — pursued me to Hampshire in a letter redirected from home and I wrote to her from the Hall, telling her what had happened, and she wrote back to me saying That was very nice and Hampshire was lovely in the spring. I had the sense to realise that it would be pointless to write to Muriel saying that, for me, Hampshire in the spring was one long winter of discontent where, in spite of the beauty of the surrounding country, I found the atmosphere in the house so sterile that I could not put pen to paper, so I wrote back to Muriel and said, Yes wasn't it, but this was only temporary and I was looking forward to a move.

A completely absurd thing had happened at the beginning of my stay with the Islingtons. On my first evening in the house

Lady Islington made a longish speech to me which I found extremely embarrassing, to the effect that she quite realised that I was not 'a normal servant' and ending, after much circumnavigation, with the announcement that she and Sir Adrian had decided that I must descend from the nursery and have my evening meals with them in the dining-room. Nothing could have pleased me less. One of my reasons for taking the job had been the prospect of undisturbed evenings, but when I tried, with tact, to indicate that I would prefer to dine alone it was taken that I was overwhelmed by her gracious condescension and I was coyly admonished: 'Oh, come now, you mustn't be shy, Miss Sandison, and we don't dress elaborately!' I could have slain her. So evening after evening I listened to diatribes on the iniquitous character of my fellow-servants in the house while the butler was out of hearing, and when he was in the room I listened to details of all the golf handicaps in the district. Now, I am a person like this: a trigonometric slide-rule is a thing I can understand and can use, but I have never been able to whip up a jot of interest in the mathematics of golf. I think I have an over-simple mind or something, but to me a game is a game and a mathematical formula a mathematical formula, and that is that.

At intervals of five days or a week, however, there would be dinner-parties when we had bigger and better discussions about servants and more plentiful details and finer shades of golf, and at one of these I told the young man on my left that I was leaving the Hall next week as the real nurse was coming back. I probably made the remark because my imminent departure was my Favourite Thought at the time. He asked out of politeness where I was going when I went away, and before I could reply my employer bawled merrily down the table as was her wont: 'I've begged and *begged* her to stay but she won't! She wants to be a secretary. Does anyone want a highly commended secretary?'

I felt like a goldfish in a great big bowl. Raw red rage filled me — I was one of the very red sort of goldfish — and then a man across the table said: 'By Jove! The very thing! Just the very thing! My cousin's husband — you know old Eddie — *he* wants a secretary! Funny how things are, aren't they?'

A storm of talk broke out and my goldfish character disappeared and I became a straw in a gale. Before anyone could wink a telephone call had been made to 'Old Eddie' in his home in Devon, I was led to the instrument like a beast to the slaughter, and I turned into Eddie's secretary at the third lot of 'pip-pip-pip' from the telephone exchange.

Now, I hope I am a person like this: I hope I give credit where credit is due. These Islington people and their friends were kind, and an inexperienced youngster like me was very lucky to have opportunity dropped into her lap by people for whom I had done nothing except what I was well paid to do, which was to keep their offspring from interfering with their golf. But I fear I am also a person like this: I find it difficult to accept help from people I do not like. This is probably due to an ungracious stand-offishness which is a characteristic of my race, for as Robert Burns said of the Highlands:

'There's nothing here but Heilan' pride, Heilan' scab an'
    hunger,
And surely when he sent me here, the Lord was in His
    anger.'

At all events, I went to bed that night a committed secretary to Old Eddie and in high dudgeon.

My Friend Monica (remember her?) and I once had a long discussion about dudgeons, high and low. Monica was educated in a convent in Paris, was bilingual and quite often seemed to me to think like a Frenchwoman. She maintained that high dudgeon was a state that applied to women only and that it was the mental equivalent of being 'en grande tenue' sartorially, and for Monica 'en grande tenue' had a meaning that was not translatable into English. A woman 'en grande tenue' is not a woman in full evening dress and diamonds; she is not a woman in her best clothes; she is very seldom any woman but a Frenchwoman and usually a Parisian at that, and she is a woman who is out to make a kill. Thus, for Monica, high dudgeon was a suit of mental clothing that was assumed for the kill. Logical enough, I granted after the fourth drink or so, but I maintained that Highland high dudgeon was quite different. Having headed Monica off a number of rude references to Macbeth, I told her about it. It is my conviction that high dudgeon is a dollop of visible silence, something like ectoplasm, of a riotous tartan pattern, that you step inside, with which it goes bump-bump-bump up a wide flight of bare wooden stairs, giving off the while a smell of brimstone. The higher the dudgeon, the brighter the tartan, the more numerous the stairs and the more overpowering the smell. So Monica said something vulgar in French and ordered another drink.

A week or so later, when I departed for Devonshire and Eddie, I had slid down the banisters and come out of my dudgeon (you bump up the stairs *in* it and slide down the banisters when you come out of it, I should have mentioned), for I had thought things over, had decided that I was an ungrateful wretch, and the fact that Eddie was a dentist had endeared him to me, for I still thought with affection of Cockabendy. When he met me at the station with his car, though, he was not a cheery bouncer like Cockabendy at all, but a small, dark, harassed-looking person, whose eyes darted about in a worried-looking way as if they feared that he had gone and pulled out the wrong tooth *again* and somebody was bound to catch him out this time. I felt sorry for him in that very first moment.

Before the first evening was over I felt more sorry for him than ever. The house was a large, forbidding, grey villa on the outskirts of town, and it was full of grey carpets, brown furniture, buff wallpaper, tan curtains, slate and chocolate paint and black fireplaces. It was of an infinite dreariness, and even the dusty feeling had a heavy weightiness that seemed to burden the body as well as the spirit. Eddie's wife was a large woman, taller than he was, with sallow skin and a tendency to pimples, but that may have been her condition, for she was heavily pregnant. Before the evening meal was over, a meal which was served by a skinny resentful-looking parlourmaid in an atmosphere of napkins in tight, yellowed-ivory, numbered rings and hissed complaints as to the food and service by the mistress of the house, I was painfully aware of three things:

(1) Eddie and his wife had five daughters and were now imminently expecting their sixth child which was to be a son.

(2) The house, the furniture and most of the family money belonged to Eddie's wife, who was a woman who took pride of ownership of possessions.

(3) Eddie's wife disapproved of me wholeheartedly.

In explanation of how I arrived at the above knowledge I have to tell you that I think I must be a person like this: I think I am person with long ears that are sensitive to all sorts of intonations that people do not intend to put into their voices at all and hardly a word is spoken in my hearing that goes unheard.

In a 'backward area' of the world I have visited, where the native population speaks an English that is still partly that of the Authorised Version of the Bible in certain meanings, a man will say: 'I do not hear you.' When this was first said to me, I used to raise my voice a little, enunciate more clearly and speak more slowly, only to be encountered with the repeated: 'I do not hear you, ma'am.' Eventually I discovered that what was meant was: 'I do not understand you.'

I think that there are two kinds of listeners in the world. There are those who hear the words that are spoken, attribute to them a single familiar meaning and no more, and there are those who hear with an understanding, greater or less, of what lies behind the words. The number of people with this latter type of hearing seems to be on the decrease and that is probably, as My Friend Twice says (he is a new one but more of him later), because 'there is far too much speaking goes on in the world'. Twice has a very intricate, detailed attitude to words, perhaps because he is an engineer and has an intricate, detailed sort of mind, and 'speaking' to him is merely a noise made by the human voice, 'talking' is social intercourse between man and man of a trivial kind and the human voice is only, for him, of any permanent value when it is 'saying something'. He complains frequently of the amount of 'speaking' that is done and claims, I think with justification, that it prevents people from 'hearing' when someone 'says something'.

Well, during the First Supper Eddie and Eddie's wife were 'talking' in Twice's sense and I was sitting there 'hearing' in the Authorised Version sense, and what I have told you is what I heard. And also, forbye and besides, I can prove that I heard aright, for about six weeks later we came to the Last Supper and that was really something. But here we have to go back and recapitulate my six weeks at 'Sandringham', for that was the name of the Villa.

A fortnight after my arrival two things happened. I had a letter from My Friend Muriel, redirected from the Hall, and Eddie's wife gave birth to her sixth daughter. During this first fortnight, which was very much of a 'lying-in' period for Eddie's wife, I had learned the rudiments of my job, which, in truth, consisted of nothing other than rudiments which were very easily learned. I was required to do nothing except answer the telephone and keep the appointment book for Eddie and his young assistant in order, type a few letters, attend to the ordering and maintaining of a few stocks of supplies, send out the accounts and keep in order a very simple book-keeping system and a card-index record of the patients' teeth. It left plenty of time to write poetry, for anyone who could write poetry in a buff-coloured room with a dusty paper fan in the fireplace, surrounded by the smell of disinfectant and anaesthetics, with the words molar and incisor echoing from every wall and complete sets of false teeth grinning from glass cases, not to mention a natty drawing of a human skull, cloven from helm to halse as was the skull of De Bohun by Robert the Bruce, to show all the teeth, the palate and the passages to nose, throat and ears, which hung in a frame over the mantelpiece. It was a cheery sort of place, this room where I worked, and very spiritual and that, right down to the monkey puzzle tree (and if you do not understand my slang, read auricaria) which grew and spread its macabre branches right outside the window.

About the second day that the curtain went up 'discovering' me, as they say in the theatre world, sitting at this table in this room with the telephone in front of me, the said telephone rang and it was, the voice said, the Nurse in charge of Lady Somebody who was asking, at the instructions of Lady Somebody's doctors, that Eddie should appear at Lady Somebody's house that afternoon and 'consult' on the subject of Lady Somebody's teeth. In my very limited experience, people who had sore teeth went to the dentist, so I made suitable noises at the telephone, said I would call back shortly and waylaid Eddie between extractions to ask him if he felt like going, bag and baggage, out into the middle of Dartmoor — or do I mean Exmoor? — to look at Lady Somebody's teeth. The response was extraordinary. I thought Eddie was going to fall upon me and embrace me.

'Lady Somebody?' he gasped. 'Good *gracious*! Oh, my goodness! Oh dear! Oh yes! Tell them yes! Yes. Listen, you'll have to come too! Get ready!'

'Me? What for?' I asked.

'Notes!' said Eddie, very flustered. 'Yes. Oh, goodness, yes! Notes! Get ready!'

We drove about twenty miles out to a big house on the other side of the moor and I took notes. In four weeks we drove about ten times all these miles and I took masses of notes. I have never known anybody with more notes about her teeth than Lady Somebody, the hypochondriacal old cow, but what did I care? Eddie and I were doing fine. Eddie took on all the earmarks of the Man Who Was Made, and at the end of the third week I put an appointment in our book for the Hon. Mrs. Someone-Else and underlined it in red, for, slow-witted as I am, I was beginning to catch on to the fact that I was seeing a Fashion Being Born. By the end of the fifth week we were pulling all the richest mouths in the town into our surgery at 'Sandringham' hand over fist, and turning the less rich ones away with the excuse that we were sorry we had to go out to Lady Somebody's today and Eddie took an hour off to order a new suit.

But, as my grandmother would tell you, 'Pride goeth before a fall', and, as Twice would tell you, 'Whatever goes up has to come down'. Something came down and something fell.

Oh yes. Mrs. Eddie got up out of child-bed, came down and the heavens fell.

Even now, nearly thirty years later, I cannot think of that evening without a hot flush of embarrassment beginning to glow somewhere inside my chest. Eddie, as usual, rose from the supper-table and went to his office and I drifted towards the staircase and my bedroom, but Mrs. Eddie gestured towards the drawing-room and indicated that she wished to speak to me. In there, with the door closed on the buff walls, the grey carpet and the brown furniture, a dreadful change came over her — her face seemed to disintegrate like the wall of a dam that had burst, and this was precisely what had happened. She was almost inarticulate with rage, jealousy, frustration and turbulent unhappiness born of all three. She gibbered of her knowledge of all my 'tricks' of 'making up to' her husband while she, suffering and helpless, bore his children. She gibbered a great deal of many wrongs, and it was as if the stone slab that was her mind had been turned over to expose a wriggling mass of putrid corruption. I backed away from her, for I was afraid for the first time in my life, with the fear of the utterly unknown and unsuspected, and contrived to indicate that I would leave the house as early as possible the next morning. I could not have done a worse thing, for then she began to plead with me: 'No! No! If you go, he will know I have spoken to you!' She gripped my arm. I shook her off. I did not care what happened to her or to him. A mask of dreadful cunning slid over her features. 'There is no need to be precip-cipitate!' Saliva spurted with the syllables. 'As long as you realise that he is MINE!'

That made me laugh with a dreadful laughter such as devils must laugh as they look upon the tortures of the damned, but she thought it was the laughter of scorn, I think, and she sat down and started to cry, the sobs jerking out between short phrases: 'Cruel — he doesn't care — all I have given him —'

I went up to my room at the top of the house and barricaded the door by pulling a chest of drawers across it. I packed my clothes, and, of all things, I wrote a letter to My Friend Muriel, put a stamp on it and put it in my handbag. The letter said nothing at all, but I wrote it so that, after I had gone from 'Sandringham', none of Muriel's blue envelopes would arrive bearing my name. I thought it would be better for Eddie if this did not happen, although any real betterment for Eddie was, I realised, a very forlorn hope. After that, I sat on the edge of the bed and waited for the morning. I had almost seventeen pounds in money and I thought I would go to London. I had never seen London, but knew it was fairly large, with plenty of people around it, and I thought they would help me to forget Mrs. Eddie.

The servants' rooms were up a short flight of stairs from mine, and as soon as they began to move from their beds I unbarricaded my door and caught the skinny parlourmaid as she came past, drawing her into my own room.

'Ethel, will you help me down the back stairs with this stuff?'

'Coo!' she commented, looking at the packed cases. 'Goin'?' She sucked her teeth. 'Don't blame you after the way she was goin' on in the drawin'-room last night. Goin' myself when I've saved one more quid.'

'Oh?'

'Not 'arf! Sick o' bein' treated like a dawg and now this 'ere new one's a girl — cor! Well, c'm'on!'

With surprising skinny, wiry strength, she lifted one end of the trunk and took a suitcase in her other hand. We made our way down the back stairs, where she pushed her head into the kitchen. 'Hi! Ellen!'

The cook came into the passage. 'Miss Sandison's goin'. Get up an' hold that bell while I phone for a taxi!'

Their backstairs organisation was remarkable. Ellen climbed on a kitchen chair and put a finger between the hammer and the gong of the telephone bell while Ethel lifted the receiver in the front hall and called a friend named Stan at the local garage. The taxi was at the back door almost as soon as Ellen had descended from the chair.

'Why you goin'?' she asked then.

'If you'da heard old Pimple Face last night, you'd know why!' said Ethel. 'Always suspicionin' folks! Same way you an' me is goin', that's why!'

'So long as you ain't pinched anythin',' said Ellen. 'I don't 'old with pinchin'. Well, good luck!'

She returned to the kitchen with the chair.

'Is Ellen just waiting for the last pound too?' I asked Ethel. I was entranced by the whole situation and organisation.

'No. Only ten bob. She's better at the savin' than me. Well, c'm'on. I got the dinin'-room to do.'

I got into the taxi. Ellen came running from the kitchen and thrust a paper packet into my hand.

'San'wich!' she said. 'Cold beef an' marge — best I could do!'

'Cor!' Ethel sucked her teeth. 'We ain't arf goin' to 'ave fun this morning' when 'Er Nibs wakes up!'

The taxi was moving away. I thrust two of my precious pounds into Ethel's hand. 'Have *plenty* of fun!' I said. 'One's for you and one's for Ellen!'

'Jumpin' Jesus!' She stood stunned in the backyard, the money in her hand, then leaped into the air, ran after my cab and thrust an envelope through the open window. 'That came last night — was on the 'all table. An' listen, THANKS!'

As I have told you already, at that age I was a person like this: I was very down one moment and very up the next, and as the cab rattled to the station where I was going to have to wait three hours for the London train, Stan told me, I was away, away up and finding the world a wonderful place in the fine summer morning.

The station was a particularly ugly and interesting one, a country junction, gay with incongruous flowers, the sort of station that is like a moth-eaten old barrister who is in retirement in his country garden most of the time and still wearing the grey 'city' suits that he has always worn, but who emerges, occasionally, to handle a case, in a blare of bustle and publicity. When the London express was half an hour away there was a girding of loins, a shaking of robes out of moth-balls and the vague country gentleman changed into a slick 'power-to-be-reckoned-with'. I am very partial to countrified railway stations because of their remarkably consistent hideousness, from the overall standpoint of their siting — how they are plonked down quite without reference to their surroundings — down to the merest detail of their decoration, the last battered tin-plate advertising the obsolete remedy for stomach trouble.

Railway stations are 'functional, of course'. I put these last three words in quotation-marks because I have decided to tell you here, although why here and not on some other page of this book unless it is part of My Art, that we are a family like this: we are a family that has 'sayings', and 'functional, of course' is one of them. And Twice is a person like this: as far as design is concerned he knows what he does NOT like, but I must say that I have never known him particularly to admire a piece of furniture or anything without it turning out to be a piece that people who really *know* will tell you is a masterpiece of its kind. It seems that Twice has 'an eye' — maybe it is on account of being an engineer and I think it is definitely because he is an engineer of Scottish training that he is so outspoken out of his quite extraordinarily coarse vocabulary.

He and I were taken once to an exhibition of fearfully arty pottery by two Friends of Mine called Miranda and Hugo — I say Friends of Mine because Twice only puts up with them because I happen to know them — and I do not think that Miranda and Hugo are their real names; I think they only chose them because they think they are 'fun'. Anyway, they take us to this exhibition and it was one of these occasions where everything is awkward. The exhibits were awkward to start with, and the people showing them to you were awkward, for they were dying for you to buy something but their code did not allow of that sort of prostitution of their art, and Twice is simply awkward, anyway, and I felt awkward, because I know about his awkwardness at awkward exhibitions. So a man with long hair led us to a table where rested an amazingly ugly poison green sort of basin with two handles which did not quite match. We all stood saying nothing, although Miranda and Hugo went in for a sort of appreciative *breathing* — you know how arty people do.

53

I heard Twice's voice say: 'What's it for?'

'Salad bowl,' said the long-haired man.

'Thought it was a chamber-pot!' Twice hissed at me, and the man heard enough to know that we did not want to buy it.

'Functional, of course!' he said, with a dismissive wave of the hand, turning to some models of dachshunds, in case we were the doggy sort.

'Functional?' Twice said, with his straight, blue-eyed stare. 'So also, I am informed, is the fundamental orifice of a donkey.'

You understand what I mean by 'awkward'?

Monica says that 'awkward' is a thing shaped roughly like a bird, but it does not sing like a nightingale or fly like a sea-gull or yield feathers like an ostrich. Instead, it moans like the wind in a chimney, paddles itself along the ground with flippers like a seal on land, gives off puffs of stuff that smell like hot mutton fat at the front door, and its natural habitat is the drawing-room when adolescents are present. That is what Monica says. I know, for a certain fact, that 'awkward' is simply Twice faced with an affectation of any sort.

Well, railway stations are 'functional, of course' and I think I must be a person like this: I do not like the unalloyed functional unless it is truly and absolutely hideous enough to have the attraction of sheer ugliness. The functional that is unobjectionable tends to be arid, like one of these kitchens that would freeze you or electrocute you or something if you started shelling peas in it instead of bringing the peas home, decently shelled already, in a frozen package. The kind of kitchen I like is one where the dog scratches himself under the table and has to be put out because of the hairs if you are about to beat an egg and with rows of jars marked 'Rice' and 'Mixed Spice', where you keep the sugar in a biscuit tin and a few odds and ends of string in the jar marked 'Sugar' because it is not really large enough for the sugar the family needs. But all this is another digression. . . .

In the end, at this station, after I had eaten Ellen's sandwiches, the London train came in and and I got on board. It was after I had been in the train for quite a time that I remembered the letter I had been given by Ethel before I left. And who *do* you think it was from? My Friend Muriel? No. You are wrong. The envelope was addressed in Muriel's indeterminate hand, which was probably why I forgot about it. Muriel was inclined, always, to get forgotten about by everybody if they had the least bit of anything else to think about or do. The letter inside the envelope was in a hand quite different, the hand of no other than Mrs. Whitely-Rollin, and a determined, bold, flourishing, almost brandishing sort of hand it was. It informed me that it had been most disappointed to discover that I had left the Hall and had taken another post, as it had had it in mind to offer me the post of second secretary to itself when my temporary engagement at the Hall ended. It had been depending on Miss Thornton, it said, to discover when this might be, but apparently I did not find any difficulty in finding posts, even in these times. (I wondered what the bold hand would think of the lack of difficulty I had in losing posts too.) It was writing now to inform me that if my present post was not to my liking it was prepared to keep its offer open for a short time. It went on to say that the Chain of Friendship, being a voluntary organisation, could not offer a high salary, but that the secretaries were treated as part of the family in what, it believed, was a very pleasant household. And it was mine sincerely. That was the gist of it. So, by the time I arrived at Paddington, I had made up my mind. I took a taxi to Victoria, caught a train to this town in Kent and took a room for the night at the Station Hotel. At eleven the next morning, I called without warning on Mrs. Whitely-Rollin.

Part II

Part II

Part II

Whitely House was another villa. If you are beginning to think that this is a tour of the villas of England, I do not blame you, but would remind you that villas are thick on the ground of England. It was of pleasanter aspect than 'Sandringham', however, enclosed by a high stone wall and with some real green grass around it. It was called 'Whitely House' and did not admit in any way to being a villa. When the front door, at which I rang, was opened by a manservant in a green baize apron, the first thing I saw was a huge suit of armour, with its arms sticking out in front of it and clutching between its hands a long weapon of the kind, I believe, which is called a halberd and which reached within a few inches of the ceiling. From the door, I followed the manservant in a semi-circular course round the armour, which took me almost into an obvious dining-room, round to the foot of the staircase and back on another tack to the door of the drawing-room on the side of the hall opposite to the dining-room. The servant opened this door to disclose a small white-haired woman at a large writing-table, spoke my name and went away.

Now, I am a person like this: I dislike all awkwardness even when it is originated by My Friend Twice, and I will 'go a bonnie length', as they say in south Scotland, to avoid it, so I went quite a length that morning. I told Mrs. Whitely-Rollin that I had been dissatisfied with my post at 'Sandringham' and had fortunately received her letter on the very day of my departure. I know that this was truth so naked as to be practically a skeleton, but already I had formed the impression that Mrs. Whitely-Rollin was a person like this: she was a person who had great faith in her own judgment, who had made up her mind that I would be a suitable second secretary for herself. Why should I create an awkwardness by telling her that I was fresh from an accusation of husband-abduction? After a pleasant chat lasting half an hour, I went back to the hotel, fetched my bags and took up residence at Whitely House, just in time to wash and come down to lunch.

In the drawing-room now, in addition to Mrs. Whitely-Rollin, was a tall, thin man of about sixty, I thought, with a wizened look, steel-rimmed glasses that hooked round his ears, and a long narrow mouth that had a toothless, concave look despite the fact that he had teeth. He took me by surprise by being Mr. Whitely-Rollin — I had somehow formed the opinion that Mr. Whitely-Rollin was decently defunct a long time ago. Then I began to get the impression that there was a lot of concavity about Mr. Whitely-Rollin and that his mind was withdrawn into itself in a way very similar to the indrawn look of his mouth. Indeed, Mr. Whitely-Rollin was giving a very good imitation of a man who was not really present, acting the part of the decently defunct.

'Where *is* Muriel?' Mrs. Whitely-Rollin asked of the air in a voice that was almost cross and added, in a voice that dripped with syrup: 'Dear silly girl, so conscientious, always working!'

And then Muriel came in. She seemed to edge her way round the door-lintel, yet it was an edging movement clumsily carried out by a large woman who could have been St. Gertrude's terror of the hockey field or St. Fanny's fast bowler. At this time, Muriel was twenty-six, being five years my senior, and her dominating feature was her wavering, dithering uncertainty. She was incapable of making a clean, clear movement and she was equally incapable of keeping still. She was irritating and pathetic at one and the same time.

At lunch Mrs. Whitely-Rollin dominated the conversation from an end, which became the head, of the table. I suppose that, in the light of my attempt to describe Mr. Whitely-Rollin, to remark on her domination is a crashing statement of the obvious. Naturally enough, I suppose, most of her conversation was directed at me as the newcomer to the household.

Now, we Highlanders are, in general, persons like this: we are persons who do not care for being enquired into too much and we hate like hell any attempt to dominate us; and next to being the dominating type, Mrs. Whitely-Rollin was very much the enquiring type. So a fine running skirmish started straight away, a sort of border raiding brought up to date. Mrs. Whitely-Rollin made a sortie by enquiring what my father's profession was, and I replied that he farmed, which was hardly a profession, I thought, and made a quick sally myself by asking if she had any interest in agriculture. She replied with a little self-indulgent laugh that she was interested in *every*thing, but her voice indicated that she was the one who was asking the questions around here. She then went through a sort of *reculer pour mieux sauter* while the pudding was served and I dug my heels into the native heath and waited. She made an onslaught by asking if my father owned the farm. I replied in the negative.

'I see,' she said. 'A tenant farmer.'

'No,' I said.

'Oh,' she said.

I said nothing. For a moment a large 'awkward' as visualised by My Friend Monica came and squatted in the middle of the table and, disliking 'awkwards' as I do, I added when it had started to smell of the mutton fat: 'It is a family farm and my grandfather, the present owner, is still alive.'

I think that was the moment when Mrs. Whitely-Rollin began to dislike me, but it took her a long time to admit it, even to herself, for she was not one to admit, if she could help it, that she had made a mistake. I, however, as a secretary and member of her household, was probably one of the biggest mistakes she ever made, and in the end she had to admit it, albeit her method of making the admission was peculiarly her own.

The next morning, after a little general talk at the breakfast-

61

table from Mrs. Whitely-Rollin, I was turned over to Muriel to be initiated into my duties and the mysteries of the Chain of Friendship. I have indicated at an earlier stage that I am not an admirer of the strictly functional, and that is true. I think the odds and ends of string that are housed in the sugar jar are symbolic of the curious genius which is an overriding characteristic of that mongrel, the Britisher. I do not know whether his genius is his because he is a mongrel but I am inclined to think so. It emerges in its full, finest and most brilliant flower in the British soldier, sailor or airman, or, rather, it emerges most strongly out of groups of them. If a group of the lowest rank of airmen, or airwomen for that matter, are set down in any building and told to live there, they will proceed to live there in a curious, clean, clever squalor which they seem to generate for their own comfort, with all sorts of devices to enable them to do the forbidden thing, such as smoking tobacco, without ever being caught in the act or having it proven circumstantially against them. This is achieved largely by adapting an unlikely instrument to an improbably use, like keeping the string in the jar marked sugar.

The above being my belief, the office of the Chain of Friendship should have positively bristled with genius of a British kind, for it was actually a room which had been originally designed as, I think, a small servants' hall, supplemented by a pantry and a small laundry of sorts. It was all semi-basement and rather dark, and rather dirty as well, for Mrs. Whitely-Rollin was an economical housekeeper, employing only the man-servant and his wife who cooked, and neither had the time to penetrate to the 'office'. This was the domain of My Friend Muriel and it was quite without genius. Here, the ruling principle of using the unlikely for the improbable was nullified, for Muriel did not ever put anything anywhere, she did what she called 'laying things down'.

'How many members are there in the Chain?' I asked, anxious to show interest and intelligence.

'Oh dear — there's a list of them somewhere. I laid it

down just yesterday. Is it over there? Well, never mind now. I must get on.'

'All right. What would you like me to do?' I asked, for she looked harassed.

'Well — well — I have to get on —' she hesitated.

I wandered through to the laundry part and viewed a heap of discarded envelopes that filled a stone sink.

'Where's the waste-paper basket?' I asked.

'It should be somewhere. I had it yesterday and laid it down. I have to get on.'

While Muriel 'got on', which meant that she sat askew on a chair and clattered away inaccurately on a rickety old typewriter, I cleaned and tidied the rooms, leaving Muriel like a tousle-headed, carbon-blacked island surrounded with a reef of jumbled papers in the middle. By the end of about a week of Muriel 'getting on' and me smoothing out and dusting papers of all shapes and sizes, I was beginning to realise how the Chain of Friendship worked. Mrs. Whitely-Rollin attended to all the men and the more 'interesting' women personally, giving them the benefit of her views on everything and sending them lots of 'heartfuls of love over the wide and stormy seas' that separated Whitely House from other places. I did not see all that she wrote in these letters, of course, for no copies were kept (and just as well, for the old laundry was at bursting point already) but I gathered from her conversation that she was all things to all men and a helping hand to the 'interesting' women, who were all woman that she felt sorry for. I came to learn that Mrs. Whitely-Rollin was not interested in, and could not like, any women that she could not feel sorry for, but I have never seen anyone with so much pity for other women as she had. Oh yes. I must say that she had plenty of pity. Muriel and I got lots of it, for we were in the category of 'poor motherless girls' and Mrs. Whitely-Rollin told us nearly every day how pathetic we were and how much she pitied us and how she was doing her very best to make us feel that we had mothers after all.

Now this suited Muriel very well, it seemed, for Muriel had a slavish devotion for Mrs. Whitely-Rollin, but the trouble was that the old dame had picked her two daughters rather carelessly, for, if there is anything in heredity at all, I do not think that any woman could have produced two people as different as Muriel and myself. I do not know what Muriel's innermost thoughts were but outwardly she and Mrs. Whitely-Rollin used to have many a sentimental wallow in each other, but I knew exactly how *I* felt. I had had a mother of my own who died when I was ten years old, and I knew that Mrs. Whitely-Rollin was no suitable substitute for her while, also, I had conditioned myself in the eleven years that had elapsed since her death to being a person like this: a person whose mother had died and that was that.

From the odds and ends of this and that that I have read from time to time I gather that an escape mechanism is quite a common psychological feature, and different people develop different mechanisms to deal with different situations. Apparently, when I was twenty-one I was a person like this: my main method of escape from a situation that annoyed, embarrassed or irked me in any way was into mischief. I had an urge to turn the thing into One Big Laugh, and at Whitely House I had a whale of a time. It was One Big Laugh from morning till night.

To begin with, the name 'Whitely-Rollin' had always amused me, and it amused me more when I discovered that Mrs. Whitely-Rollin had married plain James Rollin and had tacked her own name on to the front of his to gain 'distinction'. The rhythm of the double name linked itself in my mind with the ballad that commemorates the Battle of Hohenlinden, for some unknown reason, so that one morning when the sweetness of motherhood became the sourness of black rage when Muriel had 'laid down' a letter somewhere and it could not be found, I burst into verse as soon as our employer had waddled angrily out of the office:

The Chain of Friendship grew apace,
The secretaries lost the place,
And black with anger was the face
Of ex-Miss Whitely — rollin'.

Muriel, who was in floods of tears and looking even plainer and clumsier than usual, shook the hair out of her eyes and sobbed at me: 'I n-never *heard* a person say things like that! Oh dear, I must get on!'

'Don't be silly!' I said and gave Muriel a good shaking.

'You mustn't say things like that! She's w-wonderful and —'

'Oh, fiddlesticks! And she *does* roll. But never mind that. Listen, we're going to systematise all this junk!'

'Sys— How?'

'By card index. Come on, fetch over that heap of soul's outpourings that came in this morning.'

As if mesmerised, Muriel did as she was told and we began. It took three weeks of hard, secret work, but at the end of that time the office no longer depended on Muriel's memory, which had had all the efficiency, formerly, of the escape mechanism of a hunted beast, for that memory had been the sole bulwark between her and the rage of Mrs. Whitely-Rollin.

When I say that the work was secret, you will see the depth of my low cunning. I had no desire to run, obviously, athwart the bows of my employer, for my family had not yet recovered from my sudden departure from 'Sandringham'. In general, they thought that my excuse that I did not like the post was an impertinence on the part of an inexperienced creature like myself, a spitting in the face of the Big Depression, a gesture which they distrusted. Also, I had a suspicion that if Mrs. Whitely-Rollin and I came to too soon a parting of our ways and brass-rags my luck in finding new employment might cease to hold, so there I was, caught between the upper mill-stone of my mischievous temperament and the nether mill-stone of my socio-economic situation. I put it to you as a thought for consideration that this position of the human being is the essence of all comedy and tragedy. The only difference between Boccaccio's cuckold and me is the difference in the size and material of the millstones. But to come right down to brass tacks, though why brass I have never known, I was in constant danger at Whitely House of Going Too Far.

This would not have been difficult to do. In the intellectual life of the little town Madame X (as Mrs. Whitely-Rollin was now figuring in my mind owing to the Whitely-Rollin connection with Hohenlinden and my tendency to giggle whenever I thought of the hyphenated combination) sailed like a galleon, and Muriel and I were supposed to bob along like coracles in her wake. Nothing of any consequence took place that we did not grace with our presence, from imperialist rallies to the second-rate opera company's visit to the local playhouse. Things like meetings of the Labour Party and the films that came to the local cinema were, of course, beneath our notice, and we did not attend any church because our Chain Embraced All Creeds. Also, Madame X disliked anything that meant getting out of bed in the morning, but this was never mentioned. Come to that, beds were never mentioned either — we lived on a frightfully spiritual plane.

I was frightfully bad at this coracle-in-the-wake business and could never take it seriously, because we appealed to me as being quite extraordinarily funny. Madame X was at her best sitting at her writing-table, for when she walked it became obvious that her sedentary habits had made her too broad for her small height so that she had a waddling gait — she was literally 'Mrs. Whitely — rollin'. Next in line astern came Muriel, very large, with out-turned feet, her hat awry upon her strong, springy hair, always clutching an untidy armful of files of papers; and at the end, myself, taller and thinner than both, with my eyes cast down nun-like to conceal my giggles and my arms feeling, and no doubt looking, much too long. I was always waiting, on these public occasions, for someone to laugh at us aloud so that I might obtain release by joining in their mirth, but nobody ever did. Madame X had the pseudo-intellectual and near-political life of the town utterly subjugated.

In theory, Muriel and I 'came and went as we pleased' about the household. In practice, we were not expected to do anything of the sort, as I discovered at the end of the first fortnight. We were not 'ordinary employees', after all. We were the 'dear adopted daughters' of Madame X, and there was no need for us to 'rush about the town' to tennis and dances and these low cinemas as the other girls did when we had all of Whitely House to entertain our friends in and Madame X to go out with to all the town's most distinguished gatherings. What more could two young women want? Muriel, who had had five years of it, apparently did not want anything more, but I, ungrateful as always, found the constant shadow of Madame X something of a burden and was glad to be given the occasion of stepping outside of it, with the tacit support of my family, when the opportunity arose.

This came about through Lady Lydia having mentioned in a letter to her cousin Lady Firmantle, who lived about ten miles from Whitely House, that Janet, the girl who helped Grace while Nurse was ill, was now in Kent, and Lady Firmantle, who had a large, hearty family, aged between seventeen and thirty, boundless hospitality and a husband who was an Admiral with the Home Fleet, wrote to me and asked me to come, by bus, to tea with her. I accepted the invitation and asked for the afternoon off. Madame X regarded me with sad eyes across the lunch table, and Muriel took her cue and became sad-eyed too. There was no need to ask for time off, I was told, as if I were a servant girl, but what did I want to do with the time, anyway? I replied that I wanted to go to tea with a friend. Madame X sighed. Wouldn't it be nicer, she asked, if I brought him to tea at Whitely House? I said it was not a him and she had a house of her own and that I would like just to go there, as invited. Oh? Who was she? After all, Madame X knew the whole town — how very odd that no one else had been asked. I became very airy-fairy. Oh, this friend was not right in the Town. No. She lived quite a bit out of Town. She was Lady Firmantle, and you had to take the Ferrers-Norton bus to get to where she was, so she wasn't in the *Town*, really, not to call it the *Town* . . .

'Really, child, why must you be so round-about! Lady Firmantle! Certainly you must go. And ask her back to tea here any day that suits her. *Any* day. We live very quietly. Any day would suit us . . .'

Lady Firmantle was middle-aged, fat, untidy, with grey hair that had defied the winds of the seven seas, and as she was now past the age for breeding children she was breeding Jersey cattle instead. She had a loud, commanding voice which she used mainly for the dissemination of strong opinions about everybody and everything.

'You are Janet Sandison!' she bawled at me in the hall of her house. 'Know you by your grandmother, dreadful cussed old woman! We'll have tea alone in my office — the rest of the house is full of grandchildren and dogs. How did you get on at Grace's place — awful hole?'

I said Very well, thank you; and she said: 'Hate it myself. Nothing to do there. Grace was always a nit-wit. Here, in here.'

She threw open a heavy oak door, which bounced off some piece of furniture inside and banged shut in our faces again. She said Dammit! and threw it open again and then poked me in the ribs as we walked into the 'office'. 'Here, what you doing at that old busy-body Rollin's place?'

I tried to tell her, but her conversation had all the mighty swell of the broad Atlantic. 'Secretary? I thought that Orphan-Annie sort of girl that trails about behind her was her secretary. I've always been sorry for that girl. Not sorry for *you* though — why are you doing it?'

I indicated that I was at least earning my keep and this made her laugh with a noise like a large ship caught in a fog.

'Good God! D'you take sugar? Have some more cake and then I'll show you my milking parlour — I'm showing it to everybody just now. Very modern. Makes me wish I was a cow myself. Next time you come, though, bring that girl, Orphan Annie, you know.'

'Her name is Muriel Thornton.'

'Oh? I'll try to remember. She looks sort of unfinished always, like my Hilda, as if part of her had got mislaid. I don't mean that they're not all *there*, Annie and Hilda, but they never seem to have all the bits of themselves *with* them. Of course, Hilda's only eighteen and she'll come on when she gets over this Greek dancing stage. How old is your one?'

'Mine? Oh, Muriel? Twenty-five or six, I think.'

'Good lord! Time she was away from that old bloodsucker.

She ought to get married and collect herself. Bring her to see me. But not the old one, definitely not!'

Frequently, during the next two weeks, I thought with some bitterness how easy it was for Lady Firmantle to stand on her quarter-deck and bawl impossible orders at a poor ordinary seaman like myself, but in the end Muriel and I got on board the Ferrers-Norton bus one afternoon without the presence, but with the blessing, of Madame X. This was a triumph of diplomacy or, if we must be blunt, strategic lying on my part, but, as someone has said, it is not the lie itself that presents difficulty, it is its upkeep, so as soon as we were safely out of the town and on the country road that led to our destination I said to Muriel: 'Look here, this isn't a tennis party today and Lady Firmantle herself *is* going to be there.'

The cloud of worry settled on Muriel's face again. 'But you *told* Mrs. Whitely-Rollin—'

'Never mind that.'

'But she'll *ask* us when we get back! And *why* did you tell all these lies? When she wanted so much to call on Lady Firmantle?'

'Because Lady Firmantle doesn't *want* her calling on her!' I said brutally.

'But I never *heard* of a thing like that!' Muriel protested.

'Oh, don't be so wet, Muriel!'

'But what shall I *do*?'

'You don't have to do anything! Just have fun and leave the talking to me when we get back.'

Muriel, as always, did as she was told. We played tennis after all, because we were dressed for tennis and all the young Firmantles and their friends were home from universities, colleges, the Navy and the Army, and they were the sort of young people who were always willing to do anything active, and Muriel had tremendous fun. To my surprise, she played very well in spite of having no practice, and as her cheeks flushed up and her eyes became more blue she lost a great deal of her plainness and even made a few remarks on her own without waiting for someone to ask her a question first.

When we got back to Whitely House I did the 'talking', as

planned, and, as you know I can talk a great deal when I choose, so I chattered on guilelessly at dinner about the tennis party until Madame X suggested rather pointedly that I was a little 'over-excited tonight, dear' and changed the subject without asking a single question about Lady Firmantle.

I had been at Whitely House for some three months, giggling to myself, writing ribald doggerel in bed at night, tying the Chain of Friendship into a neat coil in the old pantry, emancipating Muriel and teasing Madame X as far as I dared before I realised that my activities were not going entirely unobserved, as I had thought they were. I had been out one evening on an illicit visit to the cinema and to the public library and was coming home with my book wrapped in brown paper under my arm, ready to hide in the syringa bush in the garden. I had found this the easiest way to obtain books of which Madame X did not approve, such as modern poetry and detective stories. I collected them from the syringa bush when I put the cat out, for that last was one of my daughterly jobs. At the end of the road, perhaps a quarter of a mile from the house, stood Mr. Rollin, smoking a small cigar in an amber holder. He was not allowed to smoke in the house, except in his study, which was a room at the back of the house that I had never been in.

'Well, Lady Flashing Stream!' he said. 'You look happy as usual!'

Several times lately, when I had seen him alone for a moment, he had called me by this name, and tonight he continued: 'You must not mind my Victorian nonsense. I read a revue of a play somewhere, a play called *Lady Precious Stream* — a pretty phrase. But you are a flashing, mountain stream — yes, indeed.'

'A hill burn, we'd call it,' I said, not quite knowing how to accept this compliment and feeling gauche, and I began to walk with him, slowly, towards the house.

'And what have you been doing?' he asked.

Now this is something I cannot explain. If Madame X had asked me I would have resented it and I would have lied to her on principle, but I did not resent *his* asking and I told the truth.

'I've been to the cinema!' I hissed in a conspiratorial whisper.

'What?' He stopped in his tracks. 'Tell me, tell me about it! What was it about?'

'About a regiment in India,' I said, and eagerly he listened while I told him the plot of the film. He sighed blissfully when I had finished, lit another of his little cigars and said: 'Don't let us go in yet. Let us walk to the other end of the road. Tell me, have you ever seen Miss Mae West?'

I replied that I had indeed once seen this epitome of the true vulgarity of the Naughty Nineties. He sighed. 'I would dearly love to see Miss West,' he said.

'There's a film of hers coming next week,' I told him. 'You should go, Mr. Rollin.'

His eyes gleamed. I now know that that was the moment when I Went Too Far, but how was I to recognise the Big Moment then? I did not, at twenty-one, have any conception of the inter-relation of events and their steady, yet hardly noticeable, roll towards an unforeseeable climax.

At dinner that night I found myself sitting at the centre of a web of conspiracy, with Madame X holding forth from the top of the table as usual, quite unaware that Mr. Rollin was living in a dream of anticipation among the curves and winks of Mae West and that Muriel was hiding under her clumsiness a trembling upspringing of love for the curate of Ferrers-Norton, whom she was now meeting regularly at the Firmantles'. I had truly kicked the pebbles that were to start the avalanche.

I think it is true when I say that I am a person like this: I am not a crier over spilt milk, and *especially* did I not cry over spilt milk in those days. I had a mind like a flea on a blanket, always jumping from hither to yon, and, indeed, I think my mind is pretty much of a flea on a blanket right now, at my present ripe age. So I did not bother myself overmuch about Mr. Rollin and Mae West and Muriel and her curate, for I had two young men of my own that I was trying to keep from finding out about each other as well as trying to keep Madame X from finding out about either, so my hands were pretty full. And, of course, there was the good old Chain of Friendship and the capers, generally speaking, of Madame X to take up a lot of my attention.

After these three months or so of detailed study, I had decided that her speciality was what I called in my own mind 'mental fornication'. I have told you that she herself wrote to all the grown males who applied to the Chain, to give them, she said, 'a feeling of association with the good, clean and pure', but her good clean purity needed further fields to do itself justice, and one of these was an old bachelor, an ex-army man, who, I think, had always been too selfish to think of marriage but who was not unwilling to come to tea once a week and make sheep's eyes across the hearth (through his eye-glass) at Madame X. All very clean and pure, of course. His name was Colonel Wise, and on *his* days Muriel and I were not supposed to enter the drawing-room, but I mostly got in there on some pretext or another for a short while, just for the hell of it.

> On Thursdays we have Colonel Wise,
> Among the pure clean flames arise
> To gaze o'er crumpets at the eyes
> Of ex-Miss Whitely — rollin'.

One of these afternoons I quite surpassed myself by dashing suddenly into the drawing-room on some excuse, but so suddenly that I startled both the occupants so much that the tea-tray, which was one of these Birmingham-Benares brass affairs on folding legs, was knocked over with a resounding crash that brought to the scene the entire household.

> Their hearts upon the hearth-rug's nap,
> When came the awful thunder-clap
> That sent the cream jug o'er the lap
> Of ex-Miss Whitely — rollin'.

The appalling ballad grew longer and longer and lived locked in a suitcase on top of my wardrobe, each dreadful stanza on odd pieces of paper, old envelopes or anything that came to hand. Even now I may open a book and have a stanza of 'Whitely rollin' ' fall out, and I merely mention it because this book is about the importance of unimportant things and it is from these careless verses that I am able to recapitulate how my country and some of its people looked to the eyes of a twenty-one-year-old in the year 1932 or so. I belong to that group of outmoded eccentrics who believe that my country and its people are important, but it seems to me that between 1930 and 1940 there were some incredibly silly people among them. In spite of the Big Depression, life was far too easy for far too many of them and, like my grandmother, when she baked scones that we did not really need, these people had to be 'at' something.

The afternoon following the crash of the tea-tray Madame X had Muriel and myself on the mat in the drawing-room after tea — literally on the mat — for it was her whimsy that we three should present, always, a tableau in that room, of the white-haired mother in a chair by the fire, with her daughters on cushions on the floor at her feet. I think perhaps that the tableau of the day before which had been disintegrated by the fall of the tea-tray was a little on her mind, or maybe she was becoming a little suspicious of our doings when out of her sight at the Firmantles', but her talk this day was all of Men as a Sex and how Women should Deal With Them. I do not remember the details — I have told you of my capacity for forgetting what strikes me as unpleasant — but it ended with a deal of Coventry Patmore and all about how it was Woman's part to 'make men of beasts, make men divine'. By this stage in the firelight talk I had reached the pitch of ill-concealed giggles, for I was aware that Mr. Rollin had slipped off to see Mae West and was conscious that either Madame X had failed in her duty to kill the beast in him or that I had run directly counter to the command of Patmore by encouraging the said beast. Whatever the reason for the talk, though, I felt certain that she was not aware of the falling from grace and taste of Mr. Rollin, and this pleased me inordinately.

There has never been any doubt in my mind that artists of all kinds have the power to confer great benefits on humanity, and Mae West, undoubtedly an artist of her kind, caused Mr.

Rollin to break the shackles of years and soar from his cage into an empyrean of freedom. It had been his habit to use a breakfast food called 'Bran-ex', which, it appeared, his wife had insisted would be good for him — it was the age, you will remember, when everyone, even the most refined, was very constipation-conscious — and around this time he pushed the packet away from him and waved away the plate that was being handed to him.

'Remember to take your Bran-ex, dear,' said Madame X.

'No, thank you, my dear,' he replied. 'I do not feel Bran-exatious this morning.' And he looked out of the window, whistling a little tune. 'Bring me two eggs,' he told the manservant.

Into the cold staring silence I dropped a hiccup of laughter and covered it immediately with: 'What a lovely word — Bran-exatious!'

It was thus that Mr. Rollin and I discovered that we could 'play at words', a game for which Madame X and Muriel had no aptitude and, looking at it all in retrospect, I can think of no mode of behaviour which I could have adopted which could have been more irritating. It seems that I was a person like this: I was a person who always had to put *both* feet into things. By this game of words, the dining-table was split in half, for Mr. Rollin, with great enjoyment, rode the hobby constantly and he and I had tremendous fun while Madame X was left with only Muriel as an audience, and even Muriel's harassed attention tended to wander with amazement at each new burst of laughter from Mr. Rollin.

In addition to this insubordination within the home — that Sacred Place, the Home — and his clandestine visits to what he was now calling in a sprightly way 'The Movies', Mr. Rollin had taken to lying in wait for me as I came in from my evening walks and we used to have most amusing, to us, conversations. There was nothing clandestine about this, and, indeed, Madame X was at pains to tell me how fortunate I was to have an adopted father as well as a mother. She would have been furious, though, had she had any idea of the sheer fun of our friendship, but neither of

74

us was at any pains to draw any diagrams for her.

Mr. Rollin had read for the Bar as a young man and had a sensitive, scholarly mind accustomed to living within itself, for, I think, his life had been lonely, and many of his very penetrating opinions were offered in a tentative way which I found most appealing from a man of his age, culture and experience to a chit like myself. One evening I found him leaning over the railway bridge watching the trains, so I too put my elbows on the parapet and we talked of engines and their beautiful names, and of ships, and I told him of the 'Five-three-fower', and he told me he would like to go to Canada some day. I said I would too. In fact, I said, I would like to go just nearly anywhere, and he said: 'Yes. And remember, child, it is better to travel hopefully than to arrive. The satisfaction lies mainly in the travelling ... Where's Miss Muriel tonight?'

'She is doing what she calls her accounts,' I said. I think that, couching my reply in that form, I was almost subconsciously asking for information on the subject of 'Muriel's accounts', which were, at that time, the only aspect of Muriel that I found in any way interesting, for never before had I seen anyone with a similar attitude to money. I had been brought up in a family that was, of necessity, thrifty and I had always been accustomed to making do with little money to spend and accustomed too, on many occasions, to doing without, but I had never been asked to account for my small pocket money, and it had never occurred to me to keep a record of what I had done with it. The record existed in the form of a book or a pair of shoes I had bought or in the memory of a concert I had heard — that was all.

Since we had begun our visits to the Firmantles and other small gatherings to which we had been invited, Muriel's accounts had come very much to the forefront. The evening after our outing, in the time after closing the office and before dinner, she would get the blue exercise book out of the locked drawer in her bedroom and with a worried air and much counting on her fingers she would enter the cost of her bus fare, the price of the sweets she had bought on the way home and any other expenses which had been incurred since she had last done her accounts. While busy with her blue book, she had a secretive, furtive, frightened look and would sigh deeply after each entry as for something lost beyond recall. I found it most extraordinary and knew what she was doing at these times only because, one evening, she was at a loss to account for a penny spent while we were at the post office that morning and I was able to help her by reminding her that she had weighed herself on the chemist's machine that stood in his doorway. When she had made the entry and had given her sigh she looked like a hunted animal that hears its pursuers run, unsuspecting, past the entrance to its hiding-place. Her accounts were obviously so much of a personal privacy of hers that I never felt that I could discuss them with her. I could not ask her why she kept them so meticulously, what satisfaction she derived from them, whether she had been trained to the habit or whether the practice had been developed by herself, but I was interested in this facet of her which was so different from anything in my own nature, or from anything I had ever observed in the limited number of people I had known.

So when I said 'what she calls her accounts' I was, as I said, seeking only half-consciously for information and enlightenment.

'And what of *your* accounts, Lady Flashing Stream?' Mr. Rollin countered.

'I don't have any. I spend it and when it's finished it's finished. Of course, Muriel has a little more salary than I have to account for.'

'Salary? My dear child, Miss Muriel is a young lady of substance.'

'Substance?'

'Some six years ago, when her father the vicar died and she came to my wife, her inheritance was some twelve thousand pounds, in property, in Essex. A very nice competence.'

'Then why on earth —' I stopped in time, I thought, but he was not so slow-witted.

'—doesn't she light out for Texas?' he finished for me in the language of the cinema. 'Not all people are travellers, Lady

Flashing Stream . . . There goes the express. Shall we walk back now?'

This new knowledge of Muriel and her accounts that she kept so religiously in her blue exercise book changed my view of her, or rather my view of her dithering way of living her life. I became impatient with her, for I said to myself: 'Good lord, if *I* had all that money I would marry my curate or do anything I wanted to do — the world would be my playground.'

You see how young I was? Money to me meant freedom and I could not see that to Muriel it was one more harassing thing, a business of keeping accounts of every penny and a wrinkling of brows over investments. Looking back, I find myself so stupid that I can hardly believe that anyone could '*get* that way', as Martha would put it. However, there it was. I became impatient and irritable with her. She seemed to like her curate, and he seemed to like her, but there she was, dithering about, I-don't-know-if-I-shoulding, wondering what Madame X would say, seemingly longing to get back into the bosom of the Church in which she had been reared, yet afraid to take a step in any direction and gradually becoming more and more of a nervous wreck.

Until I heard of her inheritance I had thought that she and her curate had decided to wait until he could improve his financial situation, and although even this would not have been *my* way of doing things I was prepared to try to understand. In the light of the 'competence', however, my understanding melted like summer snow. For me, twelve thousand pounds would have opened any door at that time and I had not the wit to see that some people have no wish to open the doors that I want to open. So, liking this young curate, I espoused his cause and prodded away at Muriel at the same time, thinking I was pushing her in a direction in which she fundamentally wanted to go, but largely because it was a direction that would annoy Madame X extremely. I may be telling you something of which you are already aware when I say that antipathy of a deep-seated kind works largely by instinct. The cobra hates and will try to kill the mongoose and the mongoose will equally try to kill the cobra. They make the

77

moves in their killing game without volition — by instinct they know how to attack and how to parry. With Madame X, I was a mangy little mongoose circling round a great big King Cobra, and without even my own full awareness I was closing in my attack on her in any way that presented itself. So great a cobra was she that I do not think she even noticed me until, to my own surprise, we were at strangle grips.

In the middle of the ebb and flow of this low drama within the walls of Whitely House, it began, in the phrase of Damon Runyon, to come on Christmas and Madame X announced that Muriel and I were to have a week's holiday, and, in the idiom of Twice, this, momentarily, stopped my laughing in church. I had nowhere to go except home to Ross-shire, and I did not have the train-fare to do that, owing to having started to buy myself a typewriter on the hire-purchase system and having invested in a very recherché evening outfit in order to go to a County Ball in January with Freddie Firmantle, who was my latest admirer. When the holiday was announced, I had my Christmas presents bought and was in a well-organised position except for the fact that my liquid resources amounted to only fourteen shillings and ninepence in the Post Office Savings Bank. The holiday was a horrid blow, until Muriel came out of the mist like an angel of sweetness and light.

'Six days is not really long enough to go away up to your home with the snow on the line and everything,' she said, and I agreed. 'I wondered if you would like to come with me to my aunt in Kensington; at least she's not really my aunt but a sort of cousin of my father's and I always go to her for holidays. You might not like it, but you said you liked London —'

'Muriel, I would love it! Thank you very, very much!' I said with fervour. If anyone had offered me a week in Holloway Prison I would have taken it so that my 'Heilan' pride, scab and hunger' need not admit its financial straits. I was filled with an uprush of gratitude to Muriel, and in a situation like that I am a person like this: I immediately cast about as to how I can do a Good Turn to Kind People like Muriel, so I got hold of Muriel's curate the next time we were at the Firmantles' and told him how she and I were going to London for Christmas and why didn't he come up and visit us and maybe he and Muriel could go to St. Paul's or the Abbey or something and have themselves a nice time. The curate thought this was a fine idea and said that he was interested in a Mission in the East End and he was sure he could get to London for about three days, so he and I went in for a nice touch of mutual congratulation and I gave him our address in Kensington before going off to find Freddie and see about a few arrangements for myself that would include an opportunity for London to have a preview of my new evening outfit.

All went merrily as a marriage bell. Muriel's Aunt Julia was a comfortable old widow, like a large fat cushion which can accommodate itself to everything and everybody, and inhabited this flat in Kensington in company with a mongrel dog called Peter that spent all its time carrying shoes from the bedrooms to the kitchen and brooms and mops from the kitchen to the bedrooms. We arrived in time for tea (out of Aunt Daisy's cups — you wouldn't remember her, Muriel — she died in 1906) from Cousin Arthur's table (you've heard of him — Enid's brother who made such a fool of himself with that girl from Avignon who stayed with the Travers's), and after Aunt Julia had told Muriel that she was looking pasty, she turned to me and said: 'And now, Janet, tell me all about your latest young man.'

I thought she must be a bit clairvoyant, but I now realise that she recognised me for the flibberty-gibbet I was, probably because she had been something of a flibberty-gibbet herself in her time. So, instead, I told her about Muriel's curate — in private while Muriel took Peter for a walk and I washed the tea-things — and all about my plans for Muriel. Aunt Julia thought the plans were excellent, and even went so far as to say that she could not have done better by Muriel herself, and we decided that the wedding would probably take place around the following June, Muriel not being the type to be hurried.

'That old Mrs. Thing won't like it, of course,' Aunt Julia said.

'Madame X?' I asked. 'Yes. That's what I call her.' And I

recited a stanza or two of Whitely-rollin', which amused Aunt Julia quite a lot. 'But Mrs. Thing is quite good too. *Why* shouldn't she like it?'

'No reason,' said Aunt Julia. 'She just *won't* because that's how she *is*.'

I conceded that this was probably true but that it would not matter. I then took this quiet opportunity of telling Aunt Julia how kind it was of her to have me for Christmas and she said: 'Rubbish! It wasn't kindness to start with, it was sheer curiosity, for you are the first friend I've known Muriel to make and I wanted to see you.' And she patted my shoulder with her fat, cushiony hand. 'I can't see in the least what you have in common, but you must be excellent for Muriel, my dear. You may rescue her from old Mrs. Thing yet.'

'What do you mean?'

'Muriel has a slave mind. Anyone can influence her, but at this stage they have to be stronger influencers than old Mrs. Thing . . . Does she still recite poetry at one?'

'Yes. Mostly Coventry Patmore to Muriel and me. I don't know what she uses for Colonel Wise though — we are not allowed to hear.'

Aunt Julia chuckled. 'What a delightful *brat* you are! My generation doesn't use the word bitch.'

'It's because I am not spiritual like Madame X,' I told her. 'Madame X says that really spiritual women are above chattering about other women.'

'I suppose,' said Aunt Julia, 'they keep all their chattering to do *to* other men?'

I said that *my* generation had been known occasionally to use the word bitch, and we both had a good laugh, and then Muriel came back with Peter.

Into that week's holiday we packed a lot of Major Events. Aunt Julia and I took to ourselves all the credit for Getting the Question Popped to Muriel on the day after Boxing Day when she came back to Kensington in the evening looking very starry-eyed, with her curate and a gold ring with a small diamond in it. After that, Aunt Julia just could *not* stop talking about everything every time Muriel was absent for a moment, and in the intervals between my piling up of my own Major Events. I had a bus ride, a walk along the Embankment, a trip in the Underground. In the realm of sheer sophistication I had my hair washed in a shop for the first time in my life (for out of the blue my father had sent me three whole pound notes for Christmas, so that I had money to burn, even after buying Aunt Julia a pot plant that she had admired for a Christmas present), I had set foot inside a London theatre, I had spent four hours in a large bookshop and bought a book for half a crown, and I had been to a night-club (with Freddie) and had drunk *champagne*. On our last evening, when Freddie had gone back to his submarine at Chatham and Muriel had gone to call on a cousin or something of her curate's, I was in the mood that comes to one who 'on honey dew hath fed and drunk the milk of Paradise' and was bawling and singing and giggling while I cooked supper for Aunt Julia and me while she sat by the fire nursing Peter in her lap.

'Tell me,' she called through to the kitchen, 'has old Mrs. Thing still got that Man in the Iron Mask in her hall?'

'You mean the Two-handed Engine?' I called back.

'*What* engine? No. This was —'

'Can't you remember your Milton, Aunt Julia? "But that two-handed engine at the door stands ready to smite once and smite no more"?' Aunt Julia had a prolonged fit of her wheezy chuckles. 'Yes, it's still there — halberd and all. I got spoken to more in sorrow than in anger only a week ago for hanging my umbrella on its cuirass or its gyves or something. Why?'

'I just wondered. I've always had a feeling about people who have those things in their halls.'

'What sort of feeling, Aunt Julia?'

'Well, I wouldn't have one in *my* hall,' she said. 'I always feel that some day they may come to life and do something awful to you, smite you, like you said. It's like that Egyptian Room at the museum that you went to see. I went once too, but I wouldn't go again.'

'Neither would I,' I agreed, and I decided then that I would not again hang my umbrella on the Two-handed Engine either, for I am a person like this: I have feelings about feelings, whether they are my own or other people's. When somebody has a feeling like that about something, I have a feeling that — well, you just never know and there might be something *in* it and I did not want any Two-handed Engine suddenly deciding that I had been rude to it or interfered with it in any way.

Aunt Julia and I talked a lot that night about all sorts of things, but there is talking and talking and the later it became the more my talking became like whistling in the dark. It was all very well for Aunt Julia to be pleased with herself for having got Muriel's Question Popped, but she did not have to go back to Whitely House with the news and I did. I was very nervous indeed, and even thought of rushing to Chatham and casting myself on Freddie's navy-blue, sub-lieutenant's bosom, but that would never have done, for Freddie had told me that I was marvellous at night-clubs and champagne and playing the fool, but not cut out to be a naval wife. I had enough sense to see that he was right. No. I had to go back to Whitely House. I then toyed with the idea that I could stay with Aunt Julia for another week and look for a job in London — that would have been nice — but I could not send Muriel back alone, not if that ring was to stick, anyhow. No. I had to go back with Muriel. So, on a cold, sleety afternoon we arrived at the station and I giggled and carried on like a maniac all the way to Whitely House in the cab, while Muriel was the colour of rather dried-up putty and so guilty-looking that you would have thought she was fresh from committing triple bigamy.

'Let me do the talking!' I said, probably from sheer force of habit, as the cab drew up at the gate, and Muriel gave me that lost drowned look that she always gave me when, through my doings, our backs were to the wall. While she paid the taxi-man I dashed through the gate, up the path, into the hall, round the Two-handed Engine (tilting its halberd and stopping to straighten it again) and threw open the drawing-room door.

'Merry Christmas! What do you think?' I bellowed in ringing tones. 'Muriel's engaged!'

How was I to remember that it was Thursday and Colonel Wise's day?

He sprang out of his chair, his eye-glass fell out on its dangling black ribbon, his tea slopped into his saucer, his knobbly knee hit the Birmingham-Benares brass, and once again down came the whole equipage with a resounding crash. Muriel appeared in the door-way, her hat awry and a suitcase in each hand, the servants appeared at the double, and Mr. Rollin walked from the dining-room through the group and said with his long, curly smile: 'Well, Lady Flashing Stream! Welcome back, my dear!'

That did it. 'Janet,' said Madame X, 'you and Muriel will have tea with Mr. Rollin in the dining-room as usual,' and as an icy obbligato to this icy cascade the last ill-balanced teaspoon fell with an icy tinkle into the fender. I backed all the way out of the room, across the hall and into the dining-room. Muriel staggered in behind me, dropped the suitcases on the floor, herself on to a chair and burst into floods of overwrought tears. Mr. Rollin came in quietly and closed the door.

'Come, come, Miss Muriel!' he said. 'No harm done. The silver doesn't break, you know. No harm done.'

'Oh, it's not that!' I burst forth. 'She's engaged, you see, and I've made such a mess —'

'Engaged? Engaged to be married? Bless my soul! How very surprising! And how delightful! Come now, Miss Muriel, you must have some tea and tell me all about it. Who is the fortunate young man?'

'The c-curate at Ferrers-Norton!' sobbed Muriel. 'His n-n-name is —'

'It's Richard Marshall!' I supplied. 'Muriel, *do* dry yourself up! We'll never get away with this if you don't pull yourself together!'

'Get away with what?' asked Mr. Rollin benignly. 'Get —'

'Oh, please! I didn't mean that! I meant —'

'Have some cake, Lady Flashing Stream. You are both very over-excited. Too many late nights, eh? You are both suffering from what would once have been called a touch of the vapours. . . . Yes, you too!' he assured me firmly. 'You are as subject to the vapours as any other young lady although you have a most individual way of demonstrating them. Mm. Yes, indeed. There, Miss Muriel, that's better.'

It was not, however, much better, for Muriel with a long breath and a high-pitched wail said: 'Oh, *why* did you have to knock down the tea-tray?'

'I did *not*!' I bawled, almost in tears myself by now. 'It was that old goat Wise that — oh, sorry!'

'Let it pass. Let it pass,' murmured Mr. Rollin. 'Yes, Lady Flashing Stream?'

'It was Colonel *Wise* who did the tea-tray! All I did was to rattle the Two-handed Engine!'

'The *what*, my dear?'

I was now in and wading about with both feet and almost past caring. 'Oh, that suit of armour thing in the hall! I sort of knocked into it and —'

'Two-handed Engine! Two-handed Engine! Very apt! Very apt indeed!' he crooned and, beating time with his long scholarly hand, he intoned: 'But that Two-handed Engine at the door stands ready to smite once and smite no more.' He beamed at me. 'You make *excellent* use of your classical education, my dear! Excellent. Very apt indeed. Oddsfish and by my halibut!'

He lapsed into his own dry, silent form of laughter and I, of course, begam to giggle, for I am a person like this: I would always rather giggle than make a fool of myself in any other way, and the amount of crying that Muriel was doing was quite enough for both of us. And so, of course, Mr. Rollin was rustling away like a grasshopper, and I was giggling, and Muriel was smiling in a watery, distraught sort of way, when Madame X came, with majesty, into the room, closed the door behind her and stood looking at us.

'What,' she said, 'do I understand to have happened?'

'You refer, my dear, to Miss Muriel's engagement of marriage?' said Mr. Rollin, exactly as if we had crises like this all the time. It must have been his early legal training, I thought, that gave him that wonderful calm. 'A most happy piece of news. I have just been offering my felicitations.

Do be seated, my dear.'

Madame X sat down. I felt that I had a ringside seat at old Canute's contest with the waves of the sea and that, contrary to history, old Canute was winning.

'That's better,' said Mr. Rollin, sitting down himself. 'Miss Muriel has just been having a touch of the vapours but she feels better now.'

'I trust,' said Madame X, 'that you, too, Janet, have regained control of yourself.'

'I am very sorry,' I said. 'Truly I am, Mrs. Whitely-Rollin. But the news was so exciting that —'

'Exciting? Hardly my view of such a serious step as Muriel seems to have taken.' She arose and turned graciously to Muriel. 'You and I must have a real talk later, my dear.' She pressed Muriel's shoulder in a soulful way, gave her a look of terrifying motherliness and understanding and rolled out of the room. Very shortly, Muriel rose and went too, like an iron filing drawn in the wake of a powerful magnet, and Mr. Rollin and I were left alone. He wished to know all about my holiday, and I gave him a blow-by-blow description of all I had seen and done in London, including details of Freddie's and my agreement as to my unsuitability as a naval wife. He was vastly entertained, and so was I, and we forgot all about Muriel and her curate.

Indeed, I forgot fairly completely about Muriel and her curate for several months, for now that she was definitely engaged our ways diverged whenever we were free of the office and Whitely House, Muriel going about with Richard and visiting his relations and spending all her Sundays at Ferrers-Norton, while I pursued my own devious ways among the Firmantles and other friends and driving about with Freddie in his little car most weekends. Even in the office we were divided, for there was only one typewriter and I was not in favour of hammering my own not-yet-paid-for-machine on Madame X's silly business, so Muriel did all the letter-writing and I was in charge of the filing and general information.

I claim the distinction that, to a great extent, it was the inhuman accuracy of my filing system that finally broke into a heap of rusted, crooked, scrap metal the good old Chain of Friendship. As I have already suggested, the basic reason for the existence of the Chain and for a good many of Madame X's other activities was the need in her that she should feel busy — she had to be 'at' something — and while she and Muriel had been messing around with this heap of papers in the old pantry and laundry and Muriel was always 'laying things down' and losing them, never a day passed without Madame X having the feeling of being a busy executive whose nerves were being torn to shreds by the inefficiency of her staff, and her having a lot of fun by turning and rending the unfortunate Muriel. I decided to alter all that. My method was extremely simple. I had a record, both alphabetical and numerical, of every member and every letter he or she had written, and I had this cross-referenced through a series of cards. This was normal office theory, learned at my Business College. But I had a special drawer which contained items that, it was my forecast, I would be asked to produce at any moment (such as the last letter from the lonely sheep farmer in New Zealand), and by watching Madame X at the breakfast-table I could almost produce what she wanted before she asked for it. This was *not* normal office theory, and I do not know where I learned it.

So, instead of the old business of Madame X saying: 'And *where*, may I ask, have you put Mr. Smith's last letter?' and then going on to have a nice, more-in-sorrow-than-in-anger, after-all-my-motherly-interest-in-you row and Muriel in tears and grovelling round her skirts, I would say: 'I'll bring it straight away, Mrs. Whitely-Rollin,' and be before her desk with the letter in ten seconds. There was, I think you must agree, no fun for her in this. Indeed, it meant that she had to write more letters than she had ever had to write before because she could no longer sit back and sigh: 'Such frustration! So *much* to do and *so* much time lost through sheer inefficiency!'

I had, by now, discovered too that I had Madame X in a beautiful cleft stick as far as the Chain was concerned. When I first went to Whitely House I had been under the impression that the Chain was a private venture of Madame X's own, but very shortly I discovered that it was subsidised by a bunch of cranks in some pacifist society in London. This society found the money to pay for stationery, stamps and Muriel's and my salaries, and they made Madame X an allowance for our food and board. It was quite a cute arrangement — or had been — for it meant that Madame X was getting all her fun for free, as my friend Martha would put it. In my organisation of the office, I had come across the draft of a letter that applied to this society for a second secretary — which was myself — and that letter put Madame X in the position where she could not get rid of me except for inefficiency or some gross misdemeanour, so there I was, very much the Viper in her Bosom. The tussle between us settled into a constant 'battle for the loose head in the scrum', as Twice would put it, and although the race may tend to go to the swift and the battle to the strong, there is a lot to be said in these circumstances for sheer Highland doggedness coupled with the toughness of healthy youth. Madame X had made something of a nervous wreck of Muriel, but I was a person like this: I did not seem to have any nerves.

Having done my efficient worst with the Chain all day, and having earned a number of compliments from the Parent Pacifists (as I thought of them) for our office organisation from time to time, I amused myself in the evenings and at weekends with my own friends and with Mr. Rollin. He had continued his illicit visits to the cinema, had discovered Greta Garbo and had become an ardent admirer of her sensitive, extraordinary beauty. He followed her films avidly, attending almost every performance, and it says much for Madame X's self-absorption that he went entirely undiscovered.

One evening, I was walking along the High Street with Mr. Rollin, who had come with me to post the day's letters, when we met My Friend Freddie. Now, it was this same Freddie who said that I was too flighty and lacking in diplomacy to make a naval wife (or words to that effect), but he was not remarkable for diplomacy and such things himself, for, although he knew perfectly well who Mr. Rollin was, he greeted me with: 'What cheer, old girl! What about the odd noggin at The Goat?'

'Not tonight, Freddie!' I said in tones that would have done credit to an admiral's lady. 'Mr. Rollin, do you know Freddie Firmantle?'

'How are you, my boy? I have heard of you from my Lady Flashing Stream here.'

'Flashing —?' said Freddie.

Freddie was a person like this — he was almost illiterate. I felt embarrassed, as I always do when a thing slips out of its context, and Lady Flashing Stream here and now was as out of context as any stocking that has slipped from its garter.

'I think it describes her lightness very well. You don't agree?' Mr. Rollin pursued.

'Flashing —?' Freddie frowned at me in deep thought and then laughed like a maniac. 'Oh, Flashing *Beam*! By Jove! Jolly good, sir! Not half, sir! Have you seen her do the Black Bottom?'

'Not so far,' said Mr. Rollin gravely. 'You mentioned The Goat just now, my boy, a very interesting old hostelry. I used to enjoy a glass of sherry before dinner, dear me, yes, indeed!'

'Fine, sir! Let's make a turn to starboard and have a noggin of The Goat's amontillado. My father swears by it!'

'Thank you, my boy. This is delightful, delightful!'

With the feeling of being present at the making of history, and not sure whether I liked the feeling, I walked between them into The Goat. When the sherry had been brought and Mr. Rollin had pronounced favourably upon it, he put his glass down, put the tips of his long thinker's fingers together and said: 'You mentioned the Black Bottom — I have seen it danced upon the cinema screen. I am old-fashioned, of course, but I prefer the waltz. I was always a devotee of the waltz.'

'Oh, Lady Flashing-What's-It can waltz too, sir!' said Freddie, as a man who would not let his friends down and all that. 'What I mean is, she is a terrific dancer, terrific. I suppose it's being Highland and all these reels and flings and things. We're going to show them a few steps at the Hunt Ball next week, aren't we, Jan?'

'The Hunt Ball! Dear me, I haven't been to a ball since I married! Bless my soul. I should like to go to a ball again — not

88

to dance, of course. Mm. Yes, indeed. Let us have a little more of this excellent sherry. Will you tell the man for me, my boy?'

For myself, I was in a nightmare of being at the Hunt Ball mounted on a runaway horse, but Freddie rang for the waiter and said: 'I'll tell my mother to send you tickets, sir. She secretaries for the Hunt or something. Anyway, she's dishing out the tickets this year — can't think why you didn't have them already, come to that.'

'I may have done, my boy, and mislaid them. Thank you, I shall be delighted to have tickets. Well, my dear, you look most thoughtful. Come, drink your sherry. This is quite a little celebration. Yes, indeed. A little wine has a tonic effect. Yes, yes, indeed.'

Well, I am a person like this: I hate waste, especially of good food or drink, so I drank my sherry and we all drank two more apiece, by which time people were playing darts in a corner and Freddie was explaining the principles of the game to Mr. Rollin. I stopped thinking what a pity it was that I had fifteen pounds invested in clothes for the Hunt Ball instead of nice and safe in the Post Office Savings Bank. To hell with tomorrow, I thought. By the time Madame X has finished with me tonight, I thought, there won't *be* any tomorrow. Shortly after seven, we debouched on to the High Street to go home to dinner, Freddie seeing us off at the door of The Goat, uncaring, before going back to play darts with his low friends. I glared at him with bitterness and a gleam of some vague intelligence crossed his face.

'I say, Jan!' he said, calling me back and thrusting a paper packet into my hand. 'Peppermints!' he hissed. 'I always use them when No. One is on below!'

'Thank you and God rot you!' I hissed back, but I accepted the peppermints.

'Like a sweet?' I said to Mr. Rollin a moment later. 'It's peppermint — sometimes sherry can cause indigestion.'

'Oh? Ah. Yes. Yes, quite. Thank you, my dear. Ah, yes. Very pleasant on a cold night.'

We sucked peppermints all the way back to Whitely House and got away with everything. God bless the Royal Navy! But that, in a nutshell, was how Mr. Rollin found one more illicit way of amusing himself.

I have pointed out to you already that these fortuitous happenings like meeting My Friend Freddie just outside The Goat have results out of all proportion, it seems, to their own importance. After all, that is largely what this book is about — fortuitous happenings and their results. Anyway, meeting Freddie outside The Goat like that led to a lot of things, some of which are as follow:

(a) It led to Mr. Rollin getting tickets for the Hunt Ball which I will tell about later.

(b) It led to Mr. Rollin getting interested in darts and renewing his interest in drink, for I think he had been interested in the latter as a young man before lapsing into marriage.

(c) It led to a definite conspiracy between Mr. Rollin and myself re peppermints, and this, honestly, was the first real conspiracy between us.

(d) It led to Freddie taking a new view about me.

(e) It led to a lot of things right up to z and a lot more after that, probably, but they are not germane to this story I am telling you.

I intend to tell you about (d) above first, not that it is germane to this story either really, but because I think it is interesting because it is all about ME, wonderful ME. But, before I tell you about (d), I would like to tell you that 'germane' is another word that My Friend Monica and I had words about.

Now, my view of germane is that it is a weed, something like what Scots gardeners call 'Tishie-laggie', a weed with creepy-crawly white roots which, no matter how you chop them up, if you leave the smallest bit in the ground, up will pop a great big lot of coarse green leaves which will choke and smother your choicest plant of Manypeeplia-Upsidedownia (developed by Edward Lear). In other words, germane is one of these weeds that once you have got it you cannot get rid of it. My Friend

Monica thought differently. (Some day, I hope, I may express a view to My Friend Monica without her thinking differently, but I fear that Monica is a person like this: she always thinks differently.) Germane, My Friend Monica says, is a woman, who is a sort of lady of the town, or, coarsely, a tart, who consorts with the most unexpected people and causes issues, mostly matrimonial. See the French name Germaine, My Friend Monica says, and she once knew a woman of this name who was just incredibly germane to nearly anything in trousers, she says. She says that this woman Germaine that she knew was germane to nearly every man and matrimonial issue in a whole suburb of Paris once. Well, I have not got Monica's experience of these things, so it is a case of everyone having their own opinion, and I repeated that in *my* opinion germane was a weed, so My Friend Monica said I wasn't so far wrong at that and what about one more for the road.

But to get back to (d) above, now that I have chopped down this weed germane that suddenly sprang up, it was like this. About three days after our sherry party at The Goat I had a letter from Freddie and I am here to tell yee-ewe that that was a very remarkable thing. I should not be surprised if I am about the only woman in the world who ever got a letter from Freddie, for, as I said before, he was practically illiterate and I am quite sure he had to put his tongue out and breathe very deeply before he could write at all. This remarkable document told me that he would be at the gate with his car at a certain time on a certain night and that if I would come out with him for an hour he would be fearfully bucked and he was mine very sincerely. For a moment I was solemnly impressed, for another moment I thought he had taken leave of his senses, and in the third moment I decided to be at the gate at the time he said and find out the exact position. He drove the car about a mile out of town, parked it at the roadside on top of a small hill, and said: 'I say, what a nice chap old Rollin is!'

Now, I am as fond of my friends as anyone, but I had not lied my way out of Whitely House on a frosty night to hold a kind of Te Deum service about Mr. Rollin, so I said: 'Yes, isn't he?' in a coolish voice.

'You know,' said Freddie with a profound air, 'I think he's got perception. Yes, perception.'

'In what particular way?' I asked, for Madame X said that Men who were Lonely valued Intelligent, Interested Companionship and I thought Freddie must be feeling lonely or something.

'Well, that name he called you — Lady Flashing Beam — I *liked* that.'

'Why?' I asked, getting really interested and not correcting his rendering of the name because that would only have led to literary trouble.

'I don't know. I just sort of liked it. It's sort of romantic and that. He's nobody's fool, old Rollin.'

Hurrah for Rollin, I thought. 'No. He's not,' I agreed.

'In fact,' said Freddie with a rush, 'I think maybe I've done you an injustice, calling you a fool and so on. After all, old Rollin doesn't think you're a fool.'

'I don't think old Rollin is a fool either,' I said.

'What's *that* got to do with it?' Freddie asked.

'Well, what's what old Rollin thinks got to do with *you* calling me a fool?'

'Here, wait a minute!' Freddie protested. 'Draw it mild. I mean —'

'Listen,' I said, 'you *are* a fool. And to you *I* am a fool and you are quite right. Old Rollin and me is quite a different thing from *you* and me, you ass. Come on, start her up! I've got to get back.'

'Oh, well, hell! If you're going to be *clever* —' he said.

'Me? Clever? Don't be a bigger ass than you can help! Come on! Home!'

'All right!' said Freddy huffily. 'But what would you say if I told you I loved you?'

'I would say you are a damned liar,' I replied.

'Honestly, you're the bottom! What sort of thing is that to say to a chap?'

'The truth,' I said. 'Holy cow, Freddie, you and I can't do anything together except dance — we can't even talk!'

'What d'ye mean — talk? We're talking now, aren't we?

What the devil d'ye want?'

'Me? I don't know. Not this, anyway. Let's go home!'

'All right. So it isn't a go?'

'No, it isn't a go, Freddie."

'What about the Hunt Ball?'

'Oh, that of *course*! A ball is different,' I said.

'You're quite right,' Freddie said solemnly. 'You *are* a fool and I was a fool for thinking you weren't. I'm glad about the ball though. No hard feelings?'

'No feelings at all, Freddie.'

'That's fine.'

'It's much more comfortable,' I told him. 'Feelings are the devil. One day when you are a three- or four-striper you'll fall in love with the Fourth Sea Lord's wife and come and tell me that feelings are the devil!'

'Don't be an ass!' said Freddie and we drove home.

I must have thought about Freddie off and on for all of a quarter of an hour that night before going to sleep, or, more precisely, I thought how odd it was how people could be influenced by other people, even people like Freddie. Now, although Freddie was illiterate in many ways and practically an idiot in many other ways, he was a very promising young submarine officer, which, if you have ever looked at the complicated insides of a submarine, you will realise argues a certain cleverness, not to say brilliance of mind. How anyone remembers which lever to pull or button to press to fire a torpedo out of one of these submarines, I do not know, which just goes to show that people have different sorts of cleverness, say what you like. Thinking all this about Freddie and coming to this conclusion about different types of cleverness, I reached the further conclusion that the trouble with people was that they were never consistently anything and that the most you could say for them was that in their mature stages they got to the point where one or two characteristics became their dominant ones. Muriel's dominant, which seemed to be dithering (as I called it to myself), had taken charge of her early in life, and Madame X was pretty well set with *her* dominant for which I had no specific name but for which I had a well-developed dislike, while it seemed that Freddie and I were still melting-pots, boiling cauldrons of this and that, sort of gypsy's stews, out of which anything might develop according to the influences that got into us, as a cook might toss in a bunch of herbs. I made a resolution to look out for these influences. I thought about what could happen to me if I got over-influenced by an influence and almost had to put the light on to stop scaring myself. I had suddenly realised that it was possible for *me* to turn into a Madame X almost without knowing it. That was a dreadful thought. I had to think of something else and quickly, and Mr. Rollin came into my mind, bless him. Then suddenly I sat up and *did* put the light on and stared at the wall. Bless my soul, I thought, there is Mr. Rollin, who must be sixty if he is a day, and he does not really have a dominant at all yet. He is as open to influence as Freddie! And he might do almost anything, for he does not even have a submarine to take up some of his attention! This was too much. I put the light out; with determination I conjured up a picture of the path through the juniper bushes that led to the spring at home, and it was a beautiful day, with the wood-pigeons gurr-gurring in the trees and the bees humming, and I went to sleep.

So as a result of our meeting Freddie outside The Goat I began to watch Mr. Rollin deliberately instead of just in a casual way, as one watches everything that happens, and I began to see that he was a Changed Man. When I had come to Whitely House he had been a poor player, a walking shadow drifting about its crowded stage without catching a glimmer of the lights, but now he had drifted off the Whitely House stage altogether on to some separate stage of his own, where, I felt, he might be building up some shattering drama, or ridiculous farce or gaudy revue or even a circus and not a soul around him was taking the slightest notice. Notably, Madame X, who should have been the most interested spectator, was taking no notice, because it was not her nature to notice people except to bend them to her own ends — and she thought she had Mr. Rollin permanently bent — and also she was too busy being the centre of her own drama.

This is where we get back, by a circuitous route, to (*a*) above, which shows you how silly it is to try to write a book about life in a business-like way, going from (*a*) to (*b*) and then on to (*c*). Life does not go from (*a*) to (*b*), but starts in somewhere around (*m*), comes back to (*b*) and then takes a violent leap down to (*t*), with pauses in between to wonder if it would not be better to use numerical designations like 3 and 5 instead of (*c*) and (*e*) or even Romans, like (iii) and (v), except that they are such a pest when you get up to the big numbers like MCLLXVIII. I have often thought that an important factor in the Decline and Fall of the Roman Empire was the complicated way the Romans had of thinking. If I had to think out all that about before or after the Ides of March before dating a letter, I could easily go into a Decline, and how young women ever spoke to their young men, with all that correct use of the gerund and positioning of the verb, without coming to a Fall passes my comprehension.

To get back to (*a*), the tickets for the Hunt Ball arrived on Mr. Rollin's breakfast plate on the very day that Madame X was announcing the New Role she had found for herself. Watch out, as the American comedians say, for thisisgonna-killya. Madame X had decided that she was a Martyr to a Cause. Out of the depth of her love for humanity, she said, she had been inspired to start something that might bring Light, Sweetness, Friendship and Spirituality into the lives of the Lonely Ones. More than that, she said, she had been a Carrier of a Small Candle in the attempt to bring the Light of Peace to all the earth, for where you had Abiding Friendship, she said, there could be No War. And what had happened? Only, she sighed, what happened to so many of those chosen people who were inspired to Work for the Weal of the World: her effort had turned into a Frankenstein, a Monster, which was destroying her. Look what was happening. There was so much work that only she could do. Oh yes, my dears — you try very hard, but you girls have not the inspiration or the experience to be able to pour yourselves out on the altar of sacrifice. You, Muriel, are a dear girl, but since you have become engaged to this — this curate, isn't it? — your work has suffered, naturally, naturally. And you, Janet, you are tremendously efficient, almost a little Frankenstein in yourself, dear — but your approach is, and always has been, the material one. Your first thought is that you have your living to earn — very natural, the struggle for survival — but if we all thought in that way, where would the world be? Where? And I am tired, so tired!

By this time Muriel was in nervous tears and I was again at the mercy of my giggles, while phrases like 'I am dying, Egypt, dying!' and ''Tis a far far better thing —' rolled sonorously through my mind, and Mr. Rollin was rootling about among his letters as usual, Mm-Mm-ing and Bless-my-soul-ing and not hearing a word she was saying.

'— and day and night,' Madame X was inspired by the devil to work up to her peroration, 'the Lonely Ones of the earth are Hunting Me Down, but the Hunt is Nearly Over!'

'Yes, my dear,' said Mr. Rollin decisively, looking up from his letters, 'I think we'll go to the Hunt Ball this year. I should like to watch the young people dance. Yes, indeed. I shall reply to Lady Firmantle's kind invitation straight away'; and, breaking into a tuneful humming of the Blue Danube Waltz, he left the room. Madame X, more in sorrow than in anger, but the sorrow winning only by a very short head as it tended to do these days, rose in silence and departed to the drawing-room and the pile of Lonely Ones' letters I had put there to await her Sweet Assuagement. I put my arms on the table, my head on my arms and laughed until I was almost deaf and blind.

'Janet!' I heard Muriel say at last, 'I never *heard* of a person like you! You *are* awful! What are we going to do?'

'Do? What do you mean, do? *I*'m going to the Hunt Ball!'

Muriel gulped and began to sob and I was sorry. I went round to her side of the table and put an arm round her and in that moment I had a dreadful, sick sense of shock as my own careless selfishness seemed to take material form and strike me a blow in the pit of the stomach. The skin of Muriel's neck was hot and dry and she was shivering as if her bones were dice in a shaken cup.

'Muriel! You're sick! You've got a temperature!'

'I kn-know!' she sobbed. 'I've had it for weeks! I can't help it!'

'You must go to bed! We must get a doctor.'

'Oh no!' It was a wailing shout. 'Oh no, I have to get on! The office —'

'The office's Aunt Fanny!' I bawled and shook her. 'I'm going to tell Mrs. Whitely-Rollin right away —'

Muriel fell on her knees on the floor and clutched at my legs. Hysteria was not a characteristic of my family. People did not behave like this.

'Muriel!' I bent and shook her. 'Muriel! Get up! Sit in that chair! You hear me? Sit in THAT CHAIR, damn you!'

'Oh, don't say that! I think I'm damned already, Richard and I, yes —'

'Shut up!' I hauled her up and practically threw her into the chair, where she dissolved into a shivering, slobbering mass, and she began to gibber. 'I'm sorry! Don't tell anyone! I'm sorry! Don't get a doctor! I'm sorry! Please don't let Mrs. Whitely-Rollin know—'

'Hold your tongue!' I snapped in the voice of my grandmother, and she did. The family voice must have been just right.

'Now, Muriel, look, you must be reasonable. People do get ill sometimes and the doctors can mostly help them. And if Mrs. Whitely-Rollin knew how you feel she would be most sympathetic.'

God forgive me for being a hypocrite, I thought, for sympathy is not *in* that old cow!

'But she d-*does* know. I t-told her, right at the beginning, when I first felt so p-peculiar and she *was* very sympathetic. I'm neurotic, she says, and all you c-can do with that is to f-fight against it and be interested in things outside yourself. I'm s-selfish, that's what I am, and wicked and doctors can't do anything for people like me and —'

I found that I had gathered up a fine, big, deep breath right to the bottom of my diaphragm. I was simply *bursting* with breath and my mind was *bulging* with vitriolic words, all fizzing and ready to reduce Madame X to an ugly cinder and you know what? I think I am a person like this: I am a person that once in a very long time has an utterly unselfish moment and this was one of them, for I let my good, big, deep breath come out through my mouth and go to waste because I felt that to say what I was going to say about Madame X would make Muriel more sick than she was already.

'Of course you're selfish!' I told Muriel smoothly. 'I've often noticed it; but, darn it, I am not going to sit here and talk about your selfishness and catch 'flu or measles or whatever you've got off of you. I'm not talking about your selfishness — I'm talking about your temperature and your slobbery nose, and I'm going to telephone the doctor.'

'Oh Janet!' she wailed. 'Oh—'

'You look a sight!' I told her. 'For Pete's sake put yourself to bed and try to look decent enough not to frighten the poor man.'

She trailed behind me to the office and watched me with drowned, swollen eyes while I spoke to the doctor.

'You'd better get to bed,' I said, putting down the receiver. 'I am Going into the Drawing-room.'

Muriel fled and scuttled up the stairs like a rabbit.

I took myself into the drawing-room with a nonchalant air. Sometime I may tell you about Monica and me and the word 'nonchalant' but not now, because I am busy. So was Madame X, of course — busy, I mean, for she was never nonchalant — when I appeared before her writing-table. She looked up.

'Janet! Must I tell you even *again* about these interruptions you make in my Time and Thought? Is it quite impossible to make a mind like yours understand that some people have nerves of more delicate balance?'

'Muriel is sick,' I said. 'I thought you would like to know that Dr. Sutherland is on his way round to see her.'

'Dr. Sutherland? Who called him?'

'I did.'

'Sometimes, my dear, you undertake things that are beyond your scope!'

'Oh, it was quite easy, Mrs. Whitely-Rollin! I just looked up the number and —'

'You did not think that *I*, in my position, might like to be informed?'

'Yes, Mrs. Whitely-Rollin. That's why I came in here just after I had —'

She snorted, put down her pen and rose. 'You have been extremely — officious, Janet. Muriel is a very silly, neurotic young woman and there is not a thing the matter with her except this — this entanglement she has got into with this most unsuitable young man. Before his advent she was a nice, normal girl — oh, you would not understand.'

'I think she must have measles or something.'

'Measles! A mind like yours *would* think of — of measles! Now, Janet, go back to the office and do not interfere any further. You are kindly disposed but young, and this situation needs a Woman with a Woman's Understanding. *I* will interview Doctor Sutherland.'

So I took my kindly-disposed young self back to the office, found myself again filled with breath right to the bottom of my diaphragm, my mind seething with words, so I sat down at the typewriter and wrote to Aunt Julia. I might as well have saved the breath, the words and the typewriter ribbon. Aunt Julia came down from London right away and tried to get Muriel moved away to a nursing home, but Madame X had the situation too well in hand. Muriel would not budge from her bedroom in Whitely House where she was having 'every Care, Kindness and Attention' and that was that. Doctor Sutherland did his best. He made out a good case for the nursing home, its night staff and other amenities, but in the face of Madame X's assurance that she Personally would have every care of Muriel, Day and Night, at No Matter What Cost to Herself, what could he do? He did what he could. He reduced Muriel's temperature to normal, he got her back into the habit of sleeping at night, he gave her a blood tonic and at his final visit a month after I had called him he made a strong final bid for her salvation.

'The worst is over now,' he said as he stood in the hall beside the Two-handed Engine.

Madame X glared at me and then, meaningly, at the office

99

door, but I put on my blankest look and stood my ground.

'I hesitate, Mrs. Whitely-Rollin, to suggest this, for I know what a busy person you are and your work has already been much disrupted, but Miss Thornton ought to have a holiday. Two months at least, if it is at all possible, and preferably out of England — Switzerland, Austria. And it would work wonders if she went with a congenial companion — like young Miss Sandison here, for instance. Someone she is at ease with, whom she knows well, so that there would be no tension.'

'I entirely agree with you, Doctor,' said Madame X, and I am here to tell yee-ewe that half a feather out of an eider duck could have laid both Doctor Sutherland and me prostrate at the feet of the Two-handed Engine. 'And I have an excellent suggestion to make,' she continued. 'I too need a holiday. I am afraid some of us are the kind who Work On without Thought of Self to Breaking Point — and I am as close to Muriel as a Mother. Indeed, you will notice that she frequently addresses me as Mother? I shall go with her Myself. I have nursed her thus far, with success I hope, and Having Set My Hand to the Plough, I will Finish the Work.'

There was a dead silence, and then Doctor Sutherland picked up his hat. 'Well, good morning, Mrs. Whitely-Rollin. Good morning, young lady. Remember the Hospital Dance next week! Good morning!'

So the next week Madame X and Muriel went off to Kitzbuhel and I went to the Hospital Dance, and Mr. Rollin came too.

While Muriel was ill, of course, the Hunt Ball had come along and Mr. Rollin had come to it with me, both of us members of Lady Firmantle's party, and Mr. Rollin had a wonderful time. It was in the course of that evening that I became aware that much of the Town and County had only been vaguely aware of the existence of Mr. Rollin, for he had come to Kent some thirty years ago as the husband of the well-known Miss Whitely and had then been heard of no more. Since I had known him, Mr. Rollin had never appeared to do anything in the way of being active about any job or business of any kind, although he occasionally spent a day in London and sometimes went out to dinner in the Town with gentlemen who seemed to be as obscure as himself. After supper at the Ball, when Mr. Rollin was going round in his courtly way paying compliments to all the older ladies and being roguish with the younger ones, and the Firmantle parents and Freddie and I were still sitting at the table, Freddie said: 'By Jove, old Rollin's having a whale of a time, isn't he?'

'Doctor Rollin to you, my lad, if every man had his due,' said Admiral Sir Hammond Firmantle.

'*I* didn't know the old man was a medico!' said Freddie.

'Not medicine. Philosophy. A lot of other things as well — a very distinguished scholar, one of the greater authorities on eastern Mediterranean languages — Turkish and all that.'

'Good Lord!' said Freddie. 'Did *you* know that, Jan?'

'Not me. I couldn't be more astonished.'

'No wonder!' said Lady Firmantle. 'Scholars! All brains and no sense! Must be, to go and attach himself to that old harridan Whitely. How he has stood her all these years I don't know.'

'Insulation,' said the Admiral. 'Scholarly insulation. Wonder what happened to the boy, though?'

'Boy?' I repeated stupidly.

'Yes. There was a boy — not hers. He was a widower when she married him. Before your time in Kent, my dear,' he told his wife. 'Clever boy, too — was at Oxford with your Uncle Paul, Freddie. Can't remember his name — he must be rising forty by now. . . . Danced with the Master's wife yet, my boy?'

'No; next but one I'm down for, sir.'

'Heavy in the hand, very,' said the Admiral. 'Janet, young Cartwright looks like a man who is looking for you. Off you go!'

Freddie and I danced the last waltz together, and Freddie said: 'I say, I *do* feel an ass, you know!'

'In what way?'

'About old Rollin — calling him no fool and all that.'

'Huh!' I said bitterly. 'What kind of an ass do you think *I* feel? I've been going around being ever so kind to him for absolute months! Giving him little treats and a little interest in life with my way of it!'

'It just shows you, doesn't it?' said Freddie.

'Doesn't it,' I agreed.

But after all, nothing was altered between Mr. Rollin and myself — which is not surprising, I suppose, for we were, in relation to one another, exactly the same two people that we had always been, and we were extremely happy together at Whitely House. Medway, the manservant, and his wife ran the house and planned the meals as they had always done; I ran the Chain as I had mostly always done, and Mr. Rollin talked delightfully at table as he had often done of late, and we went for walks and to the cinema and to The Goat with Freddie and his friends, and we did not miss Madame X and Muriel at all and hardly ever even thought about them except when Muriel sent me postcards saying how much better she was feeling and how beautiful the Tyrol was, and I would pass them to Mr. Rollin across the breakfast table.

'Ah,' he would say, 'another few words from out the eternal snows. Mmm. Yes, indeed, Innsbruck. Very nice. Innsbruck. Always connected in my mind with Browning's "My Last Duchess".'

' ". . . a rarity, which Claus of Innsbruck cast in bronze for me"?' I asked.

'Yes, indeed, child!' That I should be quick about his beloved poetical allusions delighted him and it was so easy to please him thus with my memory for words. 'So sad — to be dismissed for Neptune and a sea-horse! Poor Duchess. "Cast in bronze" — bronze, a beautiful word, soft, hard, light, dark all at once — a *princely* word!' and he would be off on a gay romp through words from a dozen languages, some ancient, some modern. He was the most delightful companion.

On the evening after Madame X and Muriel departed for Austria I was made free of his study at the back of the house, and a delightful apartment it was. There was nothing here of the rose-mad and rose-madder chintzes of the drawing-room or the flowery china ornaments, nothing of the Birmingham-Benares and what Twice calls Period-Antique-Reeproh (short for reproduction) furniture. This was a room full of things that some individual had gathered together in one place because he wished to live among them and if it was dominated by books and a gramophone whose records lived partly in an old mahogany wine-cooler and partly in an orange box, well, that was the sort of individual Mr. Rollin was and that is how the room was. It was a very satisfactory sort of room, especially when he sat in the middle of it at his big table, took off his spectacles and talked. We put the drawing-room out of use right away and sat in the study all the time that we were not in the dining-room and we talked and talked and talked.

I could not quote all that talk verbatim if I tried and you would be bored to distraction, probably, if I did, as one is by people who tell one the stories of the plays they have seen. For a play is a play and a conversation is a conversation and neither lends itself to dead reportage. But it was at this time, and largely through Mr. Rollin, that I became aware of myself as a personality.

I think that the essence of youth is its completely out-turned mind. Real youth does not look inward at all, is a mind unaware of itself, a greedy sponge for the absorption of all that comes its way from this great world in which it finds itself. It has no awareness that it is contributing anything to the world or to other people, or that it may be taking something out of the world or out of other people; it is too busy with the sheer miracle of being alive. At least, I think that that is how I was, and I think I was late of development. I had a good long run before the 'shades of the prison house began to close', before my self rose up about me.

This awareness of self was, of course, the result of a prolonged process but it seemed to me that, suddenly, the walls of the prison house solidified out of nothingness. When Madame X and Muriel had been away for about six weeks, Mr. Rollin said to me in the study one evening: 'Lady Flashing Stream, I have been feeling of late that you and I are guilty of a social lapse. Mm. Yes, indeed.' I gazed at him in silence. 'Yes. People round about, mostly *your* friends, have been extremely kind and hospitable to us and we have done nothing in return. In short, I feel that you and I should give a party.'

'A *party*?'

'Mm. Yes, indeed. Why not?'

'Here? At Whitely House?'

'Why not? The drawing-room has an excellent parquet floor for dancing, and I am told at the wireless shop, where I have made enquiries, that we may hire a selection of recordings of music for the dance for a small fee. Medway could move my gramophone into the drawing-room for the evening. Yes, indeed. I think perhaps that you and I could give a party that our friends might enjoy.'

'Of course we could, Mr. Rollin!' I was enthusiastic as soon as the first shock was over.

'I have been considering the matter for some time,' he continued, 'but was at a loss about the refreshments and the seating in the dining-room until we went to that delightful function at your friend Mrs. Carter's the other night. What was called a fork supper, I understand. Delightful, I thought. Mm. Yes, indeed. Most enjoyable.'

From there it was the merest step to the party. I was, and still am, a person like this: if I don't know how to do anything or how to find my way to anywhere, I ask people who *do* know. It is remarkable how much other people know that one does not know oneself and more remarkable still how generous they are with their knowledge. So I co-opted Lady Firmantle for her hospitality, Freddie Firmantle for his party spirit and Angela Carter for the food and drink, with the result that the party went with a bang that was heard throughout the Town and County. Mr. Rollin sent out the invitations in his own scholarly hand, almost seventy of them, and all were accepted, and then his other great contribution to the arrangements was made on the morning of the party itself.

'Medway!' he called from the front door.

'Yessir!'

'Kindly assist me to take this thing out into the back yard.'

'The h'armour, sir?' Medway was horrified.

'The Two-handed Engine, Mr. Rollin?' I was overcome too.

'A rose by any other name — ah, yes, indeed. I refer to this

104

suit of natty gent's clothing,' he said and gave it a slap on the cuirass causing its visor to open and shut again with a hollow 'Clonk!'

''Ere, look out for its 'elmet, sir!' said Medway.

Feeling my giggles getting the upper hand, I took myself off, and when next I visited the hall the Two-handed Engine was gone and Mr. Rollin was dusting his hands and saying: 'Bogus, mm, yes, very bogus,' in a satisfied voice.

By the time the guests arrived I felt like a Christmas tree with candles of excitement burning all over me, and was near to tears with happiness at Mr. Rollin and Lady Firmantle 'opening the ball' to the Blue Danube Waltz played on the gramophone. By the time the last of the guests left, I was physically a limp rag, my night's candles had burnt out, but mentally life was a clear darkness full of strange, lovely shapes as if beautiful impressions had taken concrete forms, and perhaps that is why I remember so well our talk in the study before we went to bed.

'Thank you, Mr. Rollin!' I said. 'It was a *beautiful* party!'

'Sit down, child, if you are not too tired.'

I sat down.

'That's right. I will not keep you long, but there is something I wish to say. You have thanked me for your party and that was graceful as well as perceptive. I gave the party for you and your young friends. It was my pleasure and my *thanks* to you.'

'Thanks?'

'I wonder if I can make you understand — so many words and yet so difficult to express a meaning. Yes, indeed. People are like mirrors, child. The light and the darkness play on them and they respond by throwing back a reflection which is coloured, distorted or beautified by the quality of their own glass. And mirror plays on mirror, colouring, distorting, beautifying, tarnishing, and sometimes one mirror dazzles another by its fierce, harsh light. I have called you Lady Flashing Stream, which is an old man's whimsical nonsense, but it gives a picture of the sparkling, liquid light which you brought to me. It is for that that I returned thanks in the form of a trifling thing that you would enjoy; selfish thanks, indeed, for thanks in this form meant that I could watch you in action on the mirrors of all our guests. Go to bed now, and pray that the hungry generations may never tread you down. Good night, my dear.'

I went to bed and cried and cried, for I felt for the first time that much was expected of me when, up until now, I had never thought of anyone expecting *anything* of me and thought that any expecting that was to be done was for me to do.

Our party was given on the date it was, of course, because the return of Madame X and Muriel was thought to be imminent, although this was never mentioned. The party was intended to be our Swan Song, but we were thrown into the position of the passée diva who becomes committed to one 'Farewell' concert after another. The Two-handed Engine began to spend more and more time in the back yard, and Lady Firmantle became an habituée of a house that she had hitherto refused to visit. Also, in the background, were the dear old Chain and the Parent Pacifists, but when the return of the wanderers was postponed, the latter moved forward into the foreground and announced that they intended, in the form of a committee of three, to descend upon the rural peace of Mr. Rollin and myself.

'A profoundly pompous and stupid communication,' said Mr. Rollin, handing me their letter. 'Mrs. Whitely-Rollin's letter of the sixth inst. they say — why this pretence that they are familiar with the tongue of Cicero or Horace? And why the abbreviation in the midst of such verbosity? Surely the sixth of June would be adequately comprehensible and a deal better fitted to their tongues and pens?'

'Inst. is not Latin to *them*, Mr. Rollin,' I explained.

'Nor to *me* — no, indeed!'

'I didn't mean *that*!' I protested. 'What I meant is that to them "inst." is a declension of "in", meaning "the month we are now *in*". At least, that's what *I* think about people who write inst.'

'A charming piece of reasoning, Lady Flashing Stream. And what of ult. and prox., the brothers in bastardy of inst.?'

'They are the ones before and after that they never remember which is which,' I told him.

'You speak from experience of ult. and proxers?'

'I do.'

'How utterly abysmal the human mind can be. Yes, indeed. Very well. Tell these people lunch on Wednesday, my dear, Wednesday of the week prox. or do I mean ult.?'

'Prox.'

'Very well. We may as well conclude this business.'

I did not attach any special meaning to his use of the word 'conclude', but when the Wednesday of the week prox. and the Parent Pacifists arrived I realised that 'conclude' was precisely what he meant. I ought to have realised it before, for he was never a careless spiller of words.

The Parent Pacifists (in committee) consisted of a — rather surprisingly, to me — red-faced, old, country-squirish gentleman in a Norfolk jacket and two, less surprising, weedy-looking, city-ish clerks in striped trousers and rather longish hair, and Mr. Rollin fixed all three with a beady eye over the soup and said: 'So you have heard from my wife, I imagine, that she has decided to retire from her secretaryship of the — er — the Chain of Friendship?'

I was speechless with amazement, but Norfolk jacket indicated that this was so.

'Very well advised of her, if I may express an opinion,' said Mr. Rollin. 'I understand that Miss Thornton is also resigning, also well advised. Her health has not been good. No, indeed. Well, as I see it, the withdrawal of the office from this address may take place as soon as is convenient to you. As to the mechanics of that, Miss Sandison is here and will, I am sure, attend to everything most efficiently. She is welcome to remain for as long as may suit you, and *her*, of course.'

And that was that. Norfolk jacket and his minions went away and all I had to do was pack up the odds and ends of scrap that the Chain now was, lay them in crates and send them to London. After he had seen the Parent Pacifists through the gate in the wall Mr. Rollin returned to the house, closed the door and dusted his hands. It occurred to me that this was not

107

the first time that he had cleared up a muddle left behind by his wife or had thrown in the dustbin the latest broken doll of which she had tired. It also occurred to me that he had thrown my means of livelihood into the dustbin too, and that he was completely unaware of having done so. He could think with remarkable clarity — it simply did not occur to him to think of bed, board and lodging and a few shillings a week, for such things had never come to his notice. I did not bring them to his notice now, for I am a person like this: I think the world is the better of a few people who have never had to think of getting and spending and laying waste their powers. So I watched him stump off with a satisfied air to his study, and then took myself to the office to collect my scattered wits. I had only picked up about half of them and put them back in the bag with the tape round the top where I keep my wits (My Friend Monica keeps hers all neatly pigeon-holed in a miniature rolltop desk) when the telephone rang and it was My Friend Angela (the one I mentioned as being good at food and drink for parties) to ask me to come to tea with her that afternoon but not to bring Mr. Rollin. I asked her why not and she said Just Because and I said All Right.

Angela lived in a rambling red house known as the Court, which lay about three miles out of town in the opposite direction to the Firmantles and had a husband called Hubert, who was Big Business in the City in the shipping world. Hubert was in London all the week and very often in Liverpool and Glasgow too, but at the Court Angela had three children and Hubert's old father, who had arthritis in his legs but not in his brain and who did quite a lot of business from a wheel-chair and was known to be a very, very cross old gentleman indeed. I had often heard Madame X say how sorry she was for Angela Carter with 'that selfish, trying old man', but Angela never looked as if she really needed being sorry for and was one of the gayest people I have ever known — still is, indeed, although she is a lot older now, like the rest of us. At this time I am telling about she was thirty-two.

Usually at tea at the Court there were a lot of people, mostly children and governesses, and tea was in the dining-room and very comfortable, but today it was, apparently, to be held in a rather conglomerate room known as the morning-room, and when it came it was only two cups instead of the usual dozen or more.

'Just you and me,' said Angela. 'Because I wish to speak to you.'

'Speak?'

'Yes.'

'What do you want to *speak* about?'

'Don't keep on repeating that silly word like that, Janet! Can you never be serious?'

'Yes. Why?'

'Because this *is* serious. ... When's Old Sweetness and Light coming home?'

It was amazing how everyone would say anything rather than say 'Mrs. Whitely-Rollin', for I thought I, with my Madame X, had been unique, which just goes to show you, as Freddie would say.

'That's not serious,' I said. 'That's just plain unpleasant. And nobody knows, anyway. Why are you asking?'

'Janet, I don't understand you. You're as clever as paint in some ways and so naïve in others that you slay me. Listen, the old Pussies at the Teapot are spitting and scratching like mad at the Carryings-On of you and Mr. Rollin.'

'*What*?' I was so startled that my insides turned into wire springs that jumped in all directions and then fell jangling in a heap into the pit of my stomach. The Brown Teapot was the town coffee shop run by the usual ineffectual ladies in flowered smocks and wooden beads, and Teapot Pussies was the name used by people like Angela and me for their regular clientele. 'What are they saying?' I asked.

'What do you expect? You've been alone in the house with him for weeks, you've held parties, you've been seen at the cinema, at The Goat — you've been seen in bed with him by now, I shouldn't wonder!'

'Don't be revolting!'

'There's no use getting like that, Janet! There's no use any of us getting like that. We are all so mad at ourselves we could

109

kick ourselves over it, but although we have all got quite normally dirty minds, none of us even thought of it.'

'How do you mean — *all* of us?'

'Lady Firmantle and Cissie and me and the rest of us.'

'Oh dear. Poor Mr. Rollin. What should I do, Angela? Angela, it's not *true*, you know!'

'Don't be an idiot, Janet! We know that. And don't worry about Mr. Rollin — these other-worldly old-scholar characters are tougher than you think. But I have a suggestion to make about *you* — I'd like you to come here. The Grand has fought with his secretary again.'

'Old Mr. Carter? But he has *men* secretaries. Besides, I have a job to finish at Whitely House.'

'The Grand has announced that he will try a female secretary if you are willing to come to him. As for Whitely House, you know your job there is only a not very funny joke.'

'I don't like to walk out like that, just to please the Pussies.'

'Cussed, huh?'

'No, but — I'm not ungrateful, Angela. And I would come to Mr. Carter like a shot, I'd like to. But I've got to make Mr. Rollin understand first — we're *friends*, you see.'

'Lady Firmantle said you were as Highland as peat — I see what she meant. Well, there it is. Come and talk to the Grand for a minute. I can see you are dying to get away.'

As we went into the large library which contained the Grand but was not quite large enough to contain all of his temper, he growled at us without looking up and said: 'What d'ye want? Go away!'

'Here is Janet Sandison, Grand,' said Angela.

'Janet—? Oh, that girl from Scotland who walks as if she meant it? People creeping about like that man Morris, I'm sick of it. They tell me you can read and write?'

'Yes, Mr. Carter.'

'You're with that silly woman at Whitely House that's always writing about peace on earth and subscriptions?'

'Yes, Mr. Carter.'

'Why do you work for a fool like that?'

'To earn my living, Mr. Carter.'

'That's a sane reason, anyway. As long as you don't believe in peace on earth. Leave her and come to me. Four pounds a week, live here, every weekend off from Saturday noon to go and see your mother. More money soon if you suit me.'

The salary convinced me that it was all a wonderful dream and the great thing about dreams is that you can say or do anything in them. 'Well, suit you?' he barked.

'Very well, if I would suit *you*, Mr. Carter, but I haven't got a mother for the weekends.'

'What? No mother?' He beetled his brows at me.

'Morris and all these people have mothers — Heavens come down if they can't go to see them. You mean, you'd be here on Sundays?'

'Yes, please, if you don't mind.'

He leaned forward in his wheel-chair and wagged a finger at me, very much the Chairman making an important point to his Board of Directors. 'Listen!' he said fiercely. 'Carter, Oulson & Co. was started by my old father who was a shipping clerk in the City. He was a family man, but he didn't have much time for his family through the week. He wrote to his brother in New Zealand every Sunday and we had all to keep quiet while he was doing it. I LIKE TO WRITE LETTERS ON A SUNDAY — but can I? NO. They have to go to SEE THEIR MOTHERS. All right. You can go out on Tuesdays, Thursdays and Saturdays when my message fellow comes and that will suit everybody. Angela, give her that room with the pink curtains. Girls like pink. Come the Friday after next, girl. That fellow Morris will be gone by then, thank God. I hope he goes and *lives* with his mother and she gets as sick of him as I am. Goodbye.'

In the hall Angela collapsed on to a chair and looked at me.

'Girls like pink!' she said. 'I don't know. Lady Firmantle said ought we to interfere and we decided that we ought, but I don't know. Pink curtains! Janet, *don't* start a scandal with the Grand, will you?'

I felt that life was crowding in on me much too fast. 'What on earth do you mean?' I asked.

'You and your old men!' said Angela and pushed me out of the house.

I set out on the bus journey from the Court back to Whitely House with my mind in a muddle. I think I was, and still am, a person like this: very slow-witted and able to deal with only one thing at a time at that, and too many things, all concerning me personally, had happened to me in a single day, like losing one job and being given another, being told I was a local scandal, Highland and being a 'you and your old men'. I thought about the last things first because they seemed to be more important than the losing and getting of jobs. To be a Highland local scandal whose name became linked with the names of old men made me think of a book entitled *Gentlemen Prefer Blondes* which had been having a succès de scandale in the town just before Madame X went to Austria, and she had told us at breakfast one morning that she simply could not understand why people read that sort of thing. Muriel was in bed, of course, but Mr. Rollin and I listened with interest — for neither of us had heard of this piece of literature — to what she had to say and that afternoon I went to the local library and asked my favourite assistant for a copy of the work. She said: 'Oh, I'm SO sorry — we only HAVE three copies and I've just ISSUED the last one. Oh, but just a MINUTE! It was Mr. ROLLIN who got it, so you can read it after HIM.'

So I THANKED her and came AWAY, GIGGLING and thinking in CAPITALS, which was the effect she always HAD on me. I giggled quite a lot at the artless tale told by Anita Loos' preferred blonde too, but I was not inclined to giggle at myself as her imitator. To begin with I am not a blonde, and to end with I have not got the true egocentricity of the true artist in blonde-ishment. I felt rather a fool rattling along in the bus, and extremely angry, for nothing can rouse rage, moral indignation and all sorts of other high-sounding feelings like being made to feel rather a fool. And I did not know what I was going to say to Mr. Rollin, until, just as I was opening the gate to Whitely House, I was inspired. Why say anything? I had lost one job, so I had found another. Finis. I stopped feeling rather a fool straight away and stepped into the house feeling like Voltaire, Wellington, Einstein or Napoleon or any other great brain or strategist who may happen to come to your mind (not that I think much of Einstein myself, but that is beside the point). I went upstairs to my room thinking some Great Thoughts, by which I mean that another of the great obvious truths of the ages began to be illuminated by my dim intelligence. Since my childhood, perhaps at intervals of a year, our Minister at home would choose for the text of his hour-long sermon that part of Ecclesiastes which has the words: 'There is a time to weep and a time to laugh . . . a time of war and a time of peace.' The grown-up people went to sleep while the soft, Highland voice went on, up and down the mazes of scholarship, along and around the long galleries of days and years of reading and research, and I would watch the black cherries quivering in the bonnet of old Granny Macintosh in the front pew, while she sucked her Sunday peppermints and nodded in the waking dream at the end of a long, hard life. But now I saw what the words meant. There were times for doing something, there were times for doing nothing, and it would lead to expertness in smooth living if one could decide, correctly, which time was which. So, with Ecclesiastes on my side, I made my decision and went down to dinner, with, more or less, trumpets sounding on all sides and feeling so wise that I might have had a long white beard.

Over coffee, in the study, I told Mr. Rollin where I had been that afternoon and that I was going, in less than a fortnight, to be secretary to old Mr. Carter at the Court.

'So,' he said, 'you have taken matters out of my hands, my dear. Yes. But I think that will be a very suitable and comfortable place for you. Yes, indeed. Yes. I am delighted.'

'Out of your hands?' I asked.

'I did not mean to presume, my dear. No, indeed not. But I will be candid with you. I have always deprecated this — this work of my wife's as a rather foolish undertaking. I may be quite wrong, of course, but we all have our views. At least, I have always felt it to be unsuitable for *you*, for both your temperament and your intelligence. About Miss Muriel I have no opinion — I have not studied her. But I have a number of friends up and down the country, in particular at Oxford, and I had thought that when this — er — undertaking here could be concluded I would ask you to go to one or other of these friends. They could have given you work which would have appealed to you, I feel sure. But I am extremely happy about this arrangement you have made — Carter is a most interesting man in his own field. Yes, indeed. I have been proud to give him a little assistance with this work of his.'

'Isn't he in shipping?' I asked.

'Until his retirement he was, yes. But he did not tell you? Dear me. Of course he is always in a hurry. He is at work on a history of the Port of London, a wide subject in all its ramifications. Yes, indeed. Most fascinating. Some of the earlier documents which I have been asked to translate for him are of enormous interest — the silk road to Samarkand, the poetry of commerce, the true and satisfying paradox. Yes, indeed.'

His scholar's eyes gleamed behind his spectacles. I was appalled.

'Oh, Mr. Rollin! *I* can't do a job like that! I wish I had known before!'

'Whyever not, child? All fascinating. The great days of Venice — Venice who spent what Venice earned!'

'*I* don't know anything about Venetian shipping — or any other shipping, for that matter!' I almost screamed. 'I thought I would have to write a few letters saying yours of the tenth ult. and so on! He didn't *tell* me anything about histories of ports and ancient documents and things!'

Mr. Rollin waved all this aside grandly. 'He is writing, of course, in English,' he said. 'Or, to be precise, he is collating an enormous mass of valuable but heterogeneous information about the Port of London which he will emit in your direction in a series of staccato barks. It will be your unenviable duty to commit these barks to paper, if not in the tongue that Shakespeare spoke, at least in a form that approximates to the King's English, though why His Majesty should be blamed for the mauled carcase of our language I do not understand. It will not be easy, but it will be stimulating. Yes, indeed.'

Mr. Rollin was right as usual. Life with Mr. Carter was not easy, but it was stimulating, but that came later and is not germane to this story I am telling you about My Friend Muriel, anyway. There is no need to think I had forgotten her just because she went away to Austria. No, indeed. As if Muriel would let you forget her! . . .

After he had told me more about Mr. Carter than I had thought there *was* of Mr. Carter, Mr. Rollin came to a sort of peroration or summing-up.

'Ah. Mm. Yes. You must have felt this morning, my dear, that the ground had been cut from under your feet when I concluded that — er — undertaking of my wife's with those — er — people. Yes, indeed. To be truthful, I am an old man and I had underestimated the speed of events and this aeroplane post to the Continent is very remarkable. You see, when I wrote to my wife suggesting that the — er — thing be terminated, she wrote direct to these people tendering her resignation and that of Miss Muriel, and I had no idea, until I saw them today, what their reactions were going to be. Indeed. I find myself guilty of careless thinking in the matter. Had I thought clearly, I would have known that their reaction would be a passive one, if I may speak in riddles of people who are, in the final analysis, a riddle to me. Yes, indeed. But although I did not forewarn you of my plans, child, I was not heedless of your welfare. I would not have you think that. No. You have been treated quite carelessly enough, without heedlessness on my part.'

'Carelessly?'

'In my opinion, yes. I may be old-fashioned, but it was thoughtless of my wife to depart so suddenly and leave you in a position here that might be misconstrued, socially, by some of the inhabitants of this regrettably self-satisfied though remarkably uninteresting little town. Yes, indeed. But, of course, she was worried about Miss Muriel. However, young Mrs. Carter and the Admiral and his good lady and so many charming people have been so kind in receiving me along with you that we have been spared that sort of embarrassment.'

'Yes, indeed!' I sighed at him with the last of my breath, as, inwardly, I thanked the Preacher who had counselled me that there was a time to say nothing.

'So here we are all ready to set sail for a new destination.'

'You too?' I asked, just to be friendly.

'Yes, indeed. I have a wonderful plan. Would it interest you to hear it?'

'Of course it would!'

He smiled. 'I really believe that I am going to astonish you! I have planned to go to Canada to spend a holiday with my grandchildren!'

'Your granchildren! I—'

'You didn't even know I had a child, eh?' He beamed at me. His character of the precise, distinguished scholar had faded from his face. His long tight mouth had loosened and the light in his eyes was a comfortable glow rather than the clear arc of the scholar's table. He was no longer ageless, but an oldish man; no longer withdrawn and looking out at the world, but out in it and looking at its future for his descendants. 'Ah, but I have a son. Yes, indeed. And my son is married and has two children ...' He went to his big writing-table and from a drawer he took a large, leather-covered album. 'Here they are — here they all are! That is my son William and his wife Anne, and that is young James and little Deborah.'

For the first time in many months I thought of my time at 'Sandringham', when, one day, one of the little girls had shown me what she called her 'fambly' of dolls — 'and this is Mabel an' this is Annabel an' this one here is Teddy'. Mr. Rollin showing me his family was as young as that little girl.

'And you have never told me before about all these nice people?' I asked, no doubt sounding silly because I *felt* silly.

'I would not wish to be a bore,' he said, turning the pages of the album and smiling. 'I am of the opinion that it is far too easy to be a bore about one's own enthusiasms and opinions. Were it not so, surely there would be fewer bores in the world? So I try always not to talk of anything until I am sure of a subject that will be of interest to my listener. .... William is the son of my first wife, of course. She died at his birth. We were both, she and I, very young. It is a long time ago.'

'And how long is it since you saw your son?'

'Three years now. He used to come over to this country fairly frequently and I would spend a few weeks with him in London or Oxford — and we spent two months in Berlin one year, when he was visiting the university there. But he is now tied in Montreal, so I have decided to go to him. He is a historian, by the way.'

'It will be exciting! How long since you saw little James and Deborah?'

'I have never seen my grandchildren,' he said.

It was as if he had told me the end of a story. Madame X was very strong on Chains of Friendship and Spiritual Help to Tom, Dick and Harry and Motherhood in theory, but she had no time for facts like husbands, sons, children and grandchildren.

That was the end, really, of what will go down to history as my Whitely House Period, for in the next two days events crowded in so thick and fast that I remember very few of them and of those, of course, only the most ridiculous details.

The next morning I began to drag out the files that related to the Chain of Friendship and dump them into a series of orange boxes which I had obtained while Medway nailed down these coffins of sentimentality. Medway had grasped the knowledge that I was going away and chose to be lugubrious about it so that as each box was nailed he would straighten his back and say drearily: 'Well, that's another step on your way, Miss Janet!'

To relieve the tedium of this, I said just before lunch: 'There's another thing we must do, Medway.'

'Wot, Miss Janet?'

'Get the Two-handed Engine in from the back yard.'

'The h'armour, miss?'

'Yes.'

'All right, Miss Janet.'

Without more ado Medway and his wife dragged the Engine, halberd and all, into the house and set it in its place, and when Mr. Rollin came in from his morning walk he regarded it solemnly, shook his head and said: 'Alas, poor

Yorick!' Almost at the same moment the telephone rang, and when I answered it Lady Firmantle told me that Muriel's curate had called on her that morning to tell her that Muriel had terminated their engagement. All I could think of was: 'Alas, poor Yorick!' which made Lady Firmantle bawl: 'Are you off your rocker?' to which I replied, No, and that I would come out to see her that afternoon.

So after lunch I put some more of the Chain into some more boxes and then took myself off to the Firmantles in time for tea, which Lady Firmantle and I had, drearily, by ourselves. Richard, the curate, was by way of being a protégé of hers — she had a highly developed protective instinct for most young people, probably because she had so many of her own, but it always struck me as odd that her own, such as Freddie, were the last young people to need protecting. Maybe Richard and people like him got all the protectiveness that she had left over, but she started in at the sandwiches for tea with a neat plan for the hanging, drawing and quartering of Madame X, who, she said, was entirely responsible for this dreadful thing that had been done to Richard. Privately, I was in complete agreement with her, but I knew how difficult, metaphorically, it was to hang — much less draw and quarter — Madame X where Muriel was concerned, and, still having dear old Ecclesiastes in mind, I thought perhaps this was no time for hanging, drawing and quartering.

'Muriel is free, white and twenty-one,' I said, quoting some Americanism I had read, 'and she can do as she pleases.'

'Don't pretend to be a fool!' Lady Firmantle told me. 'Muriel is a slave, yellow-livered and nearly thirty and she has no mind of her own to please!' and she fed the piece of cake she had been eating to a large black retriever as if it were the heart and liver of Madame X.

It was a most pointless discussion between us that went on and on. Lady Firmantle was a woman of clearly defined character, with a clear-cut code of thought and behaviour which had served her well through her nearly sixty years, a code that had been heated and drawn out in the fire of experience, and I was a youngster, only finding my own way,

118

but quite unable to believe that Muriel could walk, talk, clean her teeth, do her accounts and do what other things she did and still write a letter that said 'No, Richard' when what she meant was 'Yes, Richard'. After about two hours of dreary pointlessness, by which time the discussion had got down from the realms of hanging, drawing and quartering to a repetition of: 'Oh, well, Janet, we must just do what we can', I rose to take my leave.

'Sit down!' said Lady Firmantle. 'Did all Angela said to you mean nothing? Bad enough you are even sleeping there now! Have dinner here and come to the cinema with the rest of us!' And this is where dear old Ecclesiastes let me down. There is a time to resist and a time not to resist, so I thought I had resisted enough, decided not to resist about dinner and the cinema, and did not get back to Whitely House until after eleven o'clock.

When I let myself into the hall, there stood the Two-handed Engine, but, behind it on the staircase, there was movement, movement in the form of the sinuous flow of a pink satin dressing-gown on the last four steps.

'Janet.' said Madame X, with a full-stop behind the word. 'So there you are.' There was another full-stop. 'And where is Mr. Rollin?' This one was not a full stop and it was not a rhetorical question. It expected an answer.

'I don't know,' I replied.

'Indeed?'

I looked at her. She looked at me. 'The Master went out,' said Medway's voice suddenly from the green-baize door that led to the kitchen. 'I told you, madam, but you was telephonin'.'

'Medway! Go to bed!' said Madame X, and Medway went, but not before casting his eyes and eyebrows upwards in a gesture that I did not understand. Madame X gathered her pink satin skirts into one hand and with the other she held the newel-post of the stairs.

'I have been telephoning all over town,' she told me.

'What for?' I asked, taking an intelligent interest.

'— In an attempt to find you — and Mr. Rollin,' she went on. 'I have been with Lady Firmantle to dinner and to the cinema,' I told her. 'I left here about three o'clock. I don't know where Mr. Rollin may have gone — probably to dine with friends. Is Muriel here?' She merely looked at me. 'I hope she isn't asleep yet,' I said and, gathering all my courage, walked round the pink satin and up the stairs. I had intended to go to see Muriel, whose room was next to mine, but I was arrested by the thought of Medway's eyes and eyebrows which had made that curious gesture. My room looked exactly as I had left it, but I was inspired to go through the movements of coming in and going to bed before going to Muriel's room, so I placed my handbag on the dressing-table, took off the clothes I had been wearing and pulled my pyjamas from under my pillow. With them came a note in Medway's handwriting, which said: 'Dear Miss J., The Master went out about six o'clock in Master Freddie's car with two other young gentlemen. I don't know where to but they were talking about the darts championship. I tried to phone you from the papershop at Mrs. Carter's and Miss Pyne's but they did not know where you were. Madam is very angry. Yours respectfully, Medway.' *He*, in the language of America, was telling *me*. There was a discreet tap at my door and in came Mrs. Medway, saying in an unnaturally loud voice: 'I'm ever so sorry, Miss Janet — it's the milk you asked me to put in your room and I forgot till now. I'm ever so sorry, Miss Janet. . . .'

I shook Medway's letter at her and she nodded. 'Good *night*, Miss Janet!' she said and scuttled away.

I did not now feel equal to going and sitting on Muriel's bed and conducting an awkward conversation. 'The hell with the lot of them!' I thought. 'What do I care? For Madame X or for Muriel or her curate or any of them? Mr. Rollin's going to Canada and I'm going to old Mr. Carter to write a book about the Port of London! I'm a grown-up girl all on my own! I ain't got nobody and nobody cares for me! Hi-di-hi and ho-de-ho! . . .'

I was putting on my pyjama trousers when the crash came. It was bigger, better and more of a jangle than any of the noises in the 'musical' film I had heard and seen that evening — it was a crash to end all crashes, and before it had jangled itself to an

120

uneasy silence I was down on the lower flight of the staircase, but Madame X was a step ahead of me, and the Medways were in the green-baize doorway. As I arrived on the scene, however, it became, as it were, okay for further sound.

'James!' said Madame X, thus directing our eyes to Mr. Rollin, who was holding the stage in the middle of the pseudo-Persian rug that covered the hall floor. He was holding it, flat on his back, with the Two-handed Engine, halberd and all, recumbent on top of him and clasped in his arms.

'But that Two-handed Engine at the door,' he was intoning, 'stands ready to smite once and smite no more.' He peered round its helmet. 'Medway, I had forgotten you had brought the accursed thing back. Dear me. Yes, indeed.' And then he saw Madame X. 'Why, bless my soul, my dear! I thought you were in Austria!'

'Alas, poor Yorick!' said my soul.

'James!' she said. 'Get up!'

'Avaunt, knave!' said Mr. Rollin, giving a heave. 'Medway, lend a hand!' Medway jangled the armour aside and Mr. Rollin rose to his feet with suspicious ease and smoothness.

'James!' said Madame X.

Mr. Rollin walked very deliberately up the stairs until he was level with her. 'Good night, my dear,' he said gallantly and continued on his way until he came to me. 'And a very good night to *you*, Lady Strashing Fleam!' he added even more gallantly and went to his room and closed the door.

It was the only time that I ever saw Mr. Rollin under the influence of anything and this time it was alcohol. In the phraseology of the prophet Isaiah, indeed, he was as high and lifted up as a cedar of Lebanon or an oak of Bashan; and you may not believe this, but I am convinced that it is true, Madame X did not know it.

Breakfast the next morning might have been, outwardly, any breakfast in the annals of Whitely House as I had known it. Mr. Rollin was as benign as ever, Muriel as silent, Madame X as voluble and I as full of suppressed giggles as I had ever been, for Madame X had found a new way of Doing Good in the World and Muriel was again her full, if silent, lieutenant.

Austria, Madame X had found, was full of young women of irreproachable character and stuffed with the housewifely virtues whose one ambition it was to come to England to take posts as maids-of-all-work for a few shillings a week. All that was required was a liaison officer, preferably a Woman with Experience of the World yet at the same time interested in the welfare of young girls, who would establish contact between England's kitchens and the Austrian girls — a Home Finder, said Madame X, inspired. That was it. Home Finder. I watched her turn into the Home Finder right there before my eyes and in a trice there was nothing in the room but Home Finder. It was difficult to remember the scene of the night before in the hall; it was almost impossible to recall that the Chain of Friendship had ever existed, for Madame X undoubtedly had the genius of the great actor who, as he plays Hamlet for you, makes you unable to believe that a short time ago he brought Shylock to life before your own very same eyes. And she had, too, the ability of the actor to encase herself in her part to the exclusion of all else. She was not conscious of her audience. Muriel became part of her, a property of the Home Finder, as cloak and sword are properties of the actor who can make them significant or negligible in accordance with his reading of his part, but Mr. Rollin and I might not have existed. We were, in her mind, *merely* the audience. And this, My Reader, is where the difference between her and the great actor lay, a difference, which, blinded by her own ego, she did not see. The audience is never *mere* to a great actor. It is what he acts for, by and to — it is the breath of his acting life. But Madame X took her audience for granted and did not see that Mr. Rollin and I were not an audience at all. We had not paid for our seats. We did not want, even, any more the complimentary tickets she had given us. We were on our way out of the theatre, he to Canada and I to the Carters. And that is what happened. A week later the audience rose from its seats, picked up its impedimenta, and with hardly a farewell glance at the stage left the theatre where the performance was in full swing. I truly believe that, lost in her part behind the glare of the footlights, she did not at first realise that we had gone, but I did not give the matter much thought, for, like a member of any audience, I had to catch my bus, which, this time, took the form of the station taxicab which carried me and my luggage out to the Court.

Part III

Part III

I thought that I was finished with Whitely House and all the
people in it except Mr. Rollin, who said he would write to me,
and with Mr. Carter and the Port of London I had plenty on
my mind, but I did not yet know Muriel. Come to that, I don't
know Muriel even now. At the end of my first week at the
Court I had a letter from her, suggesting that we take tea
together one day in the town. My first instinct was simply to
ignore the letter, but I knew that she would be sure to write
again. My next thought was to refuse the invitation, but I felt
that that would be uncivil. In the end I made an appointment
for a certain day and went by bus to keep it, at the Teapot,
prepared for almost anything. The one thing I was *not*
prepared for happened, which was nothing at all, if it is not a
contradiction to say that nothing at all happened. Muriel, as
was characteristic of her, let me order tea, pour it out, hand her
cake and ask how she was getting along and said and did
nothing. We were just two old friends having a cup of tea
together. Wasn't that nice? Not a murmur about Madame X,
Home Finding, Mr. Rollin, Richard or any of the things or
people that were common to both our lives. She told me that
she was reading a book about Disraeli and I said: 'Oh yes?
Interesting?'

'Well,' Muriel said, 'he was a Jew.'

The rest about Disraeli, as far as Muriel was concerned,

127

was silence. She was full of silence.

I went back to the Court and Muriel went back to Whitely House, and again I thought that the thing was dead, for a relationship so inert could not possibly be alive, but not a bit of it. Three weeks later we had tea at the Teapot again, by the same routine — the letter from Muriel and my not being able to think of why we should not meet and equally unable to think why we *should* meet. At the end of about six months we had tea again and went for a walk afterwards, and when we were parting she took my breath away.

'Mrs. Whitely-Rollin is selling the house,' she said. 'We are moving to London.'

She might have been telling me that she was thinking of buying a cheap hat for wet days.

'Muriel! When?'

'We are leaving at the end of the month,' she said.

'And is Mr. Rollin going to live in London when he gets back?'

'I don't think he is coming back. All his books and things have been sent out to him in Canada.'

I thought for a moment and then walked deliberately out into No Man's Land. 'Muriel, what *about* Mrs. Whitely-Rollin?'

'What do you mean?' Muriel asked.

'Muriel.' I took a deep breath and felt as a gambler must feel who puts a very high stake on a desperate chance and, having no gambling instincts, I did not like the feeling. 'Muriel, why do you stay with Mrs. Whitely-Rollin? Don't you think she is rather an odd woman?'

Muriel looked at me without expression. 'I've never heard a person say the things you say,' she told me. That was all. We said goodbye and went our separate ways.

I think that that was an evening in the late autumn of 1934, when I looked back at Muriel over my shoulder as she walked away from me, with her dowdy hat, her dark-blue coat that dipped at one side, her thickish ankles above shoes whose heels were just not as straight as they should have been. I did not see her again until 1940, when the 1939–1945 war was well under

128

way, but the intervening years were spattered, for me, with letters in the thin, indeterminate hand which followed me, in an extraordinary way, through all my vicissitudes. Old Mr. Carter saw the publication of his history of the Port of London, dictated the sending out of the Special Presentation Edition and then died, and I, a favourite of fortune in this way, went from job to job all through the restless, inconclusive thirties, that decade destined never to be conclusive but to end in the fog of what we called the 'Phoney War'. In retrospect, it looks as if Britain's fighting potential, the people of my age who were coming up to the age of thirty in the 1930s, was waiting unconsciously for what was to come, having a good time while it could, shelving all responsibility till later, trying not to think too much, for thinking was an uneasy business with the concentration camp just round the corner, but all that may be a trick of the light of retrospect. Maybe, in truth, we were just the bunch of good-time Charlies that we seemed to be as we buzzed around on the merry-go-round, and it does not matter, for many of us gave quite a good account of ourselves when the time came.

I do not propose to give you a blow-by-blow description of my life during the six years when I did not see Muriel. I could not an I would, for many blows of many kinds were struck at all sorts of parties, with drink taken, and many of them I do not even remember, except spasmodically. After the death of Mr. Carter, my next job took me to London, to a small flat of my own in Chelsea, to be precise. From this anchorage I operated, during the hours when I was not earning my living, on a privateering principle, with no thought other than that my voyages forth should be interesting in some way. I went to theatres and rugby matches, dress parades and church services, *Hiawatha* at the Albert Hall and night-clubs in Soho, poetry readings and concerts and trips up the Thames to Hampton Court. I made a lot of friends and a vast number of acquaintances, and I was interested in everybody and everything. I ate a tremendous number of kippered herrings. Indeed, if the kippers I had eaten were laid end to end they would bridge the Atlantic. I got engaged to be married three times and three times I thought the better of it. If, instead of returning the rings, I had laid *them* end to end, they would have made a handsome bracelet, for anyone who wanted a bracelet. I used a great deal of energy without leaving a single footprint on the sands of time, and I do not regret one jot or tittle of it.

All this activity was loosely held together by one recurrent happening, very much as even the remotest tendrils of a sprawling vine are traceable back to the spot where the plant is rooted, by my visits home which I made, without fail, at least once in every year. I mention these visits here because they were one of the only two regularities in my life, and the other of these regularities was My Friend Muriel. She was no more of a friend — indeed, she was considerably less so — than many of the other people I met, but paths might cross and divide and this year's aquaintance turn into next year's faint memory, but always there would be a letter from Muriel, like this: 'My dear Janet, It is a long time since I have heard from you and I wonder if you have moved and my last letter did not reach you so I am sending this to your home address to be forwarded. I hope you are well and please write soon. Sincerely, Muriel.' I used to wonder, off and on, why she wrote them. They told me nothing, they asked for nothing. We never arranged to meet, although she and Madame X were somewhere in Wimbledon, a mere bus ride away from me. Sometimes I would not write to her for a whole year, ignoring maybe six of these letters, and then she would write home with a covering note to my father to forward her latest letter to me, and it would be 'My dear Janet, It is a long time since I have heard from you . . .' And so I would write to her again, asking after Madame X, after Mr. Rollin (but not mentioning that I was hearing from him regularly), asking how the Home Finding was going; but her next letter would come saying: 'My dear Janet, How very glad I was to get your letter and to know that you are well and busy as usual. I have a small car now and sometimes we drive out to the country for tea which is very nice. This is all my news for now but please write soon again. Sincerely, Muriel.' I would fly into a black rage over my coffee and kippers at the sight of this. So she had a small car! So they drove to the country! So this was 'all her news'! It would be a long, cold, wet Monday before *I* would write to her again, I would swear, but again the gentle, insistent letters would keep coming, and in the end I would for very shame reply to one of them.

Dear Reader, if you think that this is one of these stories where All Will Be Made Clear To You in the last chapter, in a brilliant denouement where I tell you all about the psychology of My Friend Muriel, that is where your toes turn in. I am as much at a loss as to Muriel as you are, probably more so, for it is a hundred pounds to a few small potatoes that you are a far cleverer person than I am. If I were a person like this: a person that makes neat, snap, concrete judgments about other people, a person who is never mystified by anyone, I would probably be able to be conclusive about Muriel; but I think I am a person like this: I believe that any human personality is too organically alive to be put into a neat package, labelled and put on a shelf. If you do that to it, it is going to explode and burst the paper, or leak out and stain the shelf, or ferment and make a smell that will render your storage place unusable. That, I think, is the way organic things are and that is why Lady Firmantle, for instance, was mistaken in writing Muriel off as the tool and slave of Madame X.

In that last week at Whitely House, Madame X had made it abundantly clear that I was the nastiest trick that Fate had ever played upon her. She held me morally responsible for everything that had happened. My inhuman mechanisation of the office had caused Muriel's breakdown; I had taken the 'humanity' out of the Chain of Friendship, thus leading to its dissolution; my behaviour had reacted upon Mr. Rollin who was at a Difficult Age for Men and had caused him to make this absurd trip to Canada. Indeed, Madame X said, she could not understand how some women should be born to help the world Forward and Upward by their every thought and action, while others were born under a star so ill that everything they touched disintegrated and the rest of humanity was — well, *contaminated* was the only word — by the contact with them.

131

Having made this picture of my character clear to me in the short time that I allowed her to do so, the picture as presented to Muriel down the years must have been very well defined; and knowing Madame X, every letter in my hand addressed to Muriel that arrived at Wimbledon must have caused a major crisis, but did Muriel, the slave, bend under the lash? Not Muriel. Wherever I went, however I ignored it, the faint, indeterminate hand-writing pursued me, telling me nothing, asking for nothing, giving nothing and taking nothing, and meaning, it seemed, no more than the steady drip-drip of water from a leaking pipe.

Aunt Julia died early in 1939, but during my years in London it had been my habit to visit her periodically, and I remember, shortly before she died, talking to her of Muriel.

'You never see her?' she asked.

'No, Aunt Julia. Do you?'

'No. She writes, of course. I wonder what old Mrs. Thing is up to now? She can't go on Home Finding with all these Austrian and German women with Hitler behaving like this, can she? Even *she* can hardly go on ignoring a thing like Hitler.'

'Muriel has never said anything about her to you?' I asked.

'Not a word. You know her letters. She hopes I am well. She is well herself, and the maple tree in the garden is particularly lovely this autumn.'

'So they have a maple tree?'

'Yes. Interesting, isn't it?' said Aunt Julia. 'What happened to that young man, Richard — the curate?'

'He went abroad. Darkest Africa or something. . . . Aunt Julia, is it odd that Muriel does not come to see you?'

'Odd?'

'Well, some families don't visit around a great deal although they keep in touch.'

'I find it more than odd,' said Aunt Julia. 'It *is* odd, don't you think, that *you* should come and Muriel does not. There is a thing that worries me sometimes, Janet. Maybe it is a wicked thought, but it is there nevertheless. I worry sometimes about Muriel's little inheritance — it was only a few thousands, but

132

sometimes I wonder if Mrs. Thing —?' She paused. 'Do you find me shocking?'

'No, Aunt Julia,' I told her. 'I don't. If Madame X wanted that money, she would try to get it. You are not a bit shocking. You are quite right. But I honestly don't think she needs or wants it.'

'You don't? That *is* a relief. I should hate to see her get away with that. Queer, isn't it, how family property is rooted in one's very soul?'

'Mr. Rollin was wealthy,' I said, for as far as our small family property was concerned, I felt that I was rooted in *it*, not it in *me*, but I let the matter pass. 'And unlike many scholars, he *made* some money too in his time, though why I am talking of him in the past tense I don't know. And Madame X, to give the devil her due, was not a user of money. She was a frugal sort of person, rather, and she never saw money as a source of power. It was, she said, beneath her notice. She was all for the things of the Spirit.'

'Spirit!' spat Aunt Julia.

From time to time, after that conversation with Aunt Julia, when I was sparing a thought for Muriel, I would think of her inheritance and of how, with such care and concentration, she used to 'do her accounts' in the blue exercise book and how, when we came back from a visit to Lady Firmantle, she would enter up the amount of her bus fare. It was another example, I thought, of the doggedness of Muriel, like her letters to me, a 'fast' — in her opinion, you would think — young person with whom she seemed to have nothing in common. I was as certain as if I had the information on a testified document that Madame X would not get that money away from Muriel, any more than Madame X could stop Muriel writing to me. I had no logical reason for this certainty. The reason I had given to Aunt Julia for my opinion was a false one, for Madame X was as fond of money as anyone else and had fewer scruples than most people about most things. But I knew that she would never lay hands on that money, and I was right. For lack of a better word, let us say that I knew this by intuition.

Intuition is a very interesting thing, even if you are only very

133

slightly mechanically-minded like me, for it is a long, thin, wiggly tube made of some material that I cannot name, which comes in through your ear into your mind. The other end of it goes away over your shoulder and disappears into a cloud, so that you cannot see what the other end of it is connected to, but I think it must be a large sort of vat which contains a turgid liquid which gives off a gaseous vapour, for sometimes it is a thick liquid that comes up the tube into your mind through your ear, swamping all else, and sometimes it is only the vapour that comes in and swirls about in a vague sort of way as mist does along a hillside in summer. Now, My Friend Monica says that intuition is not a mechanical contrivance like this at all, but something that is built into you, somewhere around your liver, like an extra gall-bladder, and given a certain stimulus — Monica once read a lot of Freud and that Russian who did things with dogs and their saliva somewhere on the Riviera, Pavlov, his name was — so she uses words like stimulus — *given* a certain stimulus, she says, this bladder of intuition suddenly pumps out some information into your bloodstream and up to your brain and it is usually erroneous at that. I told her I did not believe a word of it and what about another slight stimulus, and she said all right in spite of her intuition bladder pumping up that we had both had enough already.

Well, as if I were telling you something that you did not know already, in September 1939 the war came on. But here is something you really did not know — I found myself, I do not remember precisely how, in what was then known as the Women's Auxiliary Air Force, or W.A.A.F., wearing a beret that did not suit me and a mackintosh that did not fit me, because this was in the days before the women's services were Royal or even recognised properly and nobody thought of a uniform for us, much less a brain like Norman Hartnell's being engaged to consider its design.

As a Waaf I astonished even myself. On paper I was a cook — I must have mentioned kippers at some interview — and I accepted a railway warrant which took me to a very cold section of the east coast, where I found myself, at someone's instructions, handing out rather obsolescent-looking diagrams called 'Target Maps' to a lot of nice-looking young men with wings on the left breasts of their blue tunics. I did this in a place called the 'Operations Room', which was a hollow block of concrete inside a green hill which was entered through a tunnel. When I was not handing out Target Maps or putting them away again I made cocoa or tea, and I answered to the names Sandison, San-Toy, San-San and, strangely, Mimosa San, this last being developed by a young navigator who illustrated all his logs of flight with minute but lively cherubs and fishes of the kind that appear on old maps, and who bore a curious resemblance to Mr. Rollin.

It was a very dull war in those early days. Tour of duty followed tour of duty and nothing happened. I was the only female thing in this Operations Room, a sort of household pet, and I was soon instructed to sew some stripes on a tunic that had been issued to me, but I had hardly become accustomed to being Corporal San before I had more stripes to sew on and became Sergeant San. I found it all very remarkable, especially as my pay was now ahead of my drinks at the local pub and my cigarettes at the canteen for the first time since I had taken the King's Shilling. As I have told you already, I am fairly slow-witted, and my idea of His Majesty's Service was summarised vaguely in —

'Theirs not to reason why,
    Theirs but to do or die . . .'

I did not intend to die if I could help it, but was prepared to do almost anything and reason as little as possible. You would be surprised at how little you can reason if you put your mind to it as I did. In no time at all — in fact, after the first three months or so of bombing in the winter of 1940 — I found myself, still astonished and quite unreasoning, commissioned as an officer in the Air Intelligence, in a very secret branch, which had headquarters in a large country mansion in Buckinghamshire, which was surrounded by the tin huts in which we ate and slept. The work which I had to do was connected with aerial photographs of enemy territory, and the qualifications required for this work, in my opinion, were good eyesight, meticulously careful observation by the said eyesight and an unusual resistance to boredom. Nature had given me the eyesight, I can be meticulously careful if life or death depends on me, and my natural resistance to boredom is colossal. Even the Royal Air Force seemed to feel that it had fitted at least one square peg into one square hole and I spent the rest of the war in that unit. I enjoyed almost every moment of about five years of it.

England is a very beautiful country, worth fighting for even if you happen to have been born a Scotswoman. Show me anything more beautiful than a Buckinghamshire beechwood at dawn in May and my sword is yours to command, no matter where your country may be. And show me violets and primroses more lovely than those that grow by the Buckinghamshire Thames and I, personally, will never live to see an invading army trample them down. And show me a city more gallant than London in 1940 and you can have my life to preserve any one of its paving-stones. But my country did not require any of these dramatics of me. For nearly five years I never heard the sound of war, I never saw an angry enemy and neither did my colleagues. What we saw were acres and acres of photographic prints on which we had to trace and record every minute change of outline, and from this we built up reams and reams of reports and sheets and sheets of maps, and not until the heavy bombing of Germany and the advance across the Channel began did we see any fruits of our labours. Then, though, the men in the air and those on the sea and those on land made the whole thing seem worth while.

What my country did require of me, apparently, was the ability to keep sane for years of incarceration, broken by very occasional short leaves when I rushed up to London and walked about and danced and got slightly drunk, or went up to my home and walked about without benefit of drink or dance. I found it easy to do, this preserving of my sanity, always provided that my particular form of consciousness was reckoned to be sanity in the first place. I came out of the war unscathed, mentally or physically, and this is all I have to say about the war, for which I think you should be extremely grateful. If you want to read about the war, there are plenty of other books about it; and if you want to read of the effect of incarceration on human beings, there are books about incarcerations of a much more trying kind than mine. I volunteered for it all, remember, even the incarceration, and I am a person like this: I think if you let yourself in for something, well, you are *in* and you might as well shut your big mouth about it. If someone forces, or tries to force, you to do something against your will, any form of resistance from murder to sticking your tongue out is quite in order. That, after all, is why I volunteered for the boredom. It seemed to me to be the most telling way of sticking my tongue out at this Hitler person who had all these forceful ideas. Now, I am a person like this, I think: I am not a warlike or a quarrelsome person and I do not have any very strict code of morals of this and that, but I do believe very firmly in the freedom of the individual. Only this Individual, Janet Sandison, though. If other individuals do not want to be free, I do not care. They have every right not to be free if that is how they want it. I am not going to interfere with them. And it will contribute to the peace of nations if they will please not to interfere with me, either.

And so I did not interfere with Muriel. Oh no. I have not forgotten My Friend Muriel all this time I have been telling you about my gallantry in the war, and Muriel had not forgotten me either.

Just after I took up residence in my tin hut in Buckinghamshire I had a letter from her that told me that Madame X was dead. When I read this, all the Sweetness and Light and so on which had been the chosen aura of Madame X seemed very far away as, on the desk in front of me, I had a series of photographs of some of the big guns that the Germans were emplacing on the Channel Coast, and I was drawing red rings round every gun and my desk looked like a good-going case of measles, so I thought that maybe these guns had soured Madame X's sweetness and put out her light and conceded that it was probably the only good thing the guns would ever do, and then I began to think about Muriel while I put blue rings round the next size of gun I could see on the photographs. Her letter ended with: 'I have failed the medical for all the women's services so don't know what I am going to do yet. Please write soon. Sincerely, Muriel.'

This time I did 'write soon', as soon as I was off duty, and told her that I would be in London at the end of the month and suggested that we should meet. Why I did this I do not know, and after we had duly met I knew still less why I had done it, but, in spite of all that, I arranged to spend my seven days' leave with her, at her room in Chelsea which consisted mainly of two divan beds, a gas ring and a sink, with a lavatory just outside the door, on the landing.

I think that when I first arranged to meet her I had the presumption to feel sorry for her, for it seemed to me that after all these years with Madame X she must be feeling a little like a plucked chicken now that death had removed her background, but there was nothing of the plucked chicken about Muriel at all. She was about thirty-six now, of course, and heavy in the hip and ankle, and as untidy and unfinished-looking as ever. She had changed very little, but I think *I* had changed. Probably my war experience — not to mention my pre-war experience — had coarsened me, but I no longer approached Muriel on mental tiptoe as I had been wont to do.

I told you in some detail of my life before I met Muriel in the flesh to try to make clear to you how very limited was my knowledge of the world and its people. I had known only a very limited number of people, mostly of my own race, plus the Islingtons and Eddie's household. One of the ideas dropped into my wobbly-jelly mind by my family and which had stuck there was that my elders were my betters in worldly wisdom of all kinds, and I think it had stuck because it was absolutely true of my own family. The Highland peasant is nobody's fool and least of all is he the fool of his own offspring. I had been brought up by a number of people who knew a great deal more about everything than I did and who had proved to me their wisdom time and again, so I made the fairly natural mistake of believing that my elders were automatically my betters and

Muriel was between five and six years my senior. So, although on the one hand she had behaved in ways that I felt were unwise, on the other hand a deep part of my mind told me that she *must* know better than I did, so that, as I said, I approached her in those early days on mental tiptoe.

In my years between leaving Whitely House, though, and taking part in the war, I had learned quite a number of things. Indeed, I had become more adult. It had been borne in upon my weak intelligence that all people were not like my family. The child lives in a secure little world which, it thinks, is a miniature of the big world outside and its vision of growing up is a stepping out into this large world which is exactly the same as the world it has always known, except that the people in it are more numerous, the vistas wider, the trees taller and the grass greener. At least, this is the sort of child I was, and if I was half-witted, there it is, for I had no idea that people had racial and other differences of thought that would make them impossible for me to understand, that the vistas of the outside world could close in to culs-de-sac, that there were so many different trees that no man could name all the varieties and that in Kentucky there is a grass that is more blue than green. Least of all did I know that everybody else was not like me and that I was not like everybody else and that I would find myself having to make decisions as to thinking thus and remaining myself or thinking so and being like someone else.

The stage I had reached then, by the date of this next meeting with Muriel, was that I had come to the conclusion that every living being was a separate, different entity, who might think or move or otherwise have their being in a way that did not in the lease conform to my way of having my being, but alongside this I had the idea that my way of being had carried me to the age of thirty through a variety of experiences with much enjoyment and no serious mishap, and that maybe I was coming on for the age when I might be, in living, an elder to someone who had spent her life with Madame X and that, conceivably, I might be attaining that divinity of my youth, the stage of being myself an elder and a better at this business of living. The outward manifestation of all this was that I now had no compunction in 'speaking my mind' to Muriel. If I thought of a question I wanted to ask her now, I asked it, which led me to say:

'What did Old Madame X die of in the end?'

'Who?' said Muriel.

'Mrs. Whitely-Rollin. I call her Madame X.'

'Why?'

'Just because,' I replied. Who, I wanted to ask, was asking the questions — Muriel or I?

'I never heard of a thing like that. . . . It was her heart.' Muriel was not sad or anything. It was just straight like that. 'It was her heart.'

'Oh,' I said, and, never having been a subscriber to the De Mortuis Nil Nisi Bonum line of thought, I added, 'Wouldn't have thought she had a heart. Dreadful old woman.'

'Did you think so?' Muriel asked as if she were saying: 'Do you think it might rain today?'

'Yes,' I said firmly. 'I did. Can't think why you stuck to her all these years. By the way, did she leave you anything in her will?' I did not know why I asked the question.

'Yes,' said Muriel.

'Well, that's something!' I was genuinely pleased. 'I hope it was a good lot. You worked for it!'

'Oh, she didn't leave me any *money*,' Muriel said.

'Huh? Then *what*, for pity's sake?'

'The suit of armour,' she said.

I stared at her, trying to find my cue for mirth, commiseration, scorn or anything which Muriel thought would be fitting in the circumstances, but Muriel required no reaction on my part, having, apparently, no reaction of her own for me to sympathise with. 'A friend is storing it for me,' she added. Well, I thought, some of Muriel's friends get things really hard. What have I been complaining about? At least, *I* had not been asked to board the Two-handed Engine, which was rather a pity, for it would have brought a nice touch of the macabre into my tin hut in Buckinghamshire, when I came to think of it.

'I have got a job in the Auxiliary Fire Service,' Muriel told

140

me next. 'Telephone operator — at least I am doing *some-thing.*'

'That's a damn' fine effort!' I told her in the jargon of those days. 'What failed you for the Services?'

'Heart. It never got over that illness before we went to Austria.'

'Muriel, have you ever heard any more of Richard?'

'No,' said Muriel.

It was not a stone wall. It was a bank of fog with the road to nowhere on the other side and I confessed myself beaten, but in spite of all that I arranged to spend my leave with her, partly because seven days was too short for the trip to the north of Scotland with the railways running at wartime speed.

It has come to my notice that if my motives for doing things were ever completely pure, my life would be a much less puzzling affair to me. Now, people like Madame X are never in the least puzzled by their lives and do not get into muddles like me, for Madame X would have known she was Doing Good to Muriel by spending seven days with her and Relieving her Loneliness, which is a Good, Pure Motive. But I do not appear to be a person like that. I decided to spend seven days with Muriel for a whole conglomeration or gallimaufry of reasons and motives, such as trains to Scotland being too slow, London being fun, Freddie Firmantle being home on leave from his submarine as well as several other Freddies and Bills and Johnnies being around and about within reach. In case you are interested, Freddie by this time was married to My Friend Georgina, who takes size two in shoes and was in Canada with her twin babies, and I took the dog watch of duty over Freddie for her, at her instructions, when his submarine surfaced him anywhere around the British coast. I also wrote to Georgina after these meetings and reported on Freddie's health and the condition of his socks, for Freddie, although older, was no more literate than he had ever been.

And so this seven days' leave comes along and I go to London and meet Freddie and take him along to Muriel's room in the afternoon, and we all talk about Old Times for a bit until Freddie's six o'clock reflex gets working and he says: 'Is there still a noggin to be had in this town? How's your Intelligence, Jan?'

In my mild way I am quite the Intelligence Officer, for much of this type of intelligence is based on stored experience. If you see a thing like a minute starfish on an aerial photograph and it turns out on enquiry to be a new kind of wireless station, the next time you see that thing on another aerial photograph you say: 'That's another of those damned wireless stations!' Equally, if one time you are in London in the black-out and someone takes you round a few corners and down a few steps and at the end of it you get a drink, next time you are in London in the black-out and want a drink, you go round the nearest similar pattern of corners and down the nearest similar pattern of steps and it is a thousand to one that you will find a drink. So that is what I did, with Freddie and Muriel behind me, and sure enough we found a cellar where they had some whisky which Freddie said must have come out of Vesuvius and have been exchanged by Mussolini for machine guns before the war started, except that he doubted if it was that old, and they also had some gin, but we did not sample it, for Freddie, being a naval man, is a little fussy about his gin, even in wartime.

I think I started out on this evening with some idea of turning the clear, white light of my intelligence on Muriel reacting to the stimulus of what was probably her first drink other than medicinal, but sometimes, especially in Freddie's company, I have difficulty in finishing things I start out to do, and as the evening wore on my light of intelligence became less white and far from clear. One of the things that Freddie and I have in common is that a lot of people seem to know us, and when we went out in wartime London people were always coming up to bars and saying to Freddie: 'Weren't you in the Three Tuns at Pompey the night the piano went on fire? God, what a night!' Or people would be coming up to me and saying: 'Weren't you in the Sergeants' Mess at Middle Cussed the night the Adjutant fell through the big drum? God, what a night!' and then we would all have another noggin on the strength of whatever it was. If I thought *this* night was going to be any different just because Muriel was there, I was quite mistaken, for we had not finished the first glass of Dew of Vesuvius when an Army captain came up to us and said to Freddie: 'Freddie, isn't it? Remember Folkestone in May?'

'I'll never forget it,' said Freddie. 'What are you drinking? Better have the whisky. What's your name again?'

'Robertson,' the man said, bowing to Muriel and me. 'Pierre Robertson.'

'Another bloody Scotsman, Miss Thornton,' said Freddie, always polite.

'Scotsman my foot!' I said, equally polite. 'I'm Janet Sandison. I go about with Freddie Firmantle because my mind is weak. Cheers.'

In the teeth of the evidence of this history I am writing for you, I wish to say that I am a person like this: I am in the main disposed to like people until they give me what I feel to be just cause to *dis*like them, but in the case of Captain Robertson I was not prepared for one instant to give him one chance of any kind whatsoever. I would have preferred to get into the nearest air-raid shelter with a large boa constrictor, and before the end of this Dew of Vesuvius we were having with him I could see that Freddie felt very much as I did. So, with nothing said, we decided to seek another pattern of corners, some more steps and a different cellar to drink in, but this is where Muriel the Spineless suddenly turned into a solid, granite, immobile monolith right there before our eyes. She would not budge. We had another drink. She would not move. We said we were hungry. The barman brought us beans on toast. We said we were sleepy. She said Nonsense. And all this time we were having the other odd drink and Muriel had mislaid her hat, which was really a blessing, and was getting as high as a steeple, which was quite a worry.

Freddie and I went out into the hallway and had a planning meeting just outside the men's lavatory, which was most inconvenient, and rather pointless anyhow, for it ended with me saying: 'Look, I'm taking her home if it means starting a riot!' and Freddie saying: 'I couldn't agree more. Let's at it!' so we went back to the table, where she and this Pierre were gazing in drunken soulfulness at one another, and I said: 'Muriel! We're going home. You're potted to the eyebrows!'

'What?'

'You're *drunk*!' I bellowed at her.

'I never heard a pershon shay a thing like that!' said Muriel. 'Bu' lesh go home if thass wha' you wan'!'

It was as easy as that, and I wondered what I had been in such a tizzy about. I began to wonder if the photographs and the tin hut were giving me war-weary nerves after all. Muriel was violently sick, slept like a top and rose the next morning, a giantess refreshed, all ready to go on duty at her fire station. We had breakfast together before she left.

'I'm sorry about last night,' I said. 'It was unfortunate meeting that French-Canadian man like that. It spoilt the whole evening.'

'I thought he was quite nice,' Muriel said. 'But we must have drunk too much.'

'I couldn't take much of dear Pierre myself,' I told her. 'Extraordinary the people Freddie picks up. Pick up some pretty queer ones myself, come to that,' I added.

'Me, you mean?' said Muriel, and it was the first time I ever 'heard her say a thing like that'. 'Never mind, I won't get drunk on you another time. I'll be back about five,' she said, as she picked up her tin hat. 'But don't stay in. I'm going out myself and you've got your key.'

I put on my eternal uniform and went off to meet Freddie and some other people and thought no more of Captain Pierre Robertson, but on the last night of my short leave while Muriel was on night duty and Freddie and I were having a noggin or two in the comparative peace of the Ritz so that we could talk about Georgina and after we had dealt with her and the twins, I said: 'By the way, in what snake-pit did you dredge up that man Robertson who was with us the night Muriel got drunk?'

'He was part of a bunch Our Lot took off the French coast at the evacuation. There were a lot of *them* and not many of us, so they all remember *us*, if you see what I mean.'

'You don't know him?'

'Not from Adam, old girl. Don't want to, either. Do you?'

'Don't be obscene, Freddie. I was just wondering. What's he doing now?'

'Something with the Free French, I gathered. He has the lingo — a lot of these Canadians have. Funny thing. Before the war I thought that chaps were just chaps, you know — people you knew and liked and had a noggin with or a game of tennis or something. But it isn't like that. You meet the odd cove you don't *take* to, somehow. It just shows you. Listen, let's have one more here and then go somewhere and find a band.'

'Yes, let's,' I said. So we danced till four in the morning and I caught a train out of Paddington at eight and my leave was over.

Now this unit in Buckinghamshire, where my tin hut was, was not the sort of place where you could sit down, even if you wanted to, and think for long hours about Your Friend Muriel. The war began to warm up and we were kept extremely busy, but in the day-to-day life of the unit this war that we were supplying Intelligence for was a sort of back-drop behind the numerous wars that my colleagues and I could generate among ourselves. I do not mean that we suffered from low morale, or lack of patriotism, or that we wanted to mutiny or anything, but one of the qualifications for work at this unit was what the Service called 'an alert and enquiring mind'. If you are eccentric enough to want a hobby that no eccentric has yet tried, try taking about five hundred alert and enquiring minds and setting them down in a wood in the middle of Buckinghamshire and give them a year or two to ferment. The results will astonish you.

We had arguments about everything, and sometimes these ended in a near-riot with a university don and a civil engineer lined up shoulder to shoulder vis-à-vis a little man who lived, in peace-time, by forecasting the future movements of herring shoals with me as his heavy artillery. A week later, the university don and I would be calling to drastic account a mediaeval archaeologist and a professor of botany on the subject of their views on the works of Marcel Proust. We argued about everything in our so-called leisure hours, but, in retrospect, I think that James Joyce and his works probably caused more trouble than anything else. When we got on to the agenbite of inwit, the number of broken glasses in the mess always went up by leaps and bounds. The only subjects that were beneath our notice and not worth talking and fighting about were the Royal Air Force, Adolf Hitler and anything to do with the war.

What I was saying, then, was that I did not give Muriel much thought, although, of course, she kept on writing to tell me that she was still with the Fire Service, that the weather was better or worse, that she hoped I was well and, occasionally, when the fight going on in the mess did not happen to interest me (which was seldom), I would write back.

Now, that is an interesting word, if you like, that word 'seldom'. An old man up at home who was going very bald once told My Friend Tom that 'his hairs wass getting ferry seldom' and in the fullness of time I told My Friend Monica of this use of the word, and added that, as a word, seldom was, for me, nothing but a word that one used very seldom. Monica said I was quite wrong — I should have mentioned that Monica found herself in the W.A.A.F. at the same time that I did and she was now also a member of this tin-hut unit — and that she was a particularly proficient starter of battles in the mess with this way she had of throwing out 'You are quite wrong!' as if the phrase were a very ornate, be-tasselled, heavy leather gauntlet which hit the floor with a resounding 'Slap!' She has brilliant red hair too, and fiery bright-blue eyes and strong views about morality, and if you have met a battle-starter with better qualifications than Monica has got you have met a prince among battle-starters. No, she said, I was quite wrong. Seldom was, she said, a world, very much like this one we were in, in everything except its time scale. No, it did not work on Bergson's Time or Dunne's Time or any of the philosophers' times or even Double Summer Time — don't be a fool, she said — it had a different pulse or rhythm, that was all, which meant that its tides went in and out very seldom, and people breathed very seldom — by *our* standards, that was, for, after all, everything was a question of scales of standards, take this question of morality — No, I said, but the drinks were very seldom so let's have another couple.

Well, maybe you can understand that what with Intelligence and being surrounded by people like My Friend Monica, not to mention the man who discovered that he could grow edible fungi on the damp cement floor below his bed and used to eat them with gusto at breakfast, and my own temperament being what you must have by now gathered that it is, I did not think a great deal about Muriel so that, at Christmas 1941, I was fairly dumbfounded when I got a letter that hoped I was well and added that she knew I would be pleased to hear that she and Pierre — I *must* remember Pierre Robertson? — were married last week. The letter went on to say that Pierre had been invalided out of the Service on account of his stomach ulcers but he was now with the Ministry of Supply and that they had a three-room flat above the room she used to have in Chelsea and they were very happy. I was so dumbfounded that My Friend Monica noticed it although she had letters of her own that she was reading, and she, at that time, having very temporarily an attitude to men of courtesy and no more, and disapproving of my continued sporadic forays into the fields of dalliance, said: 'Well? Has that colonel with the hairs in his ears caught up with you? I told you he would. You can't hide a light like the one you had on that night even in a bushel of Buckinghamshires. What does he say?'

'Don't be a fool. It's from a friend!'

'All *right*. What does he say?'

'It's a *woman* friend,' I said with dignity.

She looked suspicious. 'A *friend*, you said? I mean, it isn't somebody's wife?'

'Actually, she *is*. That's what so —'

'Now look here. I've told you time and again this would happen! I've told you again and again that a lot of coves in uniform that you put the eye on are probably married and for that very reason they are just the sort of fools that would think your eye means what it says.' She gave a hollow laugh. 'Dammit, it took *me* three months to find out that when the

147

band plays a tune you like you get that look without knowing it. And of course you always put the eye on nice fools who wouldn't have the wit to keep you a secret from their wives. All right, it's happened. What does the woman say? For she can't be your friend any longer, God knows!'

She had talked long enough to let me gather myself. 'You are a didactic ass,' I told her. 'You talk too much. All this letter says is that this friend of mine has got married —'

'Then why sit there looking like a spiked gun? People get married all the time. If you look at the statistics —'

'There are lies, damn' lies and statistics!' said a man who had quite a civilian life reputation as a criminal lawyer, clashing his beer mug down on our table. 'Anyone who quotes statistics at me —'

'You are quite wrong!' said Monica. 'No one spoke to you at all!'

'If I might express an opinion —' said another man who was an authority on oil-processing.

'You might *not*!' I said, and, one way and another, Muriel's marriage got lost among words and pre-lunch beer, for that was how we usually rid ourselves, in the unit, of anything that was irritating us.

Please do not mistake me, though. I was not irritated, in principle, at the idea of Muriel getting married. In fact, I had always been of the opinion that marriage would be the Best End for Muriel, but after Richard the curate faded from the picture and, particularly, when I remembered how left-over she looked the last time I had seen her, I had thought that Her Chances Were Past. Therefore I should have been delighted about this marriage, and, in a way, I was, except for a feeling, mentally, rather like the feeling, physically, when you put your foot into the wrong shoe in the dark. Something felt wrong, that was all.

However, there was nothing I could do about it and I have found that if you ignore uncomfortable feelings they very often go away, so that was what I did and eventually arrived at the idea that Muriel was off my hands for good, for I had noticed in the past that many women, once they are married, regard *you*, who are *not* married, either as being their inferiors or as a sort of blackleg or non-member of their union and they fade out of your life for ever. If they are the kind of women who feel like this, their fading-out is an excellent thing and everyone is happy, so I wrote a Nice Letter to Muriel, wishing her Every Happiness and hoping that Pierre's ulcers were better now, and got on with whatever I was doing at the moment.

But it turned out that Muriel was a person like this: She Did Not Forget Her Old Friends, and her letters, the hand as thin and indeterminate as ever, kept coming along, and in the fullness of time 1945 and the end of the European War came along, too, and I was due to return to what we in the unit called 'civil' life, so I mentioned this in one of my infrequent letters to Muriel, because it was my Favourite Thought at the time. She wrote again, almost at once, asking me to stay with her and Pierre in London on my way through to my home in the north, and as I could not think of a valid-sounding excuse to make to myself for excusing myself from staying with Muriel, I accepted.

Muriel and Pierre welcomed me as prettily as anyone could ever wish to be welcomed anywhere, but maybe you will remember that many pages ago in this chronical I have told you about how it is possible to 'hear' far more than the surface meaning of the words that are spoken, and on the first evening in London I heard:

(*a*) that Muriel seemed to be as much under the domination of Pierre as she had ever been under that of Madame X;

(*b*) that there was some purpose of Pierre's, to which, through Muriel, I was to be bent.

The second thing (*b*) intrigued me very much, so much that instead of staying with them for a day or so as I had intended, I stayed for over a week to get them to the point and find out what it was.

For the first five or six evenings there was so much chat this way and that about what I intended to do with myself now that the war was over that I was quite bewildered. They seemed to find this of absorbing interest — of far more interest than I did — although it was my future and not theirs that was being bandied about or at stake or however you like to put it. I found this very odd, for people are usually more interested in their own things, such as futures, than they are in those of other people, and, of course, as far as they were concerned the war was over too, for wars are like rain — they fall on or go over for both the just and the unjust — and Pierre and Muriel had a future too, but not with the Ministry of Supply and the Fire Service, any more than I had one with Air Intelligence.

'We wondered,' said Pierre at long last, 'whether you would be interested in a post in Scotland for a change.'

'I might,' I said.

I do not know if you have ever stalked deer? As you probably know, the deer is a very, very wary animal with pronounced instincts for self-preservation that inhabits, in its noblest form, the wild Highlands of Scotland. It has wide antlers and four very fast-running legs. The only differences between me and a stag royal are that I am female, ignoble, have no antlers, and my legs, though fast-running, number only two, and the great thing that the stag royal and I have in common is that we both know when we are being stalked and we know whether the stalking is skilful or stupid. Pierre and Muriel could not have stalked a pregnant tortoise.

Pierre looked down at the floor and then up at me with his dark, beautiful eyes with that frank, candid look which a Caribbean lizard gives to an insect before the kill and said: 'Muriel and I are moving to Scotland. I am taking a partnership in a small engineering firm near Glasgow and there is an opening for a good, all-round, experienced woman like you.'

I said. 'Good. All-round. Experienced. Isn't that rather a contradiction in terms?'

'Janet!' said Muriel. 'I never heard a person say a thing like that! What Pierre means is that you have experience of business and dealing with all sorts of people and all these

150

things and *every*body knows you've got brains and —'

'What's the name of this firm?' I asked.

'You won't have heard of it yet,' said Pierre quickly. 'It's a Mr. Slater who owns it.'

'What do they make?'

'Small diesel engines. They have a terrific future. They —'

'How did you get in touch with this Slater?'

The answer to this was quite a story. It appeared that in the carnage behind Dunkirk in 1940 Pierre had lent a hand to a severely wounded man who had died before they could get him aboard the ship in which Freddie Firmantle and 'his lot' were bringing the remnant of the army to England. The name of the dead soldier was Alan Slater and Pierre had taken charge of his few personal effects and, in due course, had delivered them personally to the soldier's home in Scotland. Alan Slater had been a treasured only child and the gratitude of his parents to Pierre had known no bounds, and Pierre had been told that, when the war was over, he was to think seriously of a future in Scotland if it had any appeal for him and Mr. and Mrs. Slater would see that he did not regret his decision. I was shown letters from Mr. and Mrs. Slater and photographs of them and their dog and their garden, and the more I looked at these pictures the more I liked the Slaters and the more annoyed I became with myself for my persistent, unreasoning dislike of Pierre, who was the kindest and most hospitable of hosts to me. At last I said: 'All right. If you think I am what is wanted for Mr. Slater's office, Pierre, write and tell him I'll be in Glasgow next Wednesday on my way home and I'll come to his place to see him.'

Pierre and Muriel were overjoyed and I got the shoe-on-the-wrong-foot feeling again. People do *not* go into transports over a business interview between two people of their acquaintance. But, there it was.

On the night before I left them to make the journey north they told me that they had been lucky enough to be able to buy a house in this place in Scotland where they were going and asked whether I would witness their signatures on a few documents, and when I agreed they fetched a journalist who was now occupying the room Muriel had had on the floor below and we all had a drink, and Pierre and Muriel got the papers out and signed their names and the journalist put his signature under theirs and everybody was happy and everything. Then the journalist, who was a nice sort of person with a goatee beard, handed the pen to me, and as I wrote my name on the first document I saw that the journalist's name was Otis Coates, which I thought was tremendous fun, for I had always wanted to know someone called Otis, so I hurried along with my signing in order to get down to Christian-name terms with him and be able to say: 'But, Otis, don't you think —' So one of the papers slipped out a bit from under the others and — I have told you before that I read written words in any form almost unconsciously — I read the words in legal type: '— and parcel of land and buildings thereon, in the County of Essex known as —'

'Just there, below Mr. Coates, Janet,' said Muriel.

'This one too?' I asked. She nodded. 'I ought to charge you for all these autographs,' I said and signed my name. 'Where *is* this house?' I asked after a moment.

'Just about a mile out of Ballydendran, on the Glasgow-Carlisle road. I haven't seen it yet, but Pierre has.'

I was not listening to her, for, down the years, I could hear the voice of Mr. Rollin saying: '— property in Essex. A very nice competence.'

Did Muriel, I wondered, have her competence any more? I was now really determined to see Mr. Slater and, more than that, I was determined that if Mr. Slater employed Pierre he was also going to employ one, Janet Sandison. Although I told myself I was all kinds of a fool, that none of this was any of my business, that Muriel had never responded one whit to my influence or advice and never would, I was still extremely angry. Do not ask me why. I think I am a person like this: I simply cannot bear to see getters-away-with-things getting away with them.

When I was in the train and on my way to Glasgow and Ballydendran I was still no wiser as to why Pierre wanted me there, and when I met Mr. and Mrs. Slater I was more at a loss than ever. Mr. Slater, a fair-skinned, white-haired man of about sixty-five, met me at the local station with his small car and took me to a pleasant modern little house in the middle of a small field that had been turned into a garden and which was still not very mature. He was a shy, kindly man with the keen, quiet eyes and the broad, strong hands of the Scottish craftsman, and there was a break of laughter in the tone of his voice. I had not met his like since my days on Clydeside with 'Uncle Jim'.

'Mother is fair past herself with excitement, Miss Sandison,' he told me in the car. 'It's not often we have visitors in the middle of the day. I hope you can eat a good dinner!'

'I can eat so much I should have brought my own rations!' I told him, and he laughed.

'No need for that here. Mother is a fine provider, but she likes folk to eat it!'

'Mother' surprised me by being an Englishwoman of small proportions, for, somehow, I had expected to find a large, sonsie, Scots housewife with a dab of flour on one pink cheek and a white apron.

'Lo and behold!' she greeted us. 'So here you are! Come in, Miss Sandison.'

I did not at that time feel any particular need to have job-finding luck, by which I mean that, for once, I would have been quite glad to go home for a prolonged holiday, but it was comforting to know that my luck held as firmly as ever. Mr. Slater seemed to have made up his mind between the station and the house that I was the sort of secretary his office wanted, and while 'Mother' put the soup on the table he named a good salary, shook hands with me and said: 'Well, that's settled.'

Over the very good dinner, 'Mother' decided that rooms or a house or anywhere to live was quite out of the question in the town, with the housing shortage, but she had a nice little bedroom at the back of the house that was just the place for me, with a view of the garden and the hills and warmer than upstairs, this wintry weather. I thanked her very much and added: 'But that it might be a nuisance for you. Maybe I can get a room from Pierre and Muriel at their place.' It transpired

153

that they did not know that Pierre and Muriel had a house and they asked if I knew where it was. They did not, they said, know of a single available house in the town.

'All I know about it is that it is called The Lea,' I said, 'and it is on the Glasgow-Carlisle road.'

'The *Lea*?' Mrs. Slater's voice rose in an eldritch screech.

'Are you sure, Miss Sandison?' Mr. Slater asked quietly.

'Well — that's what they said.' I felt as if I had thrown a grenade into the middle of the white table-cloth.

'But it's a *mansion* house!' protested Mrs. Slater.

'What?'

'It's a great big barrack of a place,' Mr. Slater told me. 'It used to have its own Home Farm and all but the land was sold off before the war. It's just the house and garden now, but it's *big* right enough.'

'Lo and behold! There's twenty-five rooms in it if there's one!' said Mrs. Slater.

'Oh dear!' was all I could find to say.

'I wouldn't like to have the running of it these days,' Mrs. Slater went on. 'I hope Muriel is young and strong.'

Muriel could not boil a potato or wash a dish-cloth, but I did not deem this the time to say so.

'I suppose Pierre got it cheap,' I said wanly.

'Maybe,' said Mr. Slater. 'Maybe. Cheapness is a matter of how much is in your pocket. The Lea, even cheap, would be more than I would tackle. Of course, Pierre's wife is quite wealthy — I know that.' I was liking all this less and less. 'Listen, Mother, if that's all the dinner you have for us, get your hat and we'll run out and let Miss Sandison have a look at The Lea.'

'Mother' gave vent to a loud howl of protest about the dish-washing, was persuaded in the end to go and change her clothes, and while she was doing it I washed the dishes at her spotless sink and Mr. Slater dried them.

'Lo and behold!' she said when she came back, hatted and gloved. 'The last person that washed up for me was Pierre!'

Aha, I thought. Helps you with the washing-up, the nice, kind dear boy! I would dearly like to wash *him* up, the louse!

154

And I smiled like an angel at Mrs. Slater and helped her into the car, just as, I was sure, Pierre would do.

The Lea was a Victorian Baronial Hall, turrets at the corners and everything. We drove up to it, and the old gardener-caretaker who lived at the lodge knew Mr. Slater and took us inside by way of the back door. I was appalled by the whole ghastly edifice, but the main hall was the masterpiece. It was lined with dark oak up through two stories and along one side of it ran what could only be intended as a Minstrels' gallery, although I thought that the days of the Merrie Minstrelsy must have been over long before it was built. I stood in the middle of the floor and gazed upon it all, awestruck. 'Just the place for the Two-handed Engine!' I thought, but I must have said it aloud.

'I beg your pardon?' Mrs. Slater asked.

'Big, isn't it?' I commented inanely. There seemed to be nothing else to say.

We came back to the Slaters' house and had tea, and Mr. Slater told me of his son and of the engine which he had developed just before the war came, the engine which had been taken up by the War Office and which was now on priority manufacture for the export market.

'The thing's too big and fast-moving for me,' Mr. Slater said. 'If Alan had been here — Oh, well, for his sake, I'd like to see it the success he aye knew it was. And here I am. Bookfuls of orders, folk howling for engines from all ends of the earth, and some way or another I've got to get the tools and the men to use them and folk like yourself and Pierre to help me manage things. If it wasn't Alan's engine I would retire tomorrow. But for his sake I would like to see engines with the name "Alan Slater" on them everywhere from Alaska to Timbuctoo.'

'Have you any other office staff besides Pierre and myself?' I asked.

'Office?' he snorted. 'I've got two young lassies that can type and old Willie that keeps the books, but I've taken on another fellow — he's coming at the end of this month, like you. His name's Alexander — he's from the east o' the Border. He's just back from the Army — a likely kind of lad. I knew his father long ago.'

'Oh. What's he going to do?'

'Works Manager. He's a first-class engineer, just as good as they come — but —'

'Aye? But — Mr. Slater?'

'His father was as thrawn an old devil as ever came out o' the Borders,' he told me. 'Strong as an ox, a devil to work and a fine craftsman but the fiend's own temper. And independent as be damned. When he was working for Nicholson's, old Nicholson swore at him once and Alexander up and tied a length o' piping round old Nicholson's neck and it took two gangers to get it off him. I haven't dared to tell my foremen yet that I am bringing an Alexander into the place.' Slater's Works was sounding more and more like fun to me, and I went back to Glasgow and on up to my home for a week or two wondering if, after all, I had lost the battle for my sanity in those tin huts in Buckinghamshire.

I returned to Ballydendran on a Sunday, to start work on the Monday, to find that Pierre and Muriel were installed at The Lea among the baronial furniture that they had bought along with the house. They also had acquired a 'staff' in the form of a slatternly-looking married couple with three children who lurked about the front drive picking their noses. I was approached straight away, in the office, by Pierre to share The Lea with them at a moderate charge and I refused, with thanks, saying that I must stay with the Slaters for a little while when they had been so very kind to me. It was here that the first slight chill set in. I was utterly at a loss to know why Pierre and Muriel were so anxious to have me under their feet, and the more I thought of it the more at a loss I found myself.

But, of course, it is pointless and nonsensical for me to try to tell you that one's life is taken up entirely by thinking about things like the whimsies of Pierre and Muriel, and Slater's Works on my first Monday morning was no place for whimsies, anyway. I had just refused Pierre's kind offer to be a paying-guest at The Lea when a noise of titanic proportions

156

and classic oaths broke out in the passage outside the small office allotted to me.

'An' if ye dinna ken ony better than tae muddle *me* up wi' that wee bastard frae Cambuslang that disnae ken a bee frae a bull's fit ye can tell the Boss Ah'm awa' an' he can get *three* mair o' the same kin' o' bastards tae tak' my place!' bawled a rich West of Scotland voice.

This, in the Service, would have been known as 'conduct to the prejudice of good order and discipline' and I was fresh out of the Service as an officer of sorts, so I wrenched open my door and said: 'What is going on here?'

'*Whae's* a bastard?' enquired the unmistakable voice of Cambuslang in rhetorical question that was unprepared to listen to any answer.

'Be quiet at once!' I bawled at the two men, who looked enormous in blue overalls, welding gauntlets reaching to their elbows and welding masks hinged back over the tops of their heads to show their rage-filled eyes. They swung round towards me and were quiet from sheer shock at seeing there a face which they did not know. I smiled and pressed my slight advantage: 'Well, what's up?'

'Ach—' They both looked disgusted and shame-faced all at once, like two middle-aged schoolboys, for they were both grizzled men of fifty-five or so.

'Oh, Miss Sandison,' one of the little typists began to explain through a guichet window that looked on to the passage, 'you see, a mistake got made in the pays on Saturday and Mr. Smith got Mr. Smith's packet and —'

'Ach, haud yer tongue!' one of the men told her and then turned towards me. 'Ye see, it was like this —'

They were both explaining at once when the door to the workshops at the end of the passage opened. I saw a blur of white and a flash of bright blue, and a deep, rich voice, its edge sharpened by rage said: 'What the hell do you two men think you're at? Get back on your line!'

The door swung shut before the men could reach it, but in another second they were gone and I was staring at the empty passage.

'Who was the white coat?' I enquired of the girl at the guichet.

'Mr. Alexander, Miss Sandison,' she said in a hushed voice and closed the window in my face.

When I returned to my own office Mr. Slater was there, kindly and normal-looking, and I said: 'So your new Works Manager, Mr. Alexander, is here then?'

'Aye. He started last week. Took a notion and got here a week early.'

'Oh.'

I went on then to tell him of the row in the passage and he told me that with the shortage of office staff and the rapid expansion in the number of craftsmen such muddles and rows were all too frequent.

'We'll have to get it better organised,' he said. 'You see, I was never a big employer of labour. This was just a general repair shop until Alan got started on his engine.' He seemed lost in the maze of his difficulties and I felt very sorry for him, an old man, starting something new in trying conditions which he did not begin to understand.

'We'll soon organise it, Mr. Slater,' I said as confidently as I could. 'There's nothing to it. I'll get hold of this man, Alexander —'

'Listen, lassie, be canny!' he said hurriedly and warningly. 'I'll be honest with ye! He's a clinker in the workshops — I'm anxious to keep him. You'll try and no' upset him?'

'I'll do my very best not to,' I promised, but I began to get a kind of feeling I sometimes get in the tips of my toes about this genius in the white coat who seemed to be out to make a difficult job even more difficult for me. And also, forbye and besides, I told myself, if it comes to it, Mr. Slater can choose between White Coat and me and may the best man win. Quite often I have these rushes of confidence to the head. 'He was in the Army, you said?' I asked Mr. Slater, and he nodded.

'What was his rank?'

'Major.'

'Oh? . . . Well, Mr. Slater, if you've nothing urgent you

want me to do this morning I'm going to see how I can clear up the muddles in the pay-roll.'

'You couldn't do better!' said Mr. Slater and went away.

Mr. Slater would have been very doubtful as to my method of tackling the job, but I did not intend him to know my methods, for I have always been a person like this: I believe that what people do not know will not hurt them, so I just went ahead and backed my luck or something. I put a piece of paper in my typewriter and tapped out a screed in the following form:

To Works Manager.   From Private Secretary.
Date . . .

I understand from Mr. Slater that the record of the employees in the workshops is incomplete. This is leading to muddle and general inefficiency in the office, particularly in the handling of the pay-roll. In this connection, there was lost time on your welding lines from two men called Smith this morning through no fault of their own.

I propose to rectify this situation and would ask you to co-operate with me by meeting me for a short time in my office at any hour during the present week which may be convenient to you.

I sent the scared typist into the workshops with this missive, and after fifteen minutes she returned with this:

To Private Secretary.   From Works Manager.
Date . . .

I will come to your office at 14.00 hours today.

It was written in a large sprawling hand on a roughly torn piece of stiff drawing-paper, with thick blue pencil, and it bore an oily fingermark in one corner.

Well, I thought, the ball is rolling, and a little fast at that, for it was only three hours now until 14.00 hours and I had not an idea about this 'propose to rectify' that I had written so blithely and glibly. By 14.00 hours I was in a tizzy of nervousness and I did not know why, for I had tangled with plenty of people in my time, and why I should be scared out of my wits by a few reports about an ill-natured, ex-major, Scots engineer I could not fathom. On the dot of 14.00 hours the door of my office opened, my heart stopped altogether for a moment, started again on the off-beat and I had that feeling of wonder that I had had once as a small child when I first looked into a kaleidoscope. The instrument was the property of an old man, a friend of my grandfather, and when I had mastered the trick of closing one eye and saw the pattern of crystals at the end of the tube I was dumb with amazement and wanted to be allowed to look and look and look.

'Turn it round!' the old man said.

'No! No!' I cried, tense in every muscle as I gazed, in case some careless movement would spoil the lovely symmetry of the pattern I could see; but, taking no heed of my protest, the old man turned the tube with a sharp 'Click!' and a new and even more beautiful pattern formed, like a divine miracle, before my astonished eye. Now, just as then, an astonishing change of pattern took place, as if the background of my mind, all my experience of life, had been made up of fragments of coloured glass, and, by the act of looking into this man's face, an entirely new and beautiful design had been formed for me. And I felt very much as I had felt as a child when I held the kaleidoscope, that I must take great care, such care that it made every muscle tense, to make no careless movement, speak no careless word, even, that might cause the vision to disintegrate and disappear.

Part IV

Part IV

Part IV

I do not say that I 'fell in love at first sight', for I think this is an experience of which I am not capable. I am too slow-witted to know at a first glance that this or that person can engage my emotions, or maybe it is that I am too cold emotionally to be able to love without pause to consider, first, if I even like. No. It was rather that for the first time in my life I felt vulnerable in the depths of myself with a vulnerability that could lead either to deep satisfaction or to an agonising wounding, and the sudden consciousness of this vulnerability made my breathing difficult, made my hands shake and led to all the other petty, miserable manifestations through which the human body takes advantage of its obscure link with the human spirit.

Dear Patient Reader, let me tell you here that I do not propose to rave like an adolescent about my love affair, but it is only by remembering what I myself felt and desired and by reviewing my attempts to achieve my desire that I can show you why I found Muriel so astonishing in the end.

In the past, My Friend Monica, in her own slang phrase, had been wont to accuse me of 'putting the eye' on men, but this was a convention of teasing, for Monica knew me well enough, I think, to know that what she meant by 'putting the eye' was not one of my failings. The trifling 'love affairs' I had had, including my three engagements of marriage, I had fallen into by accident, very much in the way that, long ago, I had fallen into a half-mischievous friendship with Mr. Rollin, or as I had drifted on the tide into my 'understanding' — ridiculous description — with Victor. If I thought at all about these affairs, and I was not given to thinking overmuch about them, I think my attitude was that it was very civil of dear old So-and-so to want to marry me and a great compliment, and my family was beginning to think it was time I settled down, so, in almost a surprised sort of way, I would find myself wearing an engagement ring. But, always and inevitably, came a point very like that which I had reached with Victor that night on Clydeside so long ago, when my own form of truth rose inside me, a destructive force, which always expressed itself in the same almost meaningless words — for words are a most inadequate medium for many things — 'To hell with this! This is not what I want!' But I do not think I had ever paused to formulate what it was that I *did* want. I think that I have told you somewhere that, in the realm of design, Twice knows what he does *not* like. Well, I think that, until this moment, I was a person like this: on the very brink of my fall into some pit of conventional pseudo-emotion — such an eligible man, my dear, and so charming — I knew that this was something I did not like and I would always draw back in time.

I was all unsuspecting, therefore, in the cold, grey light of a winter afternoon in my dingy little office when the sharp 'Click!' of the kaleidoscope took place in my mind, and I found that my every nerve-end was hyper-sensitised; that one instinct was urging me forward while another commanded me to turn and run; that my happiness for the first time in my life was completely at the mercy of someone other than myself. Long ago, Lady Firmantle, in company with many other people, had said that I was 'as Highland as peat'. Well, maybe they were right. The Highland fighter is not famous for his aggressive spirit in battle and he has never been accused of a tendency to take flight under fire, but he has a strong reputation for 'standing his ground', so perhaps it is not surprising that to 'stand my ground' is the course that came to me or that that is what I proceeded to do. I knew now what I wanted, which was all or nothing, and I was prepared to fight for it. So we can go back to the narrative now and I will tell you of a few of the incidents, skim the surface, of that long, hot battle between this man and me, before we discovered that we were fighting in the common cause of wanting to stand on, and share, the same piece of ground.

Well, there I was, a fairly hard-bitten old type of thirty-five, old enough to know vaguely what had happened to me, but still young enough to be having something of a job to keep my eyes, hands and voice steady. Mr. Alexander was still wearing his white dust-coat, which was three-quarter length, and had the effect of making a man, who was already the broadest lean man I had ever seen, look broader than ever. His skin still had the yellowish tan from service in the East, and against this background glittered two brilliant, impatient-looking, blue eyes.

'Mr. Alexander? I am Janet Sandison.'

'How d'you do, Miss Sandison?'

It is a beautiful voice, I thought, you angry-looking, upsetting little beast, and you *would* have those craftsman's hands.

'Sit down, please, Mr. Alexander. I'll be as quick as I can.'

'That's all right. We've got till stopping time if you like.'

I sighed with relief. At least he was not utterly hostile. Mr. Slater would be pleased about that. And I needed time — time. Even about the routine of my job I could not think straight, but my grip was coming back.

'We won't be that long! . . . What I would like to do is to set up a record of the workers more or less on Service lines — you know what I mean? Their full names, ages, trade classification, family details — half of them are not even registered for income-tax, you know.'

'I see.'

'And all I would ask you to do is to make the men available — about fifteen minutes for each man — at times when it suits the working of your shops, each man bringing with him *your* definition of his trade and class. Can that be done during the present week, do you think?'

'Certainly, Miss Sandison.'

165

It was all too easy. What *lies* I had been told about him and his temper — what *shocking* lies — so that I had got myself into this state over him, quite apart from suddenly *feeling* like this about him! I was so sorry for myself that I could have burst into tears.

'Have you had time yet to get to know all your men?'

A steely gleam came into the eyes. 'Know them? How?'

'Well enough to be able to send them in in your own time and order without missing any.'

'That? Yes.'

'H-how did you think I meant, Mr. Alexander?'

'Well, there are different points of view.' The eyes now held a gleam of amusement. 'I know them as good welders and shabby ones, good fitters and bad ones, accurate and inaccurate machinists — in fact, I know the ones to sack when I can replace them. That's the first bit of knowing that a bloke like me does in a place like this. I'm paid to get a good job and production out of the labour. So I don't know yet whether they are Presbyterian, Roman Catholic or Other Denominations.'

'And you don't care, I suppose?'

Exceeding peace had once made Ben Adhem bold and I had grown bold too, but this was no angel that was sitting in *my* room. Ben Adhem had all the luck.

'Is that relevant?' he enquired, and the eyes were now as flat and grey as their native River Tweed in a sullen mood. 'Anyway, let's get started with this thing,' he went on.

I wanted to pick him up and throw him bodily through the window and, stocky and heavy as he was, I believe that at that moment I had the physical strength to do it. I know, Dear Reader, that this was unreasonable, but that is how it was.

'What? Now?' I asked.

'Why not? I'm an employee. In the Army they told me I shouldn't ask my men to do anything I wouldn't do myself. What details do you want?'

So help me, I thought, this is another Muriel. Nothing comes out of him. Lighten our darkness, we beseech thee, O Lord! Is he being funny, or sarcastic or inimical, or does he

166

mean every word of what he says? In love? I was so exasperated I could have burst.

'As an employee under personal contract to Mr. Slater, Mr. Alexander,' I told him with great calm, and drawing a sheet of paper towards me (if I had still had a Service hat and gloves I would have put them on), 'only your name, your age and your home address will be required.'

'My name is Alexander,' he said.

'I am aware of that, Mr. Alexander. You know the name I mean, I think.'

'Alexander,' he said.

'Your *full* name, Mr. Alexander — do I make myself clear?'

'Evidently I don't make *my*self clear. My name, Miss Sandison, is Alexander Alexander.'

'What — *twice*?' I said, furious at my own inanity the moment the words were out.

'Exactly,' he said. 'Twice.'

We sat there glaring at one another, and suddenly he threw his head back and laughed, open-mouthed and uproariously, showing a mouthful of beautiful, strong, gleaming teeth. 'Beautiful teeth! Beautiful!' said the voice of Cockabendy down the corridor of my memory, and then, as suddenly, his laughter ceased. 'I'm thirty-five,' he said. 'And I'm at the Royal Hotel at the moment until I can find a place to live. I am an engineer and I am classified as Works Manager. That do?'

'Thank you. Yes.'

I wanted to ask him why he had laughed so much but decided that he was probably laughing at *me* and that he would have the impudence to tell me so; and as that was not going to do the situation any good, I indicated that the interview was at an end. He looked at a watch on his wrist as he rose from his chair.

'I'll send about twelve men in in fifteen minutes or so,' he said. 'I can let them go in batches more easily than one at a time.'

'All right, Mr. Alexander.'

He went to the door. 'If you have any trouble let me know.'

'I don't anticipate trouble,' I said.

'No, you don't,' he replied and disappeared through the doorway.

Later that afternoon Mr. Slater came into my office and found it full of operatives in blue overalls and I explained to him what was happening.

'That's the very thing!' he said, and smiled round generally at the men. As I went on writing down the family details of one, Thomas Simpson, Fitter, First-class, age fifty-three, I had a sudden warm feeling that this was a wonderful job I had found, the best and most satisfying job I had ever had. Every one of these men was a complete, round personality in his own right. They were not units of a proletariat or anything drearily mass-produced, fit only to be known by a number in order that one could tell them apart. They were not 'operatives' — they were men, conscious of their dignity in the scale of creation and carrying that dignity with pride. Out of them came a wave of fellow-feeling towards Mr. Slater and, through him, they began to extend that feeling towards me. I could feel it lapping round me as I wrote. When I had finished with the last of the batch and he had gone out, Mr. Slater said: 'How did you get them in from the Fitting Shop?'

'Mr. Alexander is sending them in to me in batches,' I told him, 'with a note of their trade and proficiency standard.'

'Oh?'

'He and I met just after lunch and came to an arrangement.'

'Oh?'

'Mr. Alexander was very helpful and co-operative, Mr. Slater.' He looked hard at me for a long moment, said nothing and went away.

During the first month, which is usually a 'settling-down, getting-to-know-the-ropes' period in any job, my post at Slater's Works was unusual, for what I had to do was to create something to settle down in and supply my own ropes, but out of chaos order began to come. It was not a case of planning to do this or that part of organisational construction on any given day, for crisis followed crisis, and a job that could be set aside even for half an hour often had to be set aside for a whole day. The promised delivery of ball-bearings had not come forward, and 'Mr. Alexander was creating the devil'; No. 2 electrodes had come in mistake for No. 3, and the storemen had not noticed it and 'Mr. Alexander was creating the devil'. Nearly every sentence spoken in my office seemed to end with 'and Mr. Alexander is creating the devil', but I had never actually seen him at this fell work until one day there was a piercing whistling of 'Scotland the Brave' in the passage, my door flew open, and he was standing there, a blue-eyed devil incarnate.

'May I use your phone, please?' he snapped.

'Certainly,' I said, and then — you know by now what a fool I am — I enquired: 'Are you about to create the devil?'

'What the hell d'you mean?'

'I've been led to believe it's your favourite pastime.'

'What?'

'Creating the devil.'

'Listen,' he said, bending threateningly over my desk and looking as if he were about to throttle me. 'It's all very well for this office to sit here on its — to sit here pushing me to get six engines to the docks by Wednesday! Where are the bloody crates for the bloody engines? Or would you like them shipped in Christmas paper with bows of red ribbon?'

I got to my feet on the other side of the desk — we were just of a height but he was about three times my breadth — and I bent towards him and hissed: 'That temper of yours won't get you bloody crates for bloody engines or my bloody telephone either, but if you'll tell me where the bloody crates are on order *I'll* bloody get them for you!' Momentarily I had him at a loss and leapt upon my advantage. 'Is Smith and Paterson making them?'

'So I'm told,' he said, straightened his back, and began to whistle 'Scotland the Brave' again.

I picked up my telephone, trembling in every joint with rage, and spoke to old Mr. Paterson, who was a kind of carpenter reproduction of Mr. Slater, engineer.

'Oh, Mr. Paterson,' I said in my most troubled-female voice. 'I'm in the most awful hole. We need six of those crates you have for us right away and the Works Manager's been in my office creating the devil about them. Please, can you help me?'

When I put the telephone down I said: 'Send a lorry to Patersons for them in half an hour. They're taking them out of a batch for somebody else.'

He stopped whistling, narrowed his eyes at me and said: 'You amoral, lawless bitch!' and turned away.

'I got your bloody crates for you!' I bawled at his back.

He wheeled round and flashed his brilliant smile. 'Aye, you did at that! Thanks!'

Thereafter, I would hear 'Scotland the Brave' coming along the passage, but when the door flew open there would be the sudden smile and: 'Hi, what about tuppence worth of the smarm on your telephone?'

'What's wrong now?'

And it would be castings, or ball-bearings, or lathe tools, or something else that had not come forward. Everything was in short supply, all firms like ourselves were driving for export production, and the result was that I developed an extension of my personality among supply firms all over Britain as a frail female who was victimised by a Works Manager who was always 'creating the devil'. It was monstrously false, but it got us the supplies we needed, and the Alan Slater engines began to come off the line more and more quickly.

All the time, while I was being bedevilled on one side of the passage, Pierre was sitting in an office on the other side, and when I had a moment I would wonder what on earth he was doing. With the aid of one of the little typists, he wrote reams of letters, but if I happened to see the copies of any of them, it always struck me that there were more urgent things that needed doing at that particular time. Mr. Slater spent a little of his time in a small office of his own, but his natural home was in the workshops and he wandered about among the lines, looking at this and that and talking to Mr. Alexander at a high stand-up desk that he had in a corner of the assembly shop. Periodically there would be mention of 'getting an office fixed up for Mr. Alexander', but something more urgent would come to our attention, and, anyway, I thought, what is the point of an office for a man who never sits down? Better to supply him with a juke-box that would play nothing but 'Scotland the Brave'.

At the end of about six months the 'key personnel' of Slater's Works seemed to me to have settled into their functions as parts of an engine as follow:

> Mr. Slater — Governor
> Mr. Alexander — Main Drive
> Self — Oil and Grease
> Pierre — Idling Wheel.

In my own capacity I touched on the other three but had special reference to Main Drive, who was a heller for getting friction hot; and as long as Idling Wheel did not actually squeak I did not pay any attention to him, and, like this, things went along quite nicely until one day Governor called a meeting and cramped the parts of the engine into too small a housing, as it were, the locale of the meeting being round my desk. The reason for the meeting was an enquiry that had come in for five hundred engines for some company in Africa, delivery to start in six months' time at the rate of twenty a month.

'Well, there it is,' said Mr. Slater, throwing the letter which he had read aloud to us back on to my desk. 'What do you all think? Pierre?'

'It's terrific, isn't it!' said Pierre. 'Five hundred! Now let me see — we'll make — '

He began to make calculations, muttering to himself, 'Five hundred times —'

'Are you off your nut?' said Mr. Alexander suddenly.

Pierre looked up. 'What do you mean?'

The Works Manager looked at Mr. Slater. 'Maybe it's none of my business, sir,' he said, 'but I don't think this is the time to calculate problematic profits.'

'Iphm,' said Mr. Slater. 'And what *do* ye think it's a time for, Mr. Alexander?'

'Capital seems to me to be important!' I said hastily, oiling and greasing like mad. 'Er — surely?'

'Exactly,' said the Works Manager. 'With the tooling I've

171

got, I can do four a week at the very outside.'

'Can ye get as much as four out of it?' Mr. Slater asked.

'We did it two weeks running last month,' I said.

'That's very good,' the old man said.

'It's not bad for the capacity,' said Mr. Alexander, who has never been heard to say that any engineering job of any kind is 'good', for that would be saying that there is no room for improvement. In case this idea is new to you, I hand it to you as a thought that it summarises the genius of the Lowland Scot for engineering.

The meeting went on. My form of oiling and greasing now took the form of what Governor and Main Drive told me to take notes of, which was mostly approximate costs of buildings, machine tools and so on, while Idling Wheel idled, and after a long time Mr. Slater said: 'Just count that up for me, Miss Sandison.'

And while I added up the row of figures on the right-hand side of the foolscap pages Main Drive said: 'That land to the north of us is yours, Mr. Slater?'

'Aye. Alan got me to buy it before the war.'

'Good.'

'Eighty-four thousand pounds odd,' I said. 'Call it eighty-five.'

'Call it anything ye like, lassie,' said Mr. Slater. 'I haven't got it.' He pushed the letter of enquiry at me. 'Write them a civil letter telling them to try some of the bigger folk.'

'Just a minute, sir,' said Main Drive.

'What? Are ye thinking of approaching the Chancellor o' the Exchequer?' Mr. Slater asked.

'No. The bank.'

'I've nothing in the bank but my current workin' capital, man!'

'Maybe. But out there' — he jerked his head in the direction of the workshops — 'you have as nice a wee engine as anybody in Britain right this minute.'

The old man was his. The Governor cut out and Main Drive took over, for a little while, the fate of 'Alan's Engine'. In the end, Mr. Slater 'saw the banker', we got our capital and, not without many 'creations of the devil' and 'tuppenceworths of smarm', twenty instead of four Alan Slater engines were coming off the assembly line every week. We filled the African order on schedule and a good many more besides.

You probably took this book out of the library because you wanted something to read and thought that the story of My Friend Muriel would do until somebody returned Tolstoy's *War and Peace*, which was what you really fancied, and now you have a sense of injury (have taken umbrage, in fact) because you are not getting a word even about Muriel and a lot of words you do not want about engines for Africa. Well, I am trying to tell you this story as it *was* and how it was was that a whole year went over my head in Slater's Works and I woke up, or came to, at the end of it to discover that the whole pattern of personalities in the scene had suffered a change. Not a sea-change into something rich and strange, though. Oh no. Not that sort of sea-change it was, but the kind when the tide goes out from a village beach where the inhabitants, from time immemorial, have dumped their rubbish and refuse. It was a very, very nasty sea-change indeed, I discovered.

Mr. Slater, that kindly old man whom the Scots-applied adjective 'decent' best describes, was very worried, because he had learned that Pierre, as far as business or engineering was concerned, was a great, big, bombastic, empty barrel, but 'Mother', lo and behold, was just as besotted about Pierre as ever, although he had been 'a rash boy to invest so much of his money in that great big place The Lea'. Mr. Alexander, who will henceforth be known as Twice, since he had begun to answer to that name in the course of one of our major crises, was as energetic, quick-tempered and enigmatic as ever about most things, but had told me, in the course of another crisis, that he 'hated the guts of that pal of yours, Pierre'. Muriel was out at The Lea with no domestic staff at all, getting untidier and more inefficient daily, while the house had a soiled look and the grounds resembled a jungle. I went out there as seldom as I civilly could, for I did not love Pierre, the host of The Lea, any more than I ever had, and every time I called he and Muriel begged me to go and stay with them, which I did not

173

want to do having now found a comfortable bed-sitting-room near the works, where I could have a little time to myself in the evenings, instead of helping Muriel to wash dishes at The Lea. I am a person like this, you think: I am extremely selfish, you think. All right, but you wait a moment until I tell you something else.

You and I, up till this moment, have been under the impression that Pierre and Muriel — but mostly Pierre — got me this nice interesting job at Slater's Works, which was very kind of them. Well, you and I are quite wrong, as My Friend Monica would say. What really happened was that *I* got *Pierre* his job at Slater's Works, and at the end of twelve months I was just beginning to realise, in my semi-conscious way, that that was what I had done. In my life, I have never had much trouble over the things I have done deliberately, but, my gosh, the things I just sort of get into and do without even being aware of it are the devil.

Anyway, here you have me coming up to my second New Year at Slater's Works, for we do not go much on Christmas in Scotland — being a pagan rather than a Christian country, we celebrate things like time passing such as the New Year coming, and the birthdays of poets such as Robert Burns, and we are awkward and John Knoxish about the Christian faith by giving a yearly thought to St. Andrew — and I am in my bed-sitting-room and in somewhat of a dither, when I stop to think of it, about Twice, who is still at the Royal Hotel, and the Slaters are in their little house and Muriel and Pierre and the Two-handed Engine are out at The Lea, the last in the position that I had long thought was made for it, just under the Minstrels' Gallery in the Baronial Hall. And Mrs. Slater and Muriel, being English and Christian, get the idea that it is time that everybody got a fresh injection of Peace on Earth and Goodwill towards Men, and Mrs. Slater hangs a bit of mistletoe from the iron lantern in the porch of her house and Muriel sticks a bit of holly in the helmet of the Two-handed Engine, and we are all invited to take part in Peace and Goodwill at the Slaters' on Christmas Day and at The Lea on Boxing Day — just the six of us, for, lo and behold, says Mrs.

174

Slater, we are three ladies and three gentlemen and isn't that nice?

However, I am getting ahead of myself again, for it actually happened like this. About a week before Christmas, one of these dollops of snow that are characteristic of the Ballydendran end of Scotland came down overnight, then a frost came, and Twice and I were sitting in my office with, out in the yard, a consignment of engines, sitting under tarpaulins, nice and warm, on six lorries, ready to catch a boat at Liverpool the next day and the entire road from Ballydendran to Liverpool was blocked with frozen snow, while the boat was busy getting ready to close her hatches. Snowploughs and bulldozers were working on the roads and all we had to do was wait until we were told that the way was clear. In the meantime, the clock ticked and the boat battened down another hatch. We were listening in imagination to her doing it when the telephone rang.

'Ker-ist!' said Twice, looking at his watch. 'We'll still make it if I drive the first lorry myself!'

He was at the door before I had picked up the receiver.

'Slater's?' I called on a questioning note.

'Lo and behold!' came the voice. It was not the County Engineer's office to tell us that the road was open, it was Mrs. Slater with her Peace and Goodwill invitation. The let-down was dreadful. I dealt with her as civilly as I could, and Twice came back across the floor, his feet dragging. When I had put the receiver back on the rest he stared at it it and said: 'Lo and be-bloody-hold!'

I stared venomously at it too. 'Mirabile bloody Dictu!' I said, for Mrs. Slater's name was Mirabel and I had been referring to her, to myself, as 'Mirabile Dictu' for a long time, because of how she was always saying 'Lo and behold' or 'Wonderful to relate'. Twice was in the middle of one of his laughs when the telephone rang again and this time the voice said: 'Priorit-ee! Both main roads south out of Ballydendran now passable! Thank yee-oo!'

'That's it!' I said.

'Ker-ist!' said Twice, and went off with the first lorry to

Liverpool. 'Phone that ship!' he bawled from the cab as he turned out of the yard.

Our convoy caught the boat and he came into my office the next afternoon, which was a Saturday and I was just going home, as if he had only been out to the workshops for a few minutes since I had last seen him, and took up his laughing where he had left it off the day before. I looked at him in a jaundiced sort of way.

'Mirabile Dictu!' he gasped at last.

'Oh, that? I thought you were starting a nervous breakdown or something. Aren't you tired? By the way, she wants you for supper on the evening of Christmas Day.'

'Who?'

'Mirabile Dictu.'

'Not me!' he said, shying like a horse.

'Better ring her up and tell her then,' I said.

He looked at the telephone and then at me. 'What can I say?'

'The accepted thing is another engagement.'

'But I haven't. I'll be *here* all Christmas Day going through these drawings with the Old Man while the place is quiet. She'll *know* I'm not going anywhere.'

'Then why the blazes not accept?' I asked, suddenly very angry. 'It will be an excellent meal, for one thing!'

'Listen!' he spat out venomously, bending towards me. 'Are you too dumb to realise *yet* that a meal eaten with your palsy-walsy Pierre would probably choke me? How you come to have a bloke like that around you, I don't know! How you square your conscience for pushing him on to the Old Man I cannot think! How you —'

'Would you arrange to keep your filthy temper and hold your horses for one damned moment?' I bawled.

'Siddown, drat you, and don't stick your neck out at *me*!' he bawled back.

'I'll stick my neck out any time I darn please!' I shouted.

In those days Twice and I were just about as calm, detached, cool, polite and fluent a pair of debaters as you could *not* meet. After we had exhausted in childish insults what little breath our tempers left us with we would stand glaring at one

176

another, gasping like fish, the veins in our necks and temples bulging and our teeth grinding.

'I apologise!' he said next, having broader lungs and more capacity for breath than I had. 'After all, your twerps of friends are none of my business. You're a free individual, free to indulge as much rotten taste in people as you've got in you! I APOLOGISE!' he repeated, highly, widely and handsomely.

'I ought to clout you right on that scrum ear of yours!' I spat. 'How dare you say that clot is to *my* taste? How dare you call that shyster a friend of mind? How —'

'Well, isn't he? Isn't —'

'NO! How stupid can you *get*?'

He sat down. 'Look here, I've got this wrong! I'm sorry. Look, sit down, Flash. Strike the old red flag for a minute. Listen, what I thought was —'

'Never mind what you thought!' I sat down. 'Why did you call me "Flash" just now?'

'Flash? I didn't!'

'You're a liar! I'm not deaf!'

'All right, Flash, I did.'

I had never seen him with the charm turned on before, but it was on now — the teeth, mouth and eyes played quite a part in it, not to mention the voice — and it was a most potent variety of the old come-hither. You cornered rat, I thought! You never use this until you are fighting in the last ditch for that enigmatic untouchability of yours, but I've got you now. I felt like an army with banners. With a sidelong glance that would have turned my heart over if I had been a female and not a victorious army at that moment, he smiled and said: 'I have a reprehensible habit of reading anything that comes under my eye. I can read upside-down, sideways or any way.'

'So can I,' I said, indicating that this was a habit so common as not to require mention and that the sidelong look was getting him nowhere. 'Well?'

The look intensified, the smile became a little more twisted up to one side. 'I was using your telephone one day. I read the heading of a letter before I realised what it was. It was upside-down. It started "My dear Lady Flashing Stream". I'm sorry.

177

I didn't read any more of course. But you became Flash, for short — in my mind, you know, like Mirabile Dictu.' He decided that the charm was not doing its work and his face became suddenly naked-looking as he looked straight into my eyes. 'I am very sorry about the whole thing,' he said. 'But there it is. I can read upside-down.'

'So can I,' I said. 'I do it all the time. Otherwise I'd never know what that clot Robertson is up to.'

'Do I understand us to be getting back to where we were?'

'Yes, Twice.'

'Okay, Flash. Now, would you mind telling me about *our* pal Pierre — that is, if you can do it without blowing your top again?'

'Who blew *whose* top?'

'For the love of Pete!'

'Well, shut up about people's tempers!' I said. 'I'll tell you all I know about Pierre and you won't like any of it.'

And I did. It was Saturday afternoon and Slater's Works of Ballydendran were closed. It was the local equivalent of 'all that mighty heart is lying still', so that our part of the little town was very, very quiet. In the quietness, which seemed to bcome more and more ominous as I talked, I told what I knew of Pierre from the night when Muriel got drunk right along to all I had 'heard' and otherwise gathered in conversations with Pierre and Muriel and with the Slaters.

'I don't like the stink of it a bit,' Twice said when I had finished. 'And it just shows you how wrong a bloke can be,' he continued thoughtfully. 'I got the impression that this twerp was a bosom friend of yours and that you had got him his job here. I've given the thing a lot of thought one way and another and I could never understand it.'

'But *how* did you get the impression I brought him here?'

'From the Old Man.'

'Mr. Slater?'

'Who else?'

'But *how*?'

'Listen,' said Twice, looking down at the palm of his left hand as if he were reading the words he was speaking there, which is a habit of his. 'I'm not very good at saying to people that I am such and such a sort of bloke because people are not interested in *your* view of yourself because they've got their own view of you, anyway, and they usually prefer their own. But, off and on, people have told me I'm a quick-tempered, tactless sort of cove and maybe, I sometimes think, they're right. Anyway, one day, over a year ago it was, just after we all came here and started working, this Pierre comes out to the assembly shop and says something to me, so I says something to him and one thing leads to another, and that night I go to the Old Man and tell him my resignation is his just as of as soon as it's convenient to him and possibly before. The Old Man was very civil when I think about it. I wouldn't have been as civil if I had been in his place.'

'I bet you wouldn't,' I said.

'Shut up. He was civil enough to talk me into giving the thing another whirl and then he told me he was in a helluva difficult spot with this Pierre, because Mrs. Slater was very fond of him, but, what was almost worse, this Pierre and his wife were great friends of *yours* and, says the Old Man: "I wouldn't like to do anything hasty and upset Miss Sandison" ... The Old Man thinks *you* are the backbone of this ruddy business!'

'That's nice,' I said.

'Shut up. Pierre coming to work here was Mirabile Dictu's idea in the first place — the Old Man was less keen. Then Pierre sprang on opportunity and bought The Lea. The Old Man was still uncertain about it all, but then *you* came romping in and he took such a notion to you that he thought Pierre couldn't be so bad after all, so he took a second thought and decided to give Pierre the job.'

'So help me!' I exploded.

'Now then!' said Twice. 'Temper!'

'Shut up! Didn't I tell you, you dope, that Pierre told me in London, before I ever saw Mr. Slater, that he was taking a partnership in this firm?'

'I know! The only thing is that the Old Man didn't know of Pierre's intentions — he still doesn't, I imagine. Blokes like

Pierre live largely by taking truth by the forelock. And I'll tell you another thing — when we raised that capital for the new shops from the bank I asked the Old Man if he would let me lend him a few quid.'

'Oh?'

He gave me his sidelong grin. 'Don't get the notion I'm a capitalist, Flash, but with my war gratuity and a few odds and ends I had a couple of thousand lying in the bank and the Old Man was short on confidence about raising that money. He'd never borrowed money before in his life and I thought maybe if I offered MY ALL it would help his frame of mind. It did too,' he added thoughtfully. 'He sailed into those bank fellows like the old *Revenge* in high fettle — they'd have given him a million by the time he'd said his piece. But what I was telling you was, when I offered my measly drop in the bucket to him he said: "Thank you, lad. I'll take it. But don't tell Robertson. I don't want any of *his* cash." So after we'd got the money from the bank I told the Old Man to forget about my bit because he didn't need it now and I realised that he would rather be sole owner of his business as he had always been.'

'And what then?'

'He told me a bargain was a bargain and to hand over my couple of thousand before I spent it on drink.'

'And did you?'

'Yes ... But you see what I mean about Robertson? The Old Man doesn't trust him at all. By the way, what *does* the bloke do in that office all day?'

'Oh, writes the odd letter about this and that and keeps some sort of tabs on the steel allocation and so on. Nothing very much.'

'The less he does the better,' said Twice. 'All the same, you keep an eye on him.'

'What sort of eye?'

'Think of my couple of thousand — the gallant officer's gratuity for years of blood and sweat — ha, ha, ha — heavy workshops wallah, well behind the lines, who never heard a gun go off — you wouldn't see that go up the spout, would you?'

'Don't be an ass! Pierre doesn't even touch the petty cash! — Pity the war didn't give you a better outlet for your temper though. Was it very dull?'

'Excessively. Not even an export drive. . . . No, I meant just the odd peer at his letters and that.'

'Upside-down?'

'Any way you like.'

'Official peerer at Pierre?'

'That's it.' He reached for the telephone, accepted Mirabile Dictu's invitation for Christmas Day and then said: 'That being that and it now being six of the clock on the last Saturday of this week, can I offer you a dram of whisky at the Royal before you go home?'

'Thank ye kindly,' I said. 'Ballydendran will be highly entertained.'

He narrowed his eyes at me and snapped: 'Is Ballydendran that important to you?'

'No. I was merely pointing a fact that might have escaped *your* attention.'

'Then that's all right. It hadn't escaped. Get your bonnet and tippet.'

The party at Glendale (Mr. and Mrs. Slater's house) duly came along, and Twice drove me there in his car, which was an ancient Bentley with chipped paint and scarred upholstery and an engine that ran as on the day it was new, and we felt awkward because of Pierre, but had excellent food in a room that was hot to suffocation.

The party at The Lea (Mr. and Mrs. Robertson's house) duly came along and Twice drove me there and we felt awkward because of Pierre and had execrable food in a room that was cold to freezing point.

On the way out of the jungly drive, Twice turned to the right instead of to the left and I said: 'Where are we going?'

'To a hostelry down here called the Shepherd's Crook for a dram or two. I think my feet have fallen off. How are yours?'

'I don't know. I can't feel them.'

'The only person that could be comfortable in that place was that tin man under the catwalk,' said Twice.

'Tin Man! That's the Two-handed Engine!' I said. 'A most historic piece!'

'*Engine*? Oh, Lycidas?'

That surprised me. 'Yes,' I said, and I told him of Whitely House and how Mr. Rollin finished up in the Engine's iron embrace and how, eventually, Muriel came to inherit. He laughed quite a lot during the telling and then asked: 'How long ago was all this?'

'Oh, thirteen, fourteen years ago.'

'You've known Mrs. Robertson all that time?'

'Muriel? Iphm. Why?'

'Funny. I can't think of two women more unlikely to be long-standing friends. I must be wrong in my estimate of one of you.'

This was, of course, maybe three or four drams after we had arrived at the Shepherd's Crook, where there was a dance in progress and they had a late special licence for the evening, and, if once I had the boldness of Ben Adhem while in Twice's company, this time I fell into the peace of mind that is induced by John Barleycorn.

'Probably it's your estimate of me,' I said brightly. 'As an estimator of me, you stink.'

'Are you spoiling for another fight?' he asked. 'Because don't. When we get bawling at one another, it only clouds the issue further when the visibility is already at zero.'

'What issue?'

'All this mess.' He picked up his glass of whisky and stared into it, looking as if he would like to hurl it across the roof. 'I mean, to *me* it's a mess. That's a personal point of view. Can't expect you to see it my way.'

'You could at least try to let me see your point of view — tell me where you are standing, for instance, and give me a few points of reference, as in map-reading. You'd be surprised at how a bright, efficient person like me can catch on.'

Keep the tone light, I told myself. He was watching me like a hawk, and he could be just as swift on the wing and just as deadly as any hawk. He looked down at his hands again and I relaxed slightly.

'I've never been much of a one for people,' he said suddenly. 'I've never liked intimacies and all that. It will be difficult for you to understand because you are a people-ish sort of person — you've got a gift for dealing with them. People have different gifts. I'm more at home with a nice engine or mechanical contrivance. With them, you know the way the cat's going to jump — with people you don't. You go along nicely, opening all the right valves, you think, meshing all the right gears, and then, lo and behold, as Mirabile Dictu would say, the whole blooming issue blows up in your face. That's how I see it.'

'I see your point exactly,' I told him. 'And every word you say is true. But how does one avoid all contact with people except by being a hermit in a cave or one of those blokes that sit on top of poles?'

'I've always managed nicely until now,' he said.

'And what's different now?'

I said the words thoughtlessly, but as I saw him draw breath to answer me I took fright and rushed on: 'Probably the war and the peace and Slater's madhouse. Give it a little time and you'll get back on an even keel. Seeing it's Christmas, Twice, would you let me buy you a drink for once? Just to show there's no ill-feeling?'

You yammering fool, I told myself. It will cost you months to recover the ground you have lost. Look at him. He is off back to his moated grange and the drawbridge is going up. Say something, anything, to get him back. It was too late.

'No. No ill-feeling,' he said. 'Thank you. I'll have one for the road.'

I wanted to burst into tears.

Now, when I look back, I wonder how two people of thirty-five could be such fools, but, at the same time, I know that one of the few things I have learned is that people never grow too old to play the fool about something, so, really, there was nothing extraordinary about Twice and myself. However, if you have been in the habit, since about the age of twenty, of doing some sort of work and thereby earning your living, there is a provision of nature or a conditioned reflex or something that makes you go on doing it, no matter what sort of emotional muddle you are carrying about at the bottom of the bag where you keep your wits, so we went on making and exporting Alan Slater engines, and when I had a slack moment I 'peered at Pierre' just to make sure that he was not 'up to' anything. At the same time, I tried to make it clear to Mr. Slater, but obliquely, that as far as I was concerned it would not matter if Pierre was found dead in the works lavatory, and I noticed that Mr. Slater and Pierre were having more and more 'conferences' in private, in Pierre's office, and that the Old Man came away from them looking like a man who was nearly as completely disgusted as a man can be.

Partly as a part of my 'peering at Pierre' and partly out of what My Friend Monica would call 'auld lang syne' for Muriel, and partly to get away from the things that I tended to think about when alone in my bed-sitting-room, I had begun to go out regularly, of an evening, to The Lea, for Pierre had taken to 'being out on business', mostly in Glasgow, on at least one evening of the week. This was all very dreary, and is probably equally dreary for you to be reading about when you felt like reading the latest Agatha Christie, so I will tell you about My Friend Monica and auld lang syne, although Monica is not the sort of person that a sensible woman like Agatha Christie would even know, much less put in a book.

Monica says that auld lang syne is a facial expression that is related to other facial expressions in the way that last year's hat is related to other hats. Last year's hat, she says, is recent enough to have a lot of unpleasant memories attached to it, such as how much you paid for it and what a fool you looked in it; indeed, just out-of-date enough to be embarrassing and not old enough to be nostalgically interesting and suitable for sentimental charades. I said that this was a lotta hooey and that anybody with any sense knows that auld lang syne is a wheel with buckets on it, like the water-wheels on old mills, that creaks and sighs as it turns, and every so often drops a dollop of sentiment into your mind that goes 'slosh-glug' like greasy water going down a sink. And then we did not talk about it any more because My Friend Monica called for a

184

double disinfectant, just for auld lang syne, she said.

Well, one night, just for auld lang syne, Muriel and I and the Two-handed Engine were sitting (that is not true — being a gentleman, the Engine was standing) in the Baronial Hall at The Lea, and it was a freezing cold night outside and slightly colder, if anything, in the Baronial Hall, and Muriel and I were having just about as little in common as we had ever had, and there did not seem to be much to talk about, so I said: 'I'll tell you something, Muriel —'

I suppose everybody has certain tricks of speech, although maybe not the same tricks, so I will tell you that when I open a remark with the phrase 'I'll tell you something —' it means that I am about to tell you something that I think you probably know already, but that, if you do *not* know it already, I think you must be demented, and also, forbye and besides, it means that I think it is high time you *did* something to alter the thing I am telling you about. In other words, the somethings I tell you about, prefaced by that phrase, are things you would alter without being told, in my opinion, if you had any sense. So —

'I'll tell you something, Muriel,' I said. 'This house is far too big.'

'Do you think so?' she asked conversationally, but with a blank look as if it were something that had never occurred to her, as if I had said: 'I say, Muriel, just hop into my space-ship and let's go have a cocktail at that new place on Mars.'

I felt exasperated, partly with Muriel, partly because I was feeling exasperated most of the time, anyway, what with the muddle I was in over Twice and Muriel simply made me feel ex*ase*xasperated, if you see what I mean.

'Don't be an idiot!' I said, pointing up into the echoing chasm of the Baronial Hall. 'Look at that up there! Ten big bedrooms and you are sleeping in the room off the kitchen because it is warm and I don't blame you! What *is* all that up there except a hell of a lot of Too Big?'

'It is an investment,' Muriel said.

'An investment in what?'

'Pierre says it is an investment,' she said, not vehemently or anything. She was like a tropical peasant's mule. All she

185

needed was a pair of long ears and a sunbonnet. I changed the subject.

'By the way, where *is* Pierre tonight?'

'Glasgow. On business.'

'I wonder what business?' I asked thoughtfully of the air. 'I can't think of anything at the works that would —'

'How could you?' Muriel asked. 'I suppose Pierre and Mr. Slater have all sorts of irons in the fire that people like you would never know about.'

Now, Muriel was not being nasty, you know. She was simply stating the case as she saw it, and I realised this, for, as Twice had said often, everyone has a different point of view. Had Muriel been in my post at Slater's Works, Mr. Slater and Pierre *would* have had all sorts of irons in the fire that she did not know about, for Muriel would have been too busy 'laying things down' and 'getting on' to have time for 'hearing' conversations of Mr. Slater's and for 'peering at Pierre', and, above all, I told myself, Muriel would never have got herself mixed up with Twice — or anyone else for that matter — to the extent that I had. As if the strength of Twice's image in my mind had developed a long tentacle that reached out and poked her in the ribs, she said:

'I don't like that man Alexander. I had never met him until the Christmas parties, but, of course, one had to invite him for the sake of appearances.'

Careful, now, Janet, I told myself. If you let Twice get in as a wedge between Muriel and you, you will never be able to do one more thing for her. Do things for her? What are you trying to do? Help her? Why? Why help someone who is perfectly happy according to her lights? Her lights are wrong. Wrong for whom? For her? For you? In short, why don't you mind your own business? That is what my self told me back.

'Do *you* like him?' she was asking me.

'He's all right,' I said and prayed: 'Oh, please God, don't choose *this* moment to sharpen Muriel's perceptions!' I continued: 'I get along quite well with him at the works and that's all that matters. . . . *Why* don't you like him, Muriel?'

It was easier to ask the questions in this conversation than answer them, I thought.

'Pierre doesn't like him either,' she answered me, if answer you can call it.

'I should have thought that Pierre would have valued him from a business point of view,' I said. 'I gather he is extremely able at his job.'

'Oh, that,' Muriel said. 'But the workshops are a mechanical sort of job, aren't they? I mean, just a sort of liaison between management and the workers. It's not as if it called for any initiative or anything. It's really just a case of seeing that the operatives get on with their work.' Before I could gather myself and think of something to say, she gave a sigh and continued: 'Pierre hopes that as more and more men come home from the Services and things settle down they'll be able to replace him. I hope they can, for it makes things very difficult for people like Pierre and Mr. Slater to have to work with someone uncongenial. It's just a question of personality in the end,' she finished profoundly.

'Most questions are, aren't they?' I said brightly and rose. 'I'll have to be getting home.'

'Janet, I *do* wish you would be sensible and come and board with us instead of in that poky little room with no one of your own sort to talk to!'

'Muriel, it's too far out here to walk home for lunch and things.'

'Pierre would drive you.'

'And what do I do on days like this, when he is away on business?'

'You could have sandwiches or something. Besides, there is the hotel.'

'Alexander is there,' I said wickedly.

'Oh. Well, there is the Italian café.'

'I don't like ice-cream for lunch.'

I was very tired of this recurring subject of my staying at The Lea. I was very, very cross about what Muriel had said about not liking Twice. Who was *she*, I thought, to go making rude remarks about someone who was important to me? How would *she* like it, I asked myself, if I told her exactly what I thought about her precious Pierre? She would not like it at all, my self answered me back.

People are like a whole universe of little worlds, whirling about in space-time or time-space, and some, like Muriel and me, have some pole of attraction that keeps us swimming in and out of the other's orbit. And some like Pierre and Twice have poles that are negative to each other and would never come together from choice. And some, like Twice, have a strong polar attraction for a little world like me, that keeps me swimming round about him like the moon on its orbit round the earth, only I don't have as much influence on him as the moon has on the earth. I do not make any tides go in and out on Twice. Oh no. And somewhere outside this universe of little worlds there is that Thing, that Christians call God and some philosophers call the One and gamblers call Chance, that takes a deep breath occasionally and blows, and all the little worlds dance about like thistledown, and when the wind dies away a world like me finds itself being drawn along in the wake of Twice, with My Friend Muriel chasing behind me asking me to stay with her at The Lea. I am a person like this by this time: I have made up my mind that it is of no use to say to Muriel that being a satellite to the world of Pierre is no good to her. She can no more help it, I have concluded, than I can help being drawn by the magnetic world that is Twice. But what we can *both* avoid is my stopping in my tracks through space-time and letting the world that is Muriel run slap into the world that is me, so that we both go up in a small, blue flame. I can put a little distance between us. So I did it.

'I can't think,' I said, 'why you and Pierre are so keen to have an unattached woman hanging round the house. If I were married, it's the last thing I'd want!'

'I never heard a person say a thing like that!' said Muriel, and I think she was blushing, but the light was dimmish in that Baronial Hall. 'Pierre and I had it all planned,' she went on. 'You don't look like marrying and it would have been a home and a background for you, and, you know, the Slaters like you, as Pierre always knew they would. Pierre is very clever about people. Pierre will soon have his partnership in the works now and old Mr. Slater won't live for ever.'

There it was, I thought, as I walked along the bright, frosty mile from The Lea to my bed-sitting-room. Muriel had apparently never heard how 'the best-laid plans o'mice and men gang aft agley', for I did not think that ever, until she met Pierre, had Muriel been involved in a plan. The only one she had ever tried to make for herself as far as I knew was when she became engaged to her curate and Madame X had remoulded that one for her and, on the whole, Muriel had probably been very grateful, so Muriel would not realise that this plan of Pierre's that he would eventually own Slater's Works was a mouse's plan, which had even more chance of going agley than one made by a man.

The difference between mice and men, as I see it, is that the man has been gifted with the vision to think of what other men may do. The mouse does not think of anything like that. Oh no. It goes ahead, gathering bits of straw and feathering its little nest, and never thinks at all of the other creature coming along with his plough to till the ground for food for *his* little nest and bang-ho!, as Twice would put it, the mouse's posterior is sticking out of the window. Pierre had gathered bits of straw very industriously — he had Muriel, Miabile Dictu and me (so he thought) — but Mr. Slater, unbeknownst, had gone and brought along a nasty thorny little branch called Alexander and had dumped him down in the nest, making the thing shockingly uncomfortable and not at all what Pierre had intended the cosy little place should be. In addition, Pierre had made a mistake with one of the other straws, to wit, ME. I had been intended to be the big, long, pliable piece of straw that could be twisted this way and that to knit the rest of the structure together. Iphm. Pierre as a planner was a mouse and as a mouse he was not even a good chooser of straws. The only thing I felt that I did not know about Pierre now, that I wanted to know, was whether he was a mouse with the instincts of a louse or a louse with the instincts of a mouse.

So here we all were, with spring coming to Ballydendran, the snow retreating up the hills, the daffodils coming out in the gardens, the blackbirds starting to sing, and Mirabile Dictu, though far from being a young man, had a fancy that lightly turned to thoughts of love. She opened her campaign in my office one day where she had called on her way home from buying her groceries, while Twice and I were making up a case for the Ministry of Food that would convince them that our type of industry was heavy enough to cause our operatives to need an extra ounce of cheese each week. For those readers who will be my Posterity and who were not born at the time, I would mention that food was still rationed as part of the aftermath of the 1939–1945 war.

'Lo and behold!' was her greeting, as if we were the last people she expected to see around the works. 'There you are!' Twice gave her a chair. 'My, what a lot of papers! What are you doing?'

'Getting cheese,' I said, with that sublime faith I always have that the results of my activities will be what I wish.

'Trying to get extra cheese,' Twice said, who is more accurate, not to say wiser, than I am.

'But I thought Mrs. Maitland fed you!' Mrs. Maitland was my landlady. 'I didn't know your did your own housekeeping! That's a scandal! I —'

We explained more fully and she subsided and then cocked her head like a fluffy old parrot in a coy mood.

'Mind you, it's housekeeping you *should* be, a fine upstanding woman like you. All this is all very well' — she looked round the office and sniffed — 'and I know you are a great help to Mr. Slater, but I always have and always will say that woman's place is in the home. What do *you* think, Mr. Alexander?'

Let, I thought, the oxy-acetylene plant blow up outside and toss us all to Kingdom Come! Blow, bugle, blow! Roll on, thou deep and dark blue ocean, roll! Come, ye four corners of the earth. . . . Into the charged silence came a very faint whistling of the first few bars of 'Scotland the Brave'. Twice put a file of papers under his arm and picked up the felt hat that lay on a corner of my desk.

'I suppose there are women and women, Mrs. Slater, and

190

places and places for them,' he said, smiled at her as a tiger might smile at a lamb at the United Animals' Meeting, and went out.

'He's a nice man that,' she said, when the door had closed. 'If you could only get to know him, I mean, I'm sure he would be very nice. And I'm sure he's lonely, going back to that hotel every night. I keep saying to Mr. Slater to ask him up in the evenings, and he comes sometimes, but, after all, what is there in our house for him? Old people like us? What he needs is someone of his own age, to take him out of himself. . . . You like him, don't you, Janet?'

'Like him? I hadn't thought about it,' I lied. 'I get on with him very well here at the works.'

'I know that, but that's not what I meant. I thought Christmas time — oh, well, you think about it. None of us are getting any younger, you know.'

Mirabile Dictu never objected to a nice, clear statement of the obvious. 'You can rely on *me*,' she said, as one member of the Ku-Klux-Klan or the Sinn Fein might say to another. 'You would make a fine wife and I would like to see you settled.'

That was nice, I thought, as she padded away with her basket of groceries. I would make a fine wife.

The Farmer wants a wife, the Farmer wants a wife,
Heigh-ho, my Daddy-oh, the Farmer wants a wife!

I felt a little mad, but took a pull at myself and sent one of the little typists out to tell Twice that I was now free again. We had to get the cheese. Cheese. Be normal. Act as if nothing had happened. Concentrate on the cheese. Think of nothing but cheese. After all, when a seaside photographer wanted to get a smiling picture, you had heard, he asked his subject to say 'Cheese!' Cheese! Cheese! I tried it with my head inclined slightly to the right, then slightly to the left, and was going in for a rather contorted version of cheese spoken over the left shoulder when Twice said: 'Is there a porpoise close behind you, by any chance?'

'Yes. And treading on my tail!' I snapped.

'As long as it isn't your toes. Where had we got to?'

'Thirdly,' I said. 'How many more — lies can you think up?'

'I'm afraid I'm about licked,' he confessed. 'We've cited the fat shortage in general, the bacon shortage in particular, what a cold spring we are having. Can you think up a fourthly?'

'Only the handiness of cheese as a supper-dish basis — the number of ways it can be used and that sort of thing,' I said doubtfully.

'That's brilliant!' said Twice. 'You're quite the housewife! Why, I —'

I did not know what he was going to say next and he has never been able to recall it, for I picked up the heap of papers on my desk in both hands and brought them down with all my force on top of his head, from where they scattered, fountain-wise, all over the room. He sprang at me, seized me by the shoulders and shook me till my teeth rattled, and while he did it he kept saying: 'You damned Highland vixen! You damned Highland vixen! You damned —'

'Alexander!' said Pierre's voice. 'I'm going to report you to —'

I broke away, hurled myself at Pierre and bawled: 'Report your Aunt Fanny!' kicked the door shut with Pierre on the outside of it and leaned against the inside of it to try to get my breath back.

'Now!' I said when I could speak. 'Look what you've done!'

'ME!' Twice almost screamed. 'ME? You damned —'

'You stop that, Twice Alexander! Just you stop that swearing and bawling! D'you want the whole place to hear you?'

'They can hear you right out in the assembly shop right now!' Twice shouted. 'Honestly, your temper is shot to hell. You ought to take something for it — preferably a shot of arsenic!'

'Arsenic yourself, you —'

I was getting nicely wound up when the door opened again

192

and Mr. Slater said: 'I'm told you two are having a little difference of opinion. Anything I can do?' He began to pick up the scattered papers as if it was a little job that he did every day at that time, like cleaning his teeth.

'It was nothing important,' said Twice, not at all because he has more self-control than I have. It is just that he has more of that low cunning that makes people very ready-witted. 'We were just having a slight argument about this letter about the men's extra cheese.'

'Oh, just routine,' said Mr. Slater, and he put the bundle of papers on my desk and went away, humming to himself.

'Ger-r-r-r — *out*!' I growled at Twice.

'You bet!' he said. 'And you know where you and the Ministry can *put* your ruddy cheese!'

So he went out too, leaving me to my routine.

My Friend Monica will tell you that routine is a narcotic drink made out of some sort of roots, which tastes very much like potheen although, she says, she has only tasted Irish whisky out of an ordinary bottle and does not know whether it is really potheen or not. Time and again I have told Monica what a fool she is to believe the things she does, because I have known for ages that routine is a textile material that you can get dressed in without realising it, and it is brownish-greyish in colour and stuffy-hairy like fustian on one side and shiny-smooth like cheap sateen on the other. Some people, I told Monica, have been dressed in it for so long that they get to like it, such as confirmed bachelors, who wear the sateen side next the skin and the fustian side outwards and feel quite pleased with themselves, and nobody can think why, because other people can see only the fustian side. And Monica said: 'And, in fact, it's really fust-een. Well, let's have another Scotch and try the fust-een or potheen another night, because it's bad to mix them,' and that is what we did.

So the routine went on, and Twice and I made quite a convincing job of 'keeping up appearances' and plenty of engines got built and the profits came in handsomely and everything went nicely until one day a very polite man with 'government official' written all over him arrived in my office and said: 'Good morning,' and laid a black brief-case down on the table where Twice kept a litter of sketches and progress sheets and this and that.

'Good morning?' I said, looking up from my paper with my pen poised.

'I am from the Ministry of Supply,' he said. 'May I have a few moments with whoever has charge of your vehicles?' He was as nice a man as you could wish to meet to have a quiet drink or a meal with. Here, in my office, he had Trouble with 'Slater's Works' written on it in large letters sticking out in chunks all over him. Pierre had been handling the lorries and their petrol rationing for over a year now. We had all thought it an excellent way of keeping him busy. Pierre had been busy, all right. I could feel it in the air.

'Certainly, Mr. —'

'Simpson.'

'Mr. Simpson. My name is Sandison. Do sit down. I'll just sign this letter and send for him,' I said, and Mr. Simpson thanked me and sat down.

'Trouble. Petrol. Come.' I wrote at the bottom of the letter and called the little typist. 'Please take this to the Works Manager. He is waiting for it.' I then used a little time by calling a wrong number on my telephone and then I turned to Mr. Simpson. 'Now, what can we tell you about our vehicles?'

Before he could say anything, Twice came rushing in with a broken drill in his hand and shouted: 'Look at this goddamned — Oh, sorry. Didn't know you were busy —'

I must concede that it was very nicely done. I do not think that Mr. Simpson suspected us for a moment.

'That's all right, Mr. Alexander,' I said genially. 'Mr. Simpson is just waiting to see Transport.'

'Oh. How d'you do, Mr. Simpson? You're unlucky, though. Robertson's out. But can I do anything? I'm Alexander, the Works Manager — if works and managing you can call it.'

'Well —'

Mr. Simpson opened his black brief-case and out it came. Pierre had been falsifying the transport returns, applying for more petrol than our entitlement and selling the extra ration coupons on the black market. It was the most ordinary, every-day, little swindle, so badly executed that he had been caught already after his second little sortie into it.

'I'll be frank with you, Mr. Alexander,' Mr. Simpson said, when he had finished stating the sordid little case. 'I have not a case for prosecution — it is hardly worth it. I came here to issue a warning and I appreciate how you and Miss Sandison have dealt with me. Your records are in perfect order and the firm is not involved. Just one thing, I would advise you to take this particular employee off any sort of allocation work. Once they start fiddling, they don't know where to stop. Well, goodbye.'

We watched the door closed, heard the little car drive away, staring at each other.

'Once they start fiddling! I'll fiddle him! I've a bloody good mind to go through there and throttle the greasy b —'

'Where's the Old Man?' I asked.

'In Glasgow, I think. That's what he said this morning, anyway.'

'Oh, Twice, if this had come to a prosecution it would just about have killed him! Slater's Works fiddling on the black market! Alan's engine mixed up in a petty swindle! Twice, you were marvellous! But for you —'

'Shut up, you silly twit! If you hadn't kept your head when he arrived —'

'All right, as a Mutual Admiration Society we're the cat's whiskers. What do we do next?' I asked.

'The Old Man will have to be told. *You*'d better do that.'

'ME? I couldn't! What d'you think I'm supposed to be around here? Why pick on *me*? *I* don't know how many gallons —'

'You mean *I*'m to tell him?' Twice hissed. 'That would be a fine thing! The Old Man knows I hate Pierre's guts so *I*'d look pretty going around telling tales, wouldn't I?'

'Who cares a cuss how you look?'

'Who cares a cuss how you *feel*?' he retorted.

'Not you, anyway!' I spat and took a grip of the desk blotter. 'If you dare to pick that thing up and — and *do* anything

195

with it, so help me God I'll take and throttle you!' Twice stuttered.

'My goodness gracious me!' said Mr. Slater as he came in. 'What are you two chewing the rag about *now*?'

So in strophe and anti-strophe, like a Greek chorus, we told the Old Man about Pierre and the petrol, and when we had finished he said: 'I'm not surprised. I've had an inkling things weren't all they should be, somewhere. I have to thank you both, too. I wouldn't have liked a prosecution in the firm — not for a thing like that, anyway.' He looked slyly at Twice. 'Assault and battery is different. There is nothing indecent about a straight case of provocation resulting in assault and battery.' The sly glance had passed to me. 'Well, I'll have to see Mister Pierre, that's all. It's a fair scunner, though. I'm right sorry for that Mrs. Robertson, lassie. She's a nice quiet decent soul although she's maybe not very clever.'

'Muriel?' I said. 'Don't you worry about *her*, Mr. Slater. Nobody can do anything for Muriel.'

'I wouldn't like to see her walking the streets with a man who couldn't get a job, though. Iphm. Well, I'll have to think a bittie about it. . . . By the way, when I came in here, what I came in for was to tell you two that it's time we thought about the summer holidays.'

'We were just discussing that yesterday, sir,' said Twice. 'We were going to tackle you about it when you had a spare moment.'

'Well, the now's as good as any other time,' the Old Man said. 'I'll tell you my way of it first. Now Pierre was telling me we should stagger the holidays — he must have read about this staggering in the papers, maybe. But in the old days I just used to shut the place up for a couple of weeks and I would go off to Mother and Alan at the seaside and that was that. Times are different now. You two and some of the foremen had no holidays at all last year with the new buildings and everything going on, so this year I want everybody to get a break. But I don't want all this staggering the way Pierre talks about it and never knowing who's here and who's not. So I thought a quarter of them could go in the first two weeks of July and the next quarter the next two and so on until the end of August and get done with it. What d'ye think, lad?'

'Sounds ideal to me, sir. Make them draw lots for it?'

'Aye, if ye like, and then they can swap fortnights around within reason as long as they don't upset the flow in the shops. Then I want you two to have a month apiece —'

'The hell with that!' said Twice. 'A month of idleness would drive me demented!'

'Don't swear at *me*, you ill-natured devil!' said Mr. Slater quietly. 'I said a month and I mean a month. You think I can't run these shops for a month? Old man, eh? One foot in the grave? — So Pierre and I and old Willie will go in July — Miss Janet here'll have to do the pay and accounts like she did when Willie had the bronchitis, and then Miss Janet and you can go in August. How's that?'

'It'll do,' said Twice. 'That new line should be running fairly smoothly by July. Iphm.'

'Don't be rash and say the new line will be *all right*,' I said.

'I wouldn't be surprised,' said Mr. Slater as he got up to go to lunch, 'if one day he *does* throttle you. Iphm. On the whole, maybe I wouldn't feel inclined to blame him.'

He went out and got into his car.

'You see?' said Twice. 'Official permission.'

'I'm sorry. Really, I am. I don't mean to be irritating, Twice.'

'Forget it,' he said and picked up a volume of poems which had come in by post from Mr. Rollin that morning. Mr. Rollin always sent me a birthday present and I had never got around to telling him that my birthday was in March and not in May, for old Mr. Rollin had so many more interesting and valuable things in his old head that the precise date of my birth seemed unimportant. 'What's this? Oh. T. S. Eliot.'

'A birthday present,' I said.

'Your birthday's in March,' Twice said. 'It was the day we had the fight about the drawings that got lost. I remember it distinctly, for the Old Man said it was a fine carry-on on your birthday. So it's in March your —'

'What are you beefing about? So my birthday's in March,

so I get a present this morning! So what?'

'One might as well be accurate!'

'Why?'

'Oh, horsefeathers! Listen, what about a run out in the car tonight?'

'For my birthday?' I asked, just to say something and try to cover up some of my too obvious pleasure.

'God give me patience!' he bawled, then he swallowed and said very quietly, 'All right. For your birthday. You coontermashus trollop. Other women of your age *stop* having birthdays, but not *you*. Oh no. *You* start having them every other month. Honestly, Flash, do you know where you are *at*? Apart altogether from where you are going, do you know where you are at right now?'

'Lunch-time,' I said brightly. 'On a Tuesday. And if we blether on much longer there will be no lunch-time left. . . . Seriously, Twice, I don't go around squabbling with everybody and other people don't go squabbling with *me*. Don't you think, maybe, *you* could be a little odd?'

'ME? Holy suffering cow! Do *I* go having birthdays every other month?'

'There are times when I wish you'd never had a birthday at all!' I said, and I meant it at that moment. I was sick to death of this eternal battering at my defences and, whenever I made a sortie, his retiring into the citadel of his self, leaving not one vulnerable point. He was about to retire again now, the eyes were taking on that veiled look, but suddenly he changed his mind and stepped forward, unarmed, as it were.

'Flash, am I a nuisance, asking you to come out with me occasionally? Because if I am —'

I found this unbearable. 'A nuisance?' I rushed in. 'How could the only man in Ballydendran who asks me out be a nuisance? I don't know what I'd do without you, Twice!'

He grinned at me. 'It's nice to be useful. I have a pleasant baritone voice, too, I'm told, if you'd like music along with the usefulness at any time. . . . Run and get your lunch. Don't forget your T. S. Eliot.'

'Thenks evah see-oh!' I said and fled from the office.

198

When we set off in the car that evening I asked where we were going.

'Up to the top of a hill I wot of. I've got a half-bottle, two glasses, some water and some sandwiches in the back. I like sitting on top of hills better than sitting in pubs in summer. Do you?'

'Much,' I said. 'But you still like your dram, even on the hill?'

'Certainly. Whisky lends contemplation to the view. Well-known sayings given a topical turn — all part of the general service. This barouche is making a noise like a lawn-mower. Sorry.'

'Rubbish! This car runs beautifully!'

'Look here, Flash, there are a lot of things I may not know more about than you do, but an ordinary internal-combustion engine is a thing where I've got the edge on you. She needs tuning.'

'Okay, Twice, she's a lawn-mower and a darn bad one.'

'That's better,' he said with satisfaction, and we did not speak again until we were on the top of the hill with half of Lowland Scotland spread out below, like a big patchwork quilt in the evening light. You may not have seen a large stretch of Lowland Scotland from the top of a hill — I have lots of experience of scenery and I am a Highlander who was born among some of the world's finest scenery and bred to be more or less allergic to anything to do with the Lowlands except earning your living there now that cattle-stealing is out of fashion, and I am here to tell yee-ewe that a large stretch of Lowland Scotland seen from the top of a hill is quite something, as My Friend Martha would say.

'A very fair prospect,' I said, after a few moments.

'My country, 'tis of thee and all that,' he said. 'Have a dram.'

He poured out two glasses of whisky and water and gave me one.

'Yes. This *is* your country,' I said. 'The Lowlands and Border.'

'Yes. I hate to admit this, but I'll admit it all the same. I've never been north of Stirling, where I once went to play a game of Rugby.'

'What of that? I've never been further from the parish pump than Rome, and you've been to India, haven't you?'

'Iphm.'

'Where else have you been?'

'Why?'

'Hey, Twice, I'm not starting anything. But why can't you answer an ordinary civil question without getting your hackles up and bawling WHY?'

'Because I can't think why you should *ask* me where else I have been, of course. What difference does it make to you if I habitually spend my week-ends in Reykjavik?'

'Certainly it makes a difference. A man who spends his week-ends in Reykjavik is different from a man who doesn't. It would be very interesting to meet a man who just couldn't stay away from Reykjavik every Sunday.'

'Why?'

'Aw, Twice!'

'What? Oh, the why? Sorry. But dash it — listen, what *are* we talking about?'

'You.'

'ME?'

'Yes.'

'Why?'

Do you see what I mean when I say that things were not easy for me? Or perhaps you know exactly what I should have done. I know that if we had been two people in a book by a modern American novelist I would probably have said: 'Say, I'm jest crazy about ya, bub — let's get in a huddle in the corner of the disused fish cannery'; or if it had been a book by a modern English novelist I would probably have said: '*Angel! So* inhibited! Taxi, take us to the nearest bed', and that would have been that, but I find that most of the people in modern novels are singularly unlike me, so that either (*a*) I am old-fashioned or (*b*) of the opinion that the disused fish cannery or the bed is not the ultimate answer. I am probably both (*a*) and (*b*) when I come to think about it. So I said: 'All right. Let's not bother with it. Where are you going for your month's holiday?'

'I don't know yet. What about you?'

'I'm going up home. It may sound dull, but I like the place and the people.'

'Is your mother still alive? I know your father is.'

'Mother died when I was a youngster. No — it's my father, an uncle and an aunt, on a little croft on top of a hill.'

'It sounds attractive.'

'Have *you* still got parents?'

'No. My mother died shortly after I was born. My father died while I was in India. In fact, I'm a real lone wolf — my nearest relative is some sort of cousin in Edinburgh, umpteen times removed, who is a Writer to the Signet. I always think that's a nice-sounding thing to be for those that like writing.'

'Very,' I agreed. 'Another title I'm very fond of is King's Remembrancer. I'd have liked to *be* a King's Remembrancer if I had been born in the right age. Or does His Majesty still have one?'

'I should think so. But for me, I'd have liked one of the outdoor jobs, like Keeper of the King's Forests or Shepherd of His Majesty's Hills, if there was such a thing. I am very fond of nice phrases and idioms.'

'I've noticed that,' I said. 'I've enlarged my idiomatic vocabulary quite a bit since I've known you, but it's a pity that so many of your idioms are so unladylike that I can't use them except in private.'

'I hadn't noticed that you were particularly trammelled by the bonds of the ladylike. I'll never forget that first day you opened up and had at me over the crates for those engines for Venezuela. I was dumbfounded.'

'I'm sorry, Twice. I shouldn't have —'

'Don't be sorry. You couldn't have done better. I was sick to death of the Old Man and his nonsense and coming into the office on my best behaviour and remembering to act like a gentleman in a ballroom instead of be myself, the poor bloody harassed engineer.'

'The Old Man and what nonsense?'

'Oh, all this "Be canny with Miss Sandison" stuff and so on. I was at bursting point that day with that poop Pierre beefing about the production and so on, and when you upped behind that desk and let fly I could feel the tension running out through the tips of my toes. It was wonderful. You see, I'd never had to work with a woman before, and with the Old Man always telling me to mind my p's and q's I was half-demented.'

All this explained so much that had happened in those early days that I too, now, could feel tension running out through the tips of my toes.

'Mr. Slater means well,' I said. 'But he does not really believe that there are women who can be quite efficient in industry. He thinks that I'm a sort of phenomenon, which I'm not, but you can't change him. . . . That day, though, Twice, after I'd got the crates out of old Paterson, you called me amoral. You were quite right. That feminine frailty touch to get what one wants *is* amoral, but I only use it for the sake of Slater's. I wouldn't use it in a personal relationship.'

'You're telling me?' He put his head back and indulged in one of his laughs. 'Don't worry. I have a fairly accurate estimate of your integrity, I think, even if I am only a learner.'

'A learner?'

He was not looking at me, but away over the landscape, so I could watch his face without running the gauntlet of that searching glance of his.

'About women, I mean. I've never been what is called, I believe, a ladies' man. . . . Yes, I think that's true.'

'You sound uncertain.'

'I am always chary of making statements about myself,' he told me, and went on to produce a thought which might have been my own. 'It is so easy to be wrong. I may have been going around for years with a lascivious look as if I meditated rape on every woman who crossed my path, but I don't think so.'

'No. You haven't looked like that since I've known you,' I told him gravely. 'Rather the opposite. You've gone around as if you don't notice women in your path at all — it makes things very easy and comfortable.'

'I'm glad of that,' he said smoothly — too smoothly. He

202

was retiring into himself again. 'Have another tot and a sandwich.'

We opened the packet of sandwiches and I had my mouth full of bread and very good roast beef when he said suddenly: 'Tell me, why have you never married?'

It was too sudden, too direct and I could not give a concise answer, anyway. I had a few seconds of flustered panic, swallowed my mouthful of sandwich and told the truth.

'I don't quite know,' I said.

'You have no objection to the thing in principle?'

'No. None. I have every intention of marrying the moment it suits me.'

'And how imminent is the moment?' he asked.

'I don't know,' I told him. 'These psychological moments are tricky things — like the split second when a metal reaches a certain heat. Several times in the past I have thought I had the moment but I was always wrong — the moments fizzled out like damp squibs. My experience has made me wary — instead of sailing for any port in a storm as women of my age are reputed to do, I am determined to sail only for one port and that the right one. I am too old a ship and too crusty with barnacles to settle into any berth except the one I really want.'

'As long as you know what you want.'

'I think I do.'

'I hope you get it, Flash. Have another sandwich.'

To the devil with this, I thought. I am making an ass of myself. I will leave Ballydendran tomorrow. I shall put as much distance between this man and myself as the world has in it. Have I gone mad because he is the only man in the place that I can talk to? Am I turning into one of these Crazy Spinsters who Think Things? I wanted to leap out of the car and run away down the long green hill, but the world is round, and running away only gets you back, eventually, to the point where you ran from. You might as well save your breath and see the thing out on the original spot.

'What of you?' I asked. 'Have you ever given this sex-relationship thing any thought?'

'Not much,' he replied. 'I was born, I think, with one or two fixed ideas. One of them was that I wanted to be an engineer, as good a one as I had in me.'

'You've achieved that, haven't you?'

'Not entirely. Another of my ideas is that in marriage there is no compromise.'

'Compromise?'

'Most people will tell you that it is one big compromise. But for me there is no making-do or making-shift or any of that dreariness. My father re-married after my mother's death and he made do and made shift and generally put up with a singularly sulky, unreasonable and selfish woman for twenty-five years and I consider that he was a bloody fool to do it. Maybe he was, maybe he wasn't. But I know that had I been in his place —' He paused.

'Yes. You'd have throttled her.'

'Very probably,' he agreed.

'I see what you mean — and you'd have been hanged and the world would have lost a moderately good engineer.'

'Quite a wit, aren't you, Miss Sandison?' he asked, his voice suddenly shaky with rage, his teeth bared in a gleaming snarl.

'Hold it, Twice!' I said quickly. 'I am *not* trying to be witty. I mean every word of that and I agree with every word you have said! We are both putting forward the same point of view in our different ways. We both have the same ideas — marriage as a fusing of two personalities so that if the one says Lo and Behold all the time and adores purple carpets the other is not irritated with —'

'Or put upon by —'

'Or sacrificed to —'

'Or apologetic for —'

'Or distrustful of —'

'Or in any way uncomfortable with or about or mentally or physically or spiritually or any other way — all together now —'

'THE OTHER!' we said in unison, and Twice blew the horn, causing the grazing sheep to scatter in all directions. 'Let's have another dram!'

204

'I think we're a little tight already,' I said, holding out my glass none the less.

'Must be something in the sandwiches,' he assured me.

'Not that I care,' I continued. 'With what one puts up with at the works, one *has* to get drunk occasionally.'

'Tell me, why do you stick it?' he asked.

Dear Reader, I put it to you. What would you have said if you, like me, were staying on at Slater's Works of Ballydendran simply because it gave you the best opportunity of seeing as much as possible of the man who was asking you the question? In the light of later knowledge, I could not have made a more equivocal reply, but in the light that prevailed at the time I thought I did fairly well with: 'Oh, it's as good a place as any other to wait for one's ship to come in. Cheers!' I added and raised my glass.

'To your ship!' said Twice and we both had a drink and another sandwich.

One way and another, I felt bemused, bedazed and bedevilled. I do not know how badly and incompletely I have described to you my state of mind — probably very badly and incompletely indeed — but I had reached the point where I was almost afraid to think, much less speak or move. I was still conscious of that extraordinary vulnerability, as if the man could penetrate all my most secret defences and leave me without a weapon for the safeguard of my inmost self. But now I also felt that I had the key to all his defences and was being held back only by his will. He did not want me to break through, I felt, into his private world and that barrier of unwillingness stood like an impenetrable wall between us. The silence between us, now, grew longer and longer and less and less comfortable, and I knew with a deadly certainty that my resistance was weakening towards some sort of humiliating explosion, so, in desperation, with the hollow lightness of a celluloid ball dancing on a water-spout at a fair, I said: 'Hi, I've got an idea! If I knew you better, I'd ask you to my home for the holidays! You've shown me *your* hills — I could show you mine!'

'How well would you have to know me?' he asked very

quietly and with that penetrating blue stare.

Oh, please God, I prayed, make me think of the right answer.

The answer came. 'Well enough to know that you weren't just accepting the invitation in order not to hurt my feelings,' I told him.

He set his glass of whisky carefully on the floor of the car and turned in his seat to face me. 'Flash, if I lay my hand on my heart and swear to you that I would like to see your hills more than anything in the world, would that do? Would that be knowing me well enough?'

'I think so.'

'I can't promise that I'll never hurt your feelings, but I can and will promise to try always to be honest with you.'

'No man can say fairer than that. All right. That's settled. We'll go north for the holidays. Of course, you'll have to work like a brute — the harvest will be on — but it will be very healthy.'

The tension slackened and we drove back to Ballydendran, making plans for our holiday.

So, lo and behold, we battled our way through July while Mr. Slater, Pierre and Old Willie the accountant had their holidays, and on the first of August, early in the morning, we pointed the Bentley at Stirling and waved goodbye to Ballydendran.

'After Stirling, Flash, you are i/c navigation,' Twice said.

'There's nothing to it. Keep the sun on your right till noon, then let it go down on your left, keeping straight on all the time. The higher the hills get and the more the barren rocks stick out, the nearer to my home you're getting.'

The Old Bentley, specially tuned for the occasion I might mention, soon left Slater's Works far aft on her port quarter, and I do not remember sparing much thought for the people left there during that month, for it would not have been the kind of thought conducive to a happy holiday. It was all very uncomfortable. Pierre had been 'spoken to' by Mr. Slater on the subject of his little peccadillo with the petrol, and Twice and I had gathered that he had been told that he had no real future in Ballydendran and, indeed, he was to leave Slater's Works as soon as he could find another means of livelihood. Pierre was not finding this last too easy, for, in truth, he had no qualifications to offer on the market, and Mrs. Slaters, he was finding, are rare fruits, not to be found, dripping with the juice of kindliness and sympathy for the Pierres of this world, on every other tree. Mrs. Slater was, naturally, very unhappy about Pierre's fall from grace, but, governed by kindliness as she was, she continued to beg her husband 'not to be too hard on the boy'. The Old Man, in response to these appeals, continued to pay Pierre his salary while he sat in the office making applications for all kinds of posts for which he had no qualifications, and Pierre was brash and scornful and full of bravado, so that if Twice or I met him in the passage we almost felt that we, and not he, had been caught selling Mr. Slater's petrol coupons on the black market.

The night before Twice and I left for our holiday, when Muriel had returned from hers and I knew that Pierre had gone to Sheffield for an interview, I gathered all my courage together and packed it into the tight bundle behind my solar plexus where it seems to do me most good, and went out to The Lea. This was something I had not done since Pierre had been 'spoken to' by Mr. Slater, and, like everything that one procrastinates about, it was very pro and very crass and generally a big lump in my mind as I made my way along the road.

'Hello!' said Muriel cheerily as I walked into the Baronial Hall. 'I thought you were dead, it's so long since I've seen you!'

I almost died right there at her feet. Even Muriel, I felt, must feel that the situation among us was not of the most comfortable, socially speaking. 'But I know you've been busy,' she went on. 'Job-hunting takes a lot of time and thought.'

'Job-hunting?' I asked, collapsing on to the nearest chair.

'Pierre will arrange it,' she said comfortably, and went about the room in a housewifely but ineffectual way, picking things up and 'laying them down' of course, and then looking at them with her head on one side.

'Muriel, *I* am not leaving Mr. Slater's Works,' I said, brutally, and straight out, like that.

'Not leaving?' she repeated foolishly, sitting down opposite me, with her feet in their untidy shoes wide apart. 'What do you mean?'

'What *should* I mean? Why should I be leaving? I have an interesting, well-paid job which suits me ideally. Why should I be leaving?'

'I can't think why you are staying,' she said. 'The whole thing was a great mistake, and Pierre and I should never have brought you here, but, of course, we had never dealt with people like those before and —'

'People like what?'

'The Slaters. They are simply not one's own sort. That awful little house and all those ornaments and that foolish old man calling her "Mother" all the time and all that sort of thing. We should have realised long ago that people like us have nothing in common with people of that sort. I can't understand you staying on, Janet; it's such a — well — a lowering of one's standards or — well — a mercenary reason.'

I rose to my feet and said. 'Muriel, you're crazy.' She gazed at me with those vague eyes of hers. 'You are crazy. My standards are just the same as they have been all the time you have known me and the Slaters *are* my sort of people, except that they are a great deal wealthier than my family.'

'Don't be silly, Janet!' She laughed at me in an indulgent, Madame X sort of way. 'You might be a marchioness — that fat little woman will never be anything but a cook!'

'A hell of a marchioness I'd make, you stupid idiot!' I shouted at her. 'And what have cooks and marchionesses got to do with it, anyway?'

'There's no need to shout like a fishwife!' she said.

'Marchionesses, cooks, fishwives!' I exploded, the old red rag of the temper at the masthead and streaming in the wind. 'Can't you see anything that's *essential* in people? I am a crofter's daughter with a smattering of education, and you are a vicar's daughter married to a man who's been sacked from

208

his job and serve him damned well right! Anything that we are is within that framework and nothing to do with marchionesses and fishwives! And get this into your thick skull, Muriel — Pierre has thrown away the chance of a lifetime, not to mention having bitten the hand that fed him, and I am not leaving Mr. Slater because I am not Pierre's sort of person. Is that clear?'

'I never heard a person say things like that!' said Muriel. 'I don't believe you!'

'Things like *what*? *What* don't you believe?'

'You are very, very wicked to say these things about my husband. It is just spite, because you will be the next one that these Slaters will turn against. Pierre says so, and he is right. And you are frightened and spiteful —'

'Oh, all right,' I said. 'Forget the whole thing, Muriel. I am sorry I lost my temper. I have to go now.'

'I realise that working at that place has got on your nerves,' she said. 'I'm sorry we quarrelled, Janet. But you *should* reconsider your decision to stay on there — truly, it isn't your element, and Pierre and I would be glad to do anything we can to help you until you can find a new post. You know that.'

'Yes, Muriel, I know. And thank you very much.'

I left her in the Baronial Hall and went back to my bed-sitting-room; and — will you believe this? — a week after Twice and I arrived at my home I had a letter from My Friend Muriel telling me that she hoped I was having fine weather as it was lovely at Ballydendran and that she and Pierre were arranging to sell The Lea as they were going to Sheffield at the end of September. They hoped to get a house a little way out of the city, she said, and Yorkshire was a very beautiful county, she said, and they would be glad to see me there when they were settled, she said. P.S. She hoped all the members of my family were well.

Rory Mackay the postman handed me this letter while Twice and I were having a sit-easy on the strip of herbage that separated the moor from the field whose corn we were stooking while my father and Uncle George were going round and round with the three horses in the binder. The sun was golden-hot and it was a cloak of gold-blue shot taffetas that the giant had thrown down in the valley today to make the lovely careless splash that people called the Firth.

'Letters?' my father called as the binder went past.

'Only one for me, Dad!'

'You'll be having a dram the night!' called Rory the postman, 'with this quick harvest you're having and your visitors working like galley slaves!'

'Aye, aye, Rory!' my father called back to him as the binder went on around the field.

I handed the letter to Twice after I had read it. 'Muriel seems a long, long way away,' I said.

Twice scanned the letter and handed it back to me. 'She never was all that near the earth, was she?'

'No, I suppose not. You know, Twice, you're right. Muriel never *has* seen what other people see. I wonder why?'

He knocked out his pipe on a big, grey boulder where the wild thyme marched like a purple army across a miniature continent. 'Point of view. Perspective. Standpoint. All that — we've been into it before. People usually see what they want to see —

> *The Ethiop gods have Ethiop lips,*
> *Black eyes and woolly hair;*
> *The Grecian gods are like the Greeks,*
> *As cold-eyed, keen and fair.*

But I have never met anyone who seems so determined to see as through a glass darkly as your frield Muriel. Come on, these two old boys are leaving us at the post. They've got the field littered with sheaves again.' We went back to work. 'How old are they? The boys, I mean?'

'Dad is sixty-nine. George is a year younger.'

'A fine, healthy bunch, aren't you?' Twice commented.

The holiday was a great success. Of course, with this personal point of view that people have that Twice is always talking about, I did not see why it should not be. I thought my home was a lovely place, my father and my uncle delightful people, my aunt (having got over Malcolm and having married someone else and being a widow now) a nice woman, and Twice was a charming person. Why should not all these people get on well together and the holiday be a success? That was my point of view. And, for once, things worked out as I had visualised them, which just goes to show you, as Freddie would say, though what, I cannot say for certain. I think being on your native heath and among your own sort of people, as Muriel would say, must have a great deal to do with it.

It was beautiful harvest weather and we worked a bit each day, but there was nothing dark, desperate and earthy about it like Grassic Gibbon's 'Scots Quair' or any of that high, intensive drama in a peasant setting for which writers like Thomas Hardy and Mary Webb, in their separate spheres, are so justly famous. There was not, either, any Celtic Twilight or Kailyard about it. The light is clear at my home and we grow our vegetables in neat rows in the back garden.

But thinking of writers reminds me of a story told by Twice of a family party he attended in one of the Scottish Border towns where they were playing one of these variations of charades that people dream up from time to time. The young couple giving the party were of a slightly literary turn of mind and the game consisted of someone going through a mime representing the title of a well-known book. It was Christmas, and the young couple had an old uncle who was not specially literary, much to their regret, but cheerful and harmless, so he had to be given his turn at miming the title of a book, which no one took very seriously until the old man defeated the whole assembly by coming into the room with the bone out of the Christmas ham, which he had wrapped in a shawl and to which he was crooning a lullaby. After a long time, rather irritated, the niece said: 'All right, Uncle! We give up. What *is* the title?'

' "Precious Bane", of course!' said Uncle.

He is distinguished in my mind as the only case on record of a man who could mime in his native Doric.

Well, as I was saying, we worked around during the day, and, in the evenings, we would go out driving in Twice's car, sometimes only Twice and myself, sometimes three of us, sometimes all five of us, and it was all very simple and happy and uncomplicated, and I wondered why it was that Twice and I had spent so much time quarrelling while we were at Ballydendran.

On the evening of our arrival at my home, when the car was taking the last rise between the fields and the moor to the small white-washed house on top of the hill, I had a moment of sheer panic, when my thoughtless offer to Twice to 'show him my hills' rose up inside me in a great gaseous balloon of regret and self-accusation that threatened to choke me, but when my father, my uncle and my aunt came to the door and stood there smiling in the evening sun and Twice said: 'Heavens! What a beautiful place! No wonder you're a character!' I felt that everything was all right, and it was.

' "Granny's Heilan' Hame" — glug, glug, glug!' I said. 'You should see it in the winter!'

'Bleak, eh? I can imagine it!' and then my family was all around us.

A day or two later, as we were walking around and about, Twice began to hum — it is a very pleasant baritone — the air of 'Granny's Heilan' Hame'.

'Dry up!' I told him. 'Don't waste your good breath and voice on that.'

'You no' like?'

'No.'

'Why?'

'I don't like the septic — especially about the heather bells blooming when it's probably written by a bloke when he is sitting by a good fire in a Glasgow tenement on a winter night and I *hate* it when it's sung to a sloshy audience who never saw a Heilan' Granny in their lives. There *are* no Heilan' Grannies or Heilan' Hames either.'

'Well, you *should* know.'

'Certainly I do. We have Grannies, but they live in what we call homes in the Highlands. The tongue of the Glasgow tenement is not our tongue, and I see no reason why we should be turned into stags at bay and monarchs of the glen and accused of sitting permanently on our doorsteps framed in heather bells.'

212

'— blooming,' said Twice.

'Yes. Blooming. There are plenty of accurate writers about the Highlands and the Highland character, and there is very little that's heather-bellsy about it, you take it from me!'

'I hadn't noticed any heather bells dangling around *you*!' he said, and I glared at him. 'I mean it,' he continued. 'I just had no idea you felt so strongly on the subject. I can get extraordinarily irritated by some things myself, so I know how you feel. Now, if there's one tune I can't abide, it's a thing called "Scotland the Brave".'

Dear Reader, I almost burst. The best I could do was to stay silent and try not even to breathe in case I laughed myself into a coma right there, among the heather bells, blooming.

'You know the tune I mean?' he asked. 'It goes like this — *Boom*-tah-ra-*rah*-ra-*rah*-ra — I feel my blood starting to boil with sheer rage every time I hear it. I don't mean that it makes me want to cleave Scotland's enemies from helm to halse or out with the old claymore and shout: "Christ! And no quarter!" No. It makes me wish I could get hold of the cove who wrote it and hold his head under his own bath-water until he drowns.'

'That's very interesting,' I said. 'Listen, I think a thing that has been called a functional relation exists between you and that tune.'

'What on earth do you mean?'

'Well, I don't know whether whistling it makes you angry or whether when you are angry you have to whistle it, but I *do* know that every time you *are* angry you *do* whistle it.'

'Rot,' said Twice.

'But you *do*!'

'If it wasn't you saying it, I wouldn't believe a word of it!'

'I swear to you it's the truth. . . . Hi, listen, do I give tongue with "Granny's Heilan' Hame", by any chance?'

'No. No, you don't make any sort of noise at all to start with. You make a few seconds of silence that's like a thick, black blanket first and then you hit the flash point and up she goes.'

'As long as it isn't Heilan' Hames and heather bells,' I said. 'And I'll tell you another thing that makes me mad — people

213

who say something they mean to be funny and poke you in the ribs to make you see the point —'

'Or blokes that come up to you and put their hands on your shoulder —'

'Or women who reach out and rearrange your skirt —'

'Or do something to your collar and tie —'

'Or push your hair under your hat —'

'Yes, especially touching your hair —'

We began to laugh, and then Twice said: 'Listen, I have an idea! Let's talk about things we *do* like for a change. Apart from "Granny's Heilan' Hame", do you in general like music?'

We were still finishing a conversation about music and concerts when we went in for supper and my aunt said: 'Oh, concert! Tomorrow night's the concert for the Village Hall Fund.' She looked at my father. 'At least *one* of us should go!' she said in a threatening voice.

'I,' said my uncle, 'am not going to walk three miles to listen to Farquhar Stewart's lassie practising her elocution as they call it. Did I tell you, Janet, that Farquhar's old Uncle Kenny insists on callin' it electrocution since the new hydro-electric scheme got started up the Glen?'

'The car's there,' said Twice, 'for anybody who wants to go, but why don't we *all* go?'

My family looked at each other, absorbing the idea. 'Why not?' I said.

'Och,' my father said, 'what would there be at the village hall to amuse you and Mr. Alexander, lassie?'

'You'd be surprised,' said Twice.

'And, anyway, why do you keep on saying Mr. Alexander, Dad?'

'Yes. Flash calls me Twice — it's short for Twice Alexander, my name being Alexander Alexander.'

'So that's it!' My uncle turned to me. 'Your father and me was speaking about it, it being a very odd name for a man to have and we couldn't fathom it at all. But where did *you* get the name o' Flash?'

Now, this was something that I did not want my family to

214

know. My family is not whimsical at all and would not hold with 'fancy names' like Lady Flashing Stream, but before I could think of anything to say Twice was on the ball and well over the touch-line.

'She was bound to get it,' he said smoothly, 'with that temper of hers. You should hear her at the works sometimes.' He whistled the opening bars of 'Granny's Heilan' Hame'. 'Well, we'll all go to the concert, eh?'

So we all went to the concert, and Twice and I, not great exponents of the art of self-control, were hard put to it, so thoroughly did events fall out against us.

To return to Slater's Works for a moment, my life there had many contacts with people by telephone only, so that these people had no faces but only voices. One of these voices was that of a woman in the office of a steel works in Glasgow to whom I said, at least once a fortnight: 'Oh, Miss Forbes, it's Slater's again. What about that two-and-a-half round? My Works Manager's creating the devil!'

'Ooh, Miss Sendisen,' the voice would say, 'what a skendel! Reely, does he think thet steel is made bay megic? But Ay Quayte understend. Send a lorry this efternoon. Ay'll see thet you get *some*thing!'

This woman, who was undoubtedly most obliging and very efficient, and who was probably a delightful person besides, had become known to Twice and me as 'The Skendel' and when, as the third item in the programme at the concert 'Farquhar Stewart's Lassie' appeared on the stage, clasped her hands over her diaphragm, smiled an artificial smile and said: 'The Pay-ed Paper of Hemmilin' in a conversational way to the audience I saw Twice grip his hands together so that the knuckles showed white, and by the time she had said:

> *Hemmelin Town's in Brunswick by fair Hennover City,*
> *The river Weser deep end wayde*
> *Weshes its wells on the southern sayde —*

a small muscle in his cheek was working up and down like the piston of a small engine. When she got to 'Lean retts, fet retts, brown retts, tawny retts . . . ' I could no longer observe Twice, being entirely taken up with my own affairs.

Worse was yet to come. After another item or two it was announced that 'one of our visitors from the South' would now give us a song, and a man from Edinburgh, who was working at the hydro-electric scheme up the Glen, took the stage and, in a very pleasant tenor, gave a rendering of 'Drink to me only with thine eyes'. This was enthusiastically received, not least by Twice and myself, for the voice was true and expressive, and we applauded vociferously, and achieved the encore we had encouraged. The piano began to tinkle, and lo and behold, and wonderful to relate, the voice, as true as ever but dripping with glug-glug, sang out:

'The heather bells are blooming, just outside Granny's door —' Fortunately, the interval intervened when this was over, and we all went out into the yard around the hall and Twice and I were able to recover ourselves before going back for the second half, which went without incident until the last item, when 'Murdo Fraser and his Dance Band will play a selection of tunes and *everybody*'ll get the chance to sing', said the chairman, with which Murdo Fraser said: 'One, two!' and walloped the piano and the band of two saxophones, two fiddles, an accordion and a set of jazz drums went into 'Ho-ro, my nut-brown maiden' and then via the Banks of Loch Lomond, Mary of Argyll, Dark Lochnagar and a few other ladies and places to their finale when the big drum went 'Boom! Tah!' and the whole combination at full force came out swinging with 'Scotland the Brave'.

Twice and I, after the National Anthem, came out of the hall and stood about while my father and my uncle discussed the harvest with a few neighbours and enquired after the health of Willie Macintosh's mare's feet, and while my aunt congratulated Lizzie Mackenzie on her rendering of her Gaelic song and enquired after her mother's rheumatics, and then we all got into the car and started for home.

'Well,' said my uncle, 'it was a fine concert, and Farquhar's lassie is sounding more foolish than ever, the poor craitur, and that man from Edinburgh singing Janet's favourite song an' all. Did ye know, Twice lad, that Janet's just terrible fond o' that song about Granny's Heilan' Hame?'

'So I believe,' said Twice. 'It's just the kind of song you would know she would like, isn't it?'

'What *I* thought was so nice,' I said, 'was the way they finished up with "Scotland the Brave". Twice is just crazy about it — it seemed as if they knew and it was *meant*.'

'Bitch!' said Twice, blowing the horn at the same time.

'Bitch yourself!' I hissed, with the horn not blowing at all.

'Which what?' my aunt asked from the back seat.

'Which item did you like best?' I asked loudly.

'I don't know,' said my aunt. 'I wasn't listening — I was too busy watching that wee devil Ian Macleod shooting peas at the feather in the Minister's wife's hat.'

And we all laughed. It was as happy, simple and uncomplicated as that.

Indeed, things were so uncomplicated at the end of about the third week at my home that you could more or less open your mouth and let it say what it liked, so one evening, on the way back from Dornoch, when we were sitting in the car at the roadside, watching the sun go down behind Ben Wyvis, I said to Twice: 'Look here, would you say my temper was better up here than it is at Ballydendran?'

'Getting introspective?' he enquired. 'No. I would say it is much the same.'

'Then *yours* must be better,' I told him, which seemed to me to be logical.

'No,' said Twice, 'it isn't.'

'Something has changed then,' I observed.

'The essence of life is change.'

'Don't be pontifical! Your head's the wrong shape to be a Pope.'

'Have you made a special study of Popes' heads?'

'No. But I know yours isn't the right shape — Look! "The sun's rim dips, the stars rush out, At one stride comes the dark —" It must be fun in the tropics when that happens!'

'It isn't really. Actually, the bull-frogs croak, the bazaar smells, the pi-dogs start to bark. I haven't got a poetic point of view about the tropics. I like the colder, cleaner countries.'

'Iphm. I must say I'd like to go to Canada,' I said.

'And why the bloody hell don't you?' he suddenly barked at me, turning round in his seat to face me. His eyes were red, reflecting the last light of the sun, and his fighting face seemed to have all the bones sticking out through the skin, as if they were being pushed out by something inside him. All the smooth, uncomplicated peace between us exploded in a million fragments and it was all so sudden that I could not even lay hands on the hilt of my temper, so long had it lain, like the sword of Ulysses, 'rusting unburnished' and not 'shining in use'. I sat there and stared at him.

'Don't look at me like that!' he hissed. 'Go to Canada, damn you, Lady Flashing Stream! Go to Freddie! Look at the money you'd save on letters and books of poems! Why can't you make up your dithering mind? What do you *want*? Why the hell don't you go and *leave me alone*?'

Now, I do not think that I am a hysterical person, but all the silly bits of this puzzle rattled together in my mind so suddenly, and it was all so stupid and made a picture so ludicrous, that I began to laugh and could not stop. When you laugh like that you can neither see nor hear — it is quite horrible, a sort of conscious unconsciousness — and when I came out of my spasm the first thing I saw was a large tear out of the corner of one blue eye and lie glistening on his cheek-bone.

'Well,' he said quietly, 'you've done it. Have you got what you wanted? Do you feel you *know me* well enough at last? Or do I have to tell you in short words that I am all yours, for laughing at, or pitying, or whatever you want?'

He pitched forward head and shoulders on to my lap and lay quite still. It took me a moment to realise that he had lost consciousness. Once before, at the works, I had seen him so angry, when, through a welder's carelessness, a petrol tank had exploded, that he had staggered into the office, put his head down between his knees and called for brandy from the first aid cupboard. But that was not much comfort. There never was a lonelier moor than this one we were sitting on.

There never was a road that fewer people used. There never was an inert body heavier to turn over than that one, and never hands that shook like mine as I got a little whisky out of the flask and into the glass. For the first time in my life — even counting all the landmines and explosive devices of the war — I was truly terrified.

'Twice! Twice!' I forced neat whisky into his mouth and tried to shake him. 'Twice! Wake up! Twice, I can't drive this damned car, d'you hear me? Twice! I can't even turn on its lights! Wake up — for heaven's sake, wake up!'

'Gimme a drink!' said the voice.

'Here!'

'Sorry!' he said, sitting up. 'Let that be a lesson to you on the man that loses his temper. I realise it's no good apologising. I'm going out to get on my feet for a moment and then I'll drive you home. I—I'll be all right in a moment.'

He sprang out of the car hastily, went round behind it and I heard him being violently sick. When the noise stopped, I got out and said: 'Can I be of any help, Twice?'

He came and sat down on the running-board. 'A little more whisky, please.'

I gave it to him, poured some for myself and sat down beside him. I took a big gulp of my drink, put my glass down on the grass verge of the road and took a firm hold of his free hand. I was conscious that it was the first time I had deliberately touched him and that he was looking down at our hands in my lap.

'Listen, you've got all your wires crossed, Twice. Freddie is married to My Friend Georgina and they've got twins and a singleton and are very happy in Winnipeg. Mr. Rollin is nearly eighty and he sends books to an old man's sentimental vision called Lady Flashing Stream, but otherwise he is very happy with his son in Montreal. I, Flash Sandison, am sitting in the middle of a Highland moor deeply in love with one Twice Alexander. Is that clear?'

'Clear as a h - hill burn on an April day, Flash! . . . Here, I think I'm going to be sick again!'

'You certainly are *not*!' I squealed, thrusting my own drink at him and refilling his glass for myself. 'Drink that! What do you think I am going to tell my friends about the night I got engaged? That you kept throwing up like a pregnant woman?'

'Are we engaged?'

'Certainly. Why else do you think I am sitting at this roadside? It's the modern version of following you barefoot across the world and —'

'Canny, Flash, canny!' he said, very quietly. 'Don't say things like that even in fun!'

'Huh?'

'I feel a fool, warning you like this,' he said in short jerked phrases. 'You and your people — gentle and soft, like a green hill with cloud shadows going over it. You don't know about people like me, Flash!'

'I know quite a bit already and I would like to learn the rest,' I said. I felt strangely humble — an unfamiliar feeling for me.

'By God! You'll have to!' he said and hurled the glass he was holding against a boulder on the moor.

Everybody had gone to bed when we got home and we crept up to our attic bedrooms in the dark, giggling like a pair of seventeen-year-olds, which was on the whole very silly but very enjoyable, and I fell into bed by the light of a young moon and did not know another thing until my father shouted from the foot of the stairs: 'Are you going to sleep all day, lassie? It's seven o'clock and breakfast's on the table!'

I rushed down to the kitchen, and I can see it now as it was when I went in, with the early sun striking one wall, Twice leaning on the dresser, with his shirt-sleeves rolled up, drinking tea, my aunt turning round from the fireplace with the teapot in her hand, and my father and my uncle already in their places at the table.

'Good morning, everybody!' I bellowed. 'What d'you think? Twice and I decided to get married last night!'

Everybody gaped, then slowly began to smile. It was a deeply satisfactory moment.

'What she means,' said Twice, 'is not that we got married last night, but that, last night, she asked me if I would marry her.'

220

'Janet Sandison!' said my aunt.

'And what did *you* say, Twice?' my father asked.

'I said I would see *you* about it,' Twice replied.

'Well,' my father said, 'she has waited a long time and has gone a bonnie length while she was doing it, one way and another, but I couldna be better pleased with the man she is choosing if I'd picked you myself. Eh, George?'

My uncle looked at Twice. 'I think,' he said, 'that ye are a very bold, reckless young man, my lad, in the things you undertake, but I'm pleased — I'm pleased!'

So I looked at my aunt. 'Go on,' I said. 'Say your piece. You might as well cut me up and throw me to the birds and be done with it!'

'That's no way to talk, Janet Sandison!' my aunt said and turned to Twice. 'Listen, my lad, you take a firm hand and don't have any nonsense. She's been a thrawn devil all the days of her life and it's no' better she's getting, but she's not a bad lassie at heart.'

It was the only time that I could remember that my family expressed a direct opinion of me in my hearing, and they had to do it *now*, with Twice standing there, his teeth and eyes glittering with amusement, not to say a spiteful sort of triumph. I glared at him, took a firm grip on the edges of a convenient plate and opened my mouth.

'Don't you dare!' said Twice. 'You throw that plate and, so help me, I'll smack your bottom right here in front of everybody!'

'Oh!' I said, wasting my good, deep, stored-up breath. Twice pulled the plate out of my hands and waved at me like a waiter. 'Tea or coffee, madam? And how do you like your eggs?'

Oh yes. My family all had a good laugh the morning I got engaged to be married.

They were all, indeed, having such a good laugh that it was not until we were all going out to look how the corn was drying (for it was completely cut now) that my aunt said: 'Janet, did you see that telegram that came in yesterday afternoon?'

'What telegram?'

'I put it on the dressing-table in your room — just beside your lamp.'

I had not lighted the lamp the night before. I had not seen the telegram. I ran upstairs.

'Mr. Slater ill with pneumonia cannot trace Alexander very shorthanded in works can you come back Willie.'

'Poor old Willie!' said Twice. 'We'll have to go, Flash.'

'Man, man,' said my father. 'Will Mr. Slater be bad, do you think?'

'Must be,' Twice said. 'Because *he* knew I was up here.'

'Come on!' I said.

'Can we be doing anything?' my uncle asked.

'Just check the water in the radiator for me,' Twice told him, which was clever and kind of him, for old people do not like sudden things and it was better to give them something to do.

'Sandwiches,' my aunt said, while my father and my uncle went away to the cart-shed where the Bentley was housed. 'I still have some of the ham.'

When Twice and I came down with our suitcases, the three of them were rubbing the car here and there with dusters as if, if it were clean, it would travel better, and maybe they were right at that, Twice said. We left quickly, but not quickly enough for me not to have tears in my eyes by the time we were past the last of the fir trees on the moor.

Twice stopped the car. 'Aw, Flash! I've never seen you crying before! It must be an awful big thing to make you cry!'

'I always hate leaving it,' I told him. 'And extra-specially this time, because it's the Biggest Thing in the Whole World!'

'All right. Come here and have a good bawl. I can make up the time on the straight road south of Inverness.'

We made quite good time after all, for we were in Ballydendran by about two in the afternoon and went straight to the works, where old Willie greeted us.

'How's Mr. Slater?'

'Better. The worst's over, the doctor says, but of course he's terrible weak. .... We'll go in here,' he added, opening the door of my office and closing it behind us. 'I was sorry to have to send for ye. But I didna want the responsibility o' that yin ben there and the Boss not here.'

He jerked his old head in the direction of Pierre's office.

'Is *he* still here?' Twice asked.

'Aye, and like stoppin' on for the money until he goes to this new job of his.'

'Oh.'

'I'm not one for gossip, Mr. Alexander, but things is no' what they should be out at The Lea. There's debts all round the town, they say, and in Glasgow and Edinburgh forbye. And there was a black-coated lawyer kind o' a man here askin' for him yesterday and another gey queer-like customer the day before. So I thought it might be better if I wired to Miss Sandison and now that you're both here I'm very glad I did.'

'So are we, Willie,' Twice told him. 'When did Mr. Slater go sick?'

'Let me see — this is Thursday. It would be a week past Tuesday that he first complained o' feeling bad. He didna go to his bed till the Friday, though.'

Twice looked at me. 'Oh, damn!' I said and he nodded.

'How are the shops, Willie?'

'Och, fine! The men have been fair grand, Mr. Alexander. Not one single row even about the fitba' since the Boss went off. And workin' like niggers. And five mistakes in the piece-work pays last Friday and not a bad word out of any o' them. I wouldna have bothered to bring you back but for that one thing through there.'

'All right, Willie. You don't have to worry about that any more.'

'Man, I'm glad to see ye both!' said Willie and shuffled off to his dusty office, with its old safe, its leather-bound books and his bottle of cough mixture on the shelf. I sat down at my desk and looked without interest at the heaps of papers that had accumulated in the trays. It was all very flat, I felt. Tomorrow would be time enough to start looking through that lot. I would go over to Glendale soon, I thought. There might be something I could do for Mrs. Slater, even if it was only to give her someone to talk to for a little while. I found myself thinking about old Willie. In my own mind I found I was quite proud of the contribution that Twice and I had made to Slater's Works in the short time since the war had ended, but what was our contribution compared to old Willie's years of loyal service? I had gathered that Willie, and he would have been Young Willie then, had never been robust enough to be 'put to a trade' so he had been 'put to the office work' in, it so happened, the office of a local solicitor who was factor for a number of estates, so Willie did not learn the law but book-keeping instead. Willie and Mr. Slater had been in the same class at Ballydendran School, and when Mr. Slater found that his workshop had reached the size when he could no longer pull his employees' wages out of the pocket of his overalls on Friday evenings and hand them the money out in the workshop, he had suggested that Willie leave the solicitor's office and come and 'give him a hand with the wages and that'. Willie had agreed, and since then the finances of Slater's Works had been a case of: 'Money for stamps? Go and see Willie', or 'What do we owe for steel? Willie will know'; and now it was: 'The value of Alan Slater Mark IV's on order? Willie will tell us', for Willie had all sorts of information in his dusty office, recorded in an old-fashioned way, much of it in his own beautiful copper-plate hand. When people like Mr. Slater or old Willie became ill, it made you think. It was not until then that you realised how dead the works could be when one of them was absent, although, often, you did not see either of them for days at a time.

'Come on!' said Twice. 'I'll run you round to your digs. Mrs. Maitland is probably papering your room or something, but never mind. What about later in the evening?'

'I'll see. I'm going up to Glendale first. Maybe there's something I can do.'

'You can listen, anyway,' Twice agreed. 'If you're free later, I'll be around the shops somewhere. I've a few odds and ends to look at.'

We left my suitcase with Mrs. Maitland, and Twice drove me up to Glendale, where Mrs. Slater came running out to meet us.

'Lo and behold! You're back! Mercy, I'm glad to see you!' she said and burst into tears. I put an arm round her, while Twice stood about looking all hands and feet and she kept sobbing and saying: 'I'm sorry. I've been all right till now. I'm sorry.'

Suddenly Twice came over and took her away from me, held her and pushed her head against his shoulder, and it was the most appealing thing I have ever seen. Sorry to be slushy and sentimental, but it was. 'There now, Mrs. Slater,' he told her, 'You're all right and everything is going to be all right.'

'Ye-es, Mr. Alexander, but I'm so silly and —' She began to cry harder than ever from sheer relief.

'Hi!' I said. 'That's no way to welcome us and our news!'

'News?' she sobbed as if it were a word she had never heard.

'Yes, news! Stop hugging the man I am going to marry or I'll sue you!'

'You — *what*? Lo and behold!' Her tears vanished as if by magic. 'My goodness gracious *me*! Oh my! Oh mercy! Oh — come into the house! I'm going to tell Daddy right this minute.'

'Oh, Mrs. Slater —' I began.

'Sh-sh!' she said. 'In here!' And then in a voice so lacking in lo-and-beholdishness that I did not recognise it, she said: 'Rob, are you awake?'

'Aye — and that's the youngsters,' said the faint voice from the bed.

'Yes, Rob, and, lo and behold, they're going to get married.'

'My, but I'm pleased.' The voice was, unbelievably, less faint.

'We're going now, sir,' said Twice. 'And you must go to sleep.'

'Aye. Listen though, lad!'

'Yes?'

The voice became almost as strong as that of one of the fitters at the works in a rage. 'Ye're a wicked-tempered devil,

225

and if ye're not good to that lassie you'll reckon wi' *me*!'

'I'll be good to her, sir.'

'Aye. Ye better be. Away ye go. Come and see me the morn.'

'Good night, sir.'

Well, I thought, my own family is a dead loss but I *have* got an advocate, and 'you and your old men!' said Angela's voice down the long corridor of time. Memory, what a thing it is, and what echoes it has at moments when you least expect them.

Twice went away and left me with Mrs. Slater, and I got her to make me some supper while I helped her in the feckless way that she thought suitable to a woman who had been private secretary to people like her husband for a lifetime. I am no great psychologist, but it is elementary that, if you can make someone do a thing they like doing — in Mrs. Slater's case, cook a meal — and talk to them about something they like to talk about — in Mrs. Slater's case, what she called Romance — you are well on the way to making that person feel happy. I contrived, at least, to make Mrs. Slater feel less unhappy and, incidentally, made her eat, without noticing she was doing it, what was probably the first meal she had eaten in a week. I stayed with her until about eight o'clock, but there was still time to drive out a little way somewhere with Twice, and I set out to walk round the short back way from Glendale to the works, feeling that all was well with the world, for Mr. Slater was getting better, and I had Twice, and Pierre and Muriel were going away, and everything for me, was wonderful.

Ballydendran is one of these little towns that are nowadays described as being 'near Glasgow'. In former days, however, there used to be many green fields between it and Glasgow, and Ballydendran still had a lot of its green fields left, in spite of miles of tarmacadam trunk roads going to the city, housing schemes and the 'New Extension' to Slater's Works which consisted of one big, but low, white building built in four bays, so it was by a field path that I went, with a hawthorn hedge on one side, where the berries were a greenish-bronze colour and not yet their ripe, dark red. That is how I was before I met Twice, I thought romantically, a greenish-bronze colour, all

sicklied o'er with the pale cast of immaturity. I am as empty of
Romance, as you have probably noticed, as a tapioca pudding
is full of slime. I had occasion, once, to remark to My Friend
Monica that Romance was a country I had not visited yet, I
thought.

'How do you mean — a country?' she said. 'And besides,
even if it were a country — though that's quite wrong — you
must know whether you've been there or not. *I* always know
where *I've* been.'

'Don't be a fool!' I said, for I have not got this abrupt,
impolite way that Monica has of telling people that they are
quite wrong. 'Look at that time you were Over-the-Moon with
that bloke with the D.F.C. and Bar that had the big feet. You
didn't know you had been Over-the-Moon until after you
came back, and a fine fool you looked too.'

'We are not discussing feet,' said Monica with dignity.
'What is this delusion you cherish about Romance?'

'It is a country full of forests,' I told her, 'and well furnished
with castles, like the châteaux of the Loire, and all the men
wear cloaks and swords all day and go to the jousting and —'

'In nothing but a cloak and sword?'

'Certainly. That's the way they joust in Romance. And in
the evenings the men are troubadours and sing — they are all
tenors — to the ladies, who wear wimples and chatelaines and
furbelows and martingales and —'

'Are they lady horses?'

'Shut up — you know the things I mean. And out in the
woods a voice keeps saying: "Ah que le son du cor est trist au
fond des bois." '

'Your French accent is the bottom — le perishin' fond des
bois, in fact,' Monica said. 'And, anyway, Romance isn't a
country at all. That is quite wrong. It is a disease that is
commonest among adolescents, although some people get it
when they are quite well on in years — adolescence has
nothing to do with the age you are, after all. People are quite
wrong in thinking so. Why, that hearty type you got in tow
with at that dance at Blowdown-under-Wynd — *he* was an
adolescent and he must have been forty if he was a day.'

'We are not talking about adolescence — or any other sense, come to that,' I said. 'What more about this disease?'

'Speaks for itself,' she told me. 'It's the disease of roaming after mans, or if you are a male it is rowomance — with a wolf-whistle in it — without knowing you are doing it. . . . Will your mess bill stand the shock of another drink each? If not, we might as well go over the hut to bed — and farewell, Romance.'

Iphm, I thought, as I climbed through the fence that led into the field that held the 'New Extension', I must write to Monica and tell her that I was going to marry Twice. They were bound to like each other. It was just about then, as I walked round the corner of the Assembly Shop, that I got the feeling that something was wrong. Have you ever got a feeling like that? Some people say it is a pricking in their thumbs, and some say it is a feeling in their bones, but I get it in the nape of my neck and feel as a dog must feel when the hair stands up on his shoulders. I began to move quickly, but very quietly, to the main office door, which was standing open, and so was the little guichet window that looked from the passage into Old Willie's office. Through this, as in a frame, I saw the back of Old Willie's white head, with the hooks of his glasses that went round his ears, and above the old head a raised arm and hand holding a billet of wood. I ran up the passage and pushed my head through the window in time to hear: 'You dirty bastard!' and see Pierre spin round to face Twice. Pierre went up about two feet from the floor, sailed backwards through the air until he hit the open door of the safe and fell down and Twice hurled himself on top of him.

'Willie!' I bellowed. 'Willie! Stop him! He'll kill him!'

Willie shook his dazed old head and took off his glasses as if to see better what was happening.

'Willie! Stop him! Kick him! Willie!' Twice was snarling like a beast, his face convulsed, and Pierre's head was going bump-bump-bump on the floor with a hollow sound as these broad hands circling his throat went up and down as if piston-driven. I began to yell. 'Twice! Damn you! STOP IT!'

He looked up from his murderous work, blinked once and looked down at Pierre, and then his hands loosened their grip and he rubbed them down the front of his shirt as if wiping them.

'Mester Alexander, laddie!' said Willie. 'What happened?'

Twice got to his feet and glared at me. 'Come in or stay out!' he snapped. 'Don't stand there like a horse in a loose-box!'

'I can't,' I said. 'I'm stuck in this window.'

'God Almichty me!' said Old Willie.

It took a little time to release me from the window, for Twice had to get a screw-driver and take part of the frame out, so securely had I struggled and swollen myself into position, but it gave us all an opportunity to use plenty of rude words and generally blow off steam. Then we opened up the first-aid cupboard and got out the brandy bottle.

Pierre was still lying in the corner by the safe, but he was breathing.

'This is a fine set-out,' said Willie. 'We'd better get a doctor.'

'Damn that!' said Twice. 'He'll come round.'

'Oh, Twice —'

'Shut up, you! Going getting stuck in windows. . . . What are you doing here with the safe open at this time of night anyway, Willie?'

'It's pay-day the morn, Mr. Alexander!' Willie protested. 'I was just checking the sheet and —'

'Do you mean to tell me that the cash for the men is in that safe?'

'Where else? We aye draw the money on Thursday —'

'Holy suffering cow!' Twice picked up the billet of wood from the floor and hefted it in his hand. 'See this, Willie?' Willie stared at the weapon. 'I can just see the headlines in the paper. Robbery with Violence at Ballydendran . . . Glasgow Gang Suspected . . . And another editorial on the rise in lawlessness since the war.' He swung round and looked at the inert body on the floor. 'Quite neat. I didn't think he had it in him, the rat!'

'Oh, my goodness gracious me!' said Old Willie, sitting down. 'I think maybe I'll take a droppie o' that brandy after all.'

229

'He's moving!' I said.

'I'll move him!' said Twice.

'Twice Alexander! If you —'

'Don't blow your top!' said Twice and dragged Pierre to his feet and out into the yard. Willie and I followed, like a dumb chorus with a rather ill-rehearsed routine. Twice propped Pierre against the wall of the quiet back road outside the main gate. 'Now, get home. And don't come back, for, so help me, if I see your face again I *will* kill you!'

Pierre did not say anything, but he began to move away side-wise, holding himself half-upright by clinging to the wall.

Back in the office, Twice said: 'I don't propose to say a word about this to anyone until the Old Man is better. Do you agree?'

Willie and I nodded. We both realised that there is a time to argue and a time *not* to argue.

'Will he get out to The Lea all right, do you think?' Willie asked.

'If he doesn't, somebody will find him, and it wouldn't matter if they didn't. But, Willie, this business has got to stop.' Twice waved his hand at the pay-sheet and the open safe. 'You have been lucky tonight, but only lucky enough with nothing to spare. When did you start this foolish racket of keeping that amount of cash in that old tin box overnight?'

'We've *aye* done it, Mr. Alexander! That's what we got the safe for!' Willie protested. 'Of course, in the old days the pay-sheet wasn't so big — but there's no thieves in Ballydendran!' he ended in scandalised tones.

Twice gave up. For some things, his manner seemed to say, Willie was too old and the idea of a thief in his home town was too new-fangled for absorption. 'All right, Willie, we'll think of something.'

'If the Boss hadna been no' weel,' said Willie, with much more of the accent of his countryside than usual in his speech and a remarkable amount of venom in his voice for one so mild, 'I would have phoned to the polis and *reported* that man Robertson, that's what I would have done! The very idea! It's a fair scandal, that's what it is — an incomer like that thinkin' on robbin the works safe! . . . Still, will he get out to The Lea all right, think ye?'

'Of course he will!' said Twice.

'Well, you were at the war and you should know. But I never saw a man so mishandled.'

'Mishandled be damned! He'll get home all right. And you lock up that old biscuit box and go home yourself!'

Twice looked at the safe with strong dislike. 'And we *ought* to report Robertson, you know,' he added to me.

'It would kill Mr. Slater,' I said.

'Aye,' Willie agreed. 'The disgrace o' a thing like that — aye, he wouldna get over it, no' wi' him bein' weak like he is.'

'Oh, all right. Anyway, I don't think Robertson will come back *here*. As long as he stays at home it will be all right.'

So we all went home, but Pierre, with that way people have of not doing what you estimate they will do, did not go home to The Lea. Days, a week, two weeks went past, and Mr. Slater was about the house for a few hours a day and the town was rife with all sorts of wild rumour, and towards the end of the third week Mrs. Slater sent for Twice and me to come over to Glendale, so we took Old Willie with us, judging that this was the time to tell Mr. Slater all that we knew.

'Aye. There you are — and Willie too,' he greeted us from his armchair. 'Sit down. Janet, lassie, this is a bad business I'm hearing about The Lea. Have you been out to see that poor woman?'

'Muriel? No, Mr. Slater. Why?'

'The poor soul. You'll have to go out to her. It seems that Pierre's away for good.'

'For good?'

'Aye. He flew from Prestwick yesterday.'

'Flew? How do you know?'

Mirabile Dictu began to cry. 'It was awful!' she said. 'Just awful! To think —'

'Now, Mother, stop worrying yourself. It's a good riddance, but I'm sorry for that poor woman out there.'

'What has happened, sir?' Twice asked.

'It's no' very nice,' the Old Man said. 'It seems he sold the

231

place, The Lea, to a firm in Edinburgh and as soon as he got the cheque he turned it into cash and flew away to America with the lot. That's the story as best we can get at it. The first inkling I had that something was wrong was when his wife rang up here yesterday to ask if we knew where he was. She hadn't seen him for a fortnight — he'd told her he was going down to Sheffield, but he should have been back and she was anxious. So Mother took a walk out there this morning to ask if she had heard anything, but in the meantime I had phoned these folk in Sheffield. They had never seen him since his interview when he failed for the job. He had told his wife he had *got* the job. He told me that too. Then, when Mother was there at The Lea, a man and his wife arrived from Edinburgh with a house agent man and said they had bought the house. Poor Mother didn't know what to say or do —'

'I didn't know where to *look*!' sobbed Mirabile Dictu.

'— so she came away. But there it is. If these folk paid their money, the place is theirs.'

'Poor Muriel!' I said.

Twice rose. 'I suppose you want to go out there, Flash?'

It was Muriel. I had to go. 'Yes,' I said and I rose too.

'Let me out here,' I said to Twice at the gate to the untidy, weedy drive. 'I'll walk back. I'll come to the works — or to the hotel, later.'

I went up the steps into the Baronial Hall. The Two-handed Engine was lying on its back on the floor, its hands sticking up in the air, the helmet detached from the rest of it and lying on the carpet and its halberd was lying in a long coffin-like crate. Muriel was doing something clumsy to one of its shoulders with a screw-driver, and she looked up at me, then rose from her knees and sat on the nearest chair, the screw-driver still in her hands.

'Hello, Muriel,' I said.

I do not know what I expected to find — hysteria, perhaps — but I was surprised at her calm.

'Hello,' she said.

'I came to ask if there was anything I could do,' I told her.

'Do?' she repeated.

'Yes. You see, I heard — Mr. Slater told me about —'

'About what?' Her face and voice were quite expressionless.

'About the house being sold,' I said.

'It isn't.'

'But Mrs. Slater said —'

'*That* fool?' Muriel sniffed at me and looked away into a corner.

'And — Pierre?' I faltered, feeling more than a little of a fool myself.

'Oh, *he's* gone,' she told me and her manner took my breath away and made my knees go weak so that I sank on to the nearest Period-Antique-Reproh chair.

'Gone?' I repeated after her, staring at her, and as I stared her face took on that look of furtive cunning that it used to wear so long ago when she 'did her accounts' in the blue exercise book.

'Yes,' she said, with an ugly little sniff that was almost a sneering laugh. 'With five hundred pounds that those fools in Edinburgh paid him as a deposit —' Her voice suddenly became louder and definitely scornful. '— on this house which wasn't his to sell!'

'Not *his*?' I asked, feeling that the only means of finding my way in this quagmire was to repeat things that she had already said as one uses foot-printed tussocks of grass to cross a morass.

'Why should it be his?' she asked shrilly. 'It was bought with *my* money!'

'Are the deeds in your name?'

'Of course! Do you think I am a fool?'

'But that time in London — I witnessed Pierre's signature —'

'Oh, that? The transfer of the lease of the Chelsea flat. No. The Lea is mine,' she said with satisfaction. 'At the moment, that is. I *have* agreed to sell it.'

'Oh, I see.' I was not very interested in this side of things. I was too stunned by My Friend Muriel to be interested in anything like the purchase or sale of The Lea.

'Yes. It's going to be turned into a boys' school,' she went

233

on conversationally. 'I'm making about two thousand out of it.'

'That's nice,' I said, which sounded so incredibly silly that I added hastily: 'So you will be going away?'

'Yes,' she said.

'And — and Pierre?' I asked.

A small sullen cloud crossed her face. 'He wants me to divorce him, but I won't.'

'Why not, Muriel?'

'I don't want to,' she said, and she licked her lips in a peculiar way. 'Why should I if I don't want to? He can't make me. Besides, it wouldn't be right.'

'Right?'

'You know that I am a member of the Anglican Church, Janet!' she told me reprovingly.

'Oh,' I said, and I felt cold claws of nausea twist the pit of my stomach. Had I been able, I would have walked out of the house and left her, but I was so giddily sick that I did not dare to move. 'Muriel — are you fond of Pierre?'

'Fond of him?'

'Do you still love him?'

'Still?'

'You must have felt something for him when you married him!'

'Felt something? A lot of nonsense gets talked about that sort of thing —' She looked away from me across the Baronial Hall, thinking some thoughts of her own.

'Muriel,' I persisted, 'why did you marry Pierre in the first place?'

She looked at me as if I had asked an inordinately foolish question, and then she shrugged her shoulders. 'I thought it would turn out all right,' she said. 'It *would* have too.' She looked around the Baronial Hall. 'It *looked* all right.' She seemed to be discussing the prospectus of a company that, contrary to expectation, had gone bankrupt. 'But it went wrong mostly through that silly old man Slater bringing that man Alexander into the firm.'

'Muriel, are you crazy?' I asked quietly.

If she heard me, she made no sign. 'But how was I to foresee that the old fool would do a thing like that?' she asked of the dusty air. 'I was mistaken about Alexander, too, really,' she continued thoughtfully. 'Pierre misled me about him. Pierre was an even bigger liar than I thought. I thought Alexander was just an oily engineer, but he seems to be quite smart. One has to admire him.'

That did it. Up to a point, I am a Woman of Peace, but Muriel had stepped past the point. I sprang to my feet and stood over her, no longer feeling sick or weak at the knees, but at the highest pitch of my fighting temper.

'You revolting trollop!' I spat at her.

'I *never* heard a person say a thing like that!' she said, looking up at me with her shapeless mouth slightly open and her vague eyes searching my face. 'What on earth is the matter with you?'

'The matter? Great God in Heaven! Do you think all the world is like yourself? That everyone will jump into bed with a crook — as you did — in the hope of getting a share in an engineering firm? Do you think we all live as you do? Do you see nothing ugly in yourself? You — the woman who made a couple of thousand out of marrying a man you didn't even like? No wonder Pierre stole your five hundred and ran away! It's a pity he was only a small-time crook! That old woman Rollin was more your match — all she wanted to leave you was a tin man and she was damned right!'

'Oh, she left me more than that,' said Muriel, as calmly as if she had never heard a word I had said, and probably she had not, at that. I think that Muriel always heard only the things she wanted to hear and saw only the things she wanted to see. But she had the effect now of stopping me in mid-tirade.

'More than that?' I repeated stupidly.

'Yes. She left me quite a bit,' said Muriel with satisfaction. 'I didn't like to tell you at the time because you had been her secretary too and your feelings might have been hurt at not getting anything. Of course —'

'My feelings?' I squealed. 'Holy suffering cow! My feelings —'

'Janet, what *are* you in such an uproar about?' She sounded quite hurt. 'After all, *I* am the one that's in trouble — not you. And —' She gave a sigh in the manner of Madame X. 'Of course, you always did tend to get into an uproar about things. I've got calmer since I got older, but you never seem to have settled down. Look, I'll write and let you know where I am in London and —'

'You'll *write*? You dare to write me one more of your damn' silly letters and I'll come and ram it down your rotten throat! Do you understand? I never want to see you or hear from you again as long as I live!'

'Janet! I *never* heard a person say a thing —'

I did not let her finish. I wanted to do her physical violence to make her understand my loathing, so instead of kicking *her* I took a strong place kick at the helmet of the Two-handed Engine which sent it sailing from the floor and up between two posts of the Minstrels' Gallery from whence it flew through a hideous stained-glass window in a wild jangle of metal and splintering glass. When the noise had ended, I said: 'So there!' in a loud voice and dashed out of the Baronial Hall and took a flying leap down the front steps into the weedy drive, leaving her looking after me with a glance of pained astonishment.

'Played, Sandison, played!' said Twice from the flower-bed where he stood with the helmet under his arm like a football.

'You still here?' I asked, still trembling with rage.

'Certainly,' he replied, beginning to wipe the helmet with his handkerchief. 'I wouldn't have missed a second of that for anything.'

'I didn't get anywhere with her,' I said, as I got into the car. My rage had gone, leaving behind it a dismal sense of failure.

'No,' said Twice. 'You didn't . . . Your cigarettes are in that side pocket, by the way . . . But not having got anywhere with her in fifteen years, you can hardly expect a five-minute miracle, can you?'

He started the car and it rolled down the drive and out through the rusty gates. I felt that I might be going to cry.

'People *aren't* like that, are they, Twice?'

'There are people and people.'

'People like *us*, though?'

'Like us? Well, we have it on good authority that I'm an oily engineer —'

'But quite smart!' I said, my tears receding.

'Well, I got away with something of Muriel's, anyway.'

'Huh?'

'The Tin Man's head. It's in the back.'

'Twice Alexander!'

'And if she wants it back she can come and get it.'

He turned the car towards our hilltop with the view. 'Let's get up into the wind. . . . Nobody's going to call *me* quite smart and get away with it. I didn't merely feel insulted when she said that, I felt outraged. . . .

'Outraged,' he repeated ten minutes later when he had stopped the car on the moorland hill where the clean wind blew.

That was the word. What I had felt, too, during that interview with Muriel, was a sense of outrage, and I said so to Twice now.

'Yes. Outrageous. And I thought she was just an ordinary person. All these years I have thought that she was just an ordinary person.'

'What do you mean by "ordinary"?' he asked.

I stared into his questioning eyes and, looking into that clear blueness, I said out of the new light that flooded my mind: 'Yes. I am talking nonsense. There is not such a thing as an ordinary person, is there?'

'No. Except maybe this.' He reached into the back of the car and brought forward the head of the Two-handed Engine, holding it tenderly in his lap and beginning to polish its visor with a piece of cotton waste. 'With no brains in its tin head and no heart in its tin chest. I am going to keep this as a centre-piece for the mantelpiece — the symbol of the Ordinary Person.' He continued to rub the visor with his handful of waste, not looking at me. 'Feeling sad?' he asked.

'No. I'm not sad — it is more pure blind rage. I feel that Muriel has made a fool of me, not only me, but a packet of other people as well.'

'How do you mean?'

'Well, we all — Mr. Rollin, Aunt Julia, the Slaters, Lady Firmantle — everybody who knew Muriel was always sorry for her and trying to help her. We all felt she was being Put Upon, Taken Advantage Of, and things like that. But not Muriel. When I look back on things, she took far more advantages than she ever gave — even inviting you to tea at The Teapot and letting you pay the bill! I think we all had the wrong end of the stick. After all, she ended up with Madame X's money, probably Aunt Julia's as well — I think she was the nearest relation to Aunt Julia and they were very family-property-minded. People were — were just *investments* to Muriel, damn it! I was one and Pierre was another, and there was I, pitying her like anything and thinking Pierre was making a fool of her! Golly, I *do* feel mad!'

'That's fine,' said Twice. 'I'd rather have you feeling mad than feeling hurt at the end of a long friendship.'

'Friendship! I wish I'd never laid eyes on the cow!' And then my brain went into a spinning whirl like that turn of the kaleidoscope again. 'No!' I said hastily. 'No! I take that back! But for Muriel, I would never have met *you*! That's a frightening thought. Why should someone like Muriel be so important in the lives of you and me?'

'That's enough!' said Twice. 'The water is getting too deep for the Ordinary Person and me, isn't it, chum?' He held up the helmet and stared at its hideous face. 'Your property-minded momma is gonna miss ya, honey!' he sang to it.

I laughed. 'If Muriel knew you had that, she'd write a nice letter hoping you were well and asking you to send it back.'

'And she wouldn't get it.'

'She'll probably write, anyway,' I said lugubriously, for habit dies hard and I could not imagine life unadorned by letters from Muriel. But I was wrong. I have never had another letter from My Friend Muriel.

THE END

MY FRIEND MONICA
By Jane Duncan

The My Friend books tell the story of Janet Sandison, of her Highland family, and of the fascinating and varied friends who shaped her life.

Janet and Monica became friends during the war. They didn't meet again until Janet and 'Twice' Alexander were about to marry, and then Monica, with her flaming red hair and aristocratic manner, burst on post-war Scotland determined to become a permanent part of their lives. Throughout the renovation of their old stone cottages into a home, through Janet's tragic illness, Monica clung close, creating problem upon problem in their stormy lives.

It wasn't until they all went back to Reachfar, to the family in Ross-shire that the old values of friendship were re-established.

This is the third of the My Friend books.

0 552 12876 7 £2.50

A SELECTED LIST OF FINE NOVELS
AVAILABLE FROM CORGI BOOKS

THE PRICES SHOWN BELOW WERE CORRECT AT THE TIME OF GOING
TO PRESS. HOWEVER TRANSWORLD PUBLISHERS RESERVE THE RIGHT
TO SHOW NEW RETAIL PRICES ON COVERS WHICH MAY DIFFER FROM
THOSE PREVIOUSLY ADVERTISED IN THE TEXT OR ELSEWHERE.

All these books are available at your book shop or newsagent, or can be ordered direct from the publisher. Just tick the titles you want and fill in the form below.

ORDER FORM

TRANSWORLD READER'S SERVICE, 61–63 Uxbridge Road, Ealing, London, W5 5SA.

Please send cheque or postal order, not cash. All cheques and postal orders must be in £ sterling and made payable to Transworld Publishers Ltd.

Please allow cost of book(s) plus the following for postage and packing:

U.K./Republic of Ireland Customers:
Orders in excess of £5: no charge
Orders under £5: add 50p

Overseas Customers:
All orders: add £1.50

NAME (Block Letters)..

ADDRESS ....

....